Slip

of the

Hand III

J.P. Farrell

Riverhaven Books

www.RiverhavenBooks.com

Slip of the Hand III is a work of fiction. While some of the settings are actual, any similarity regarding names, characters, or incidents is entirely coincidental.

Published in the United States
by Riverhaven Books,
www.RiverhavenBooks.com

ISBN: 978-1-937588-80-9

Printed in the United States of America
by Country Press, Lakeville, Massachusetts

Edited and designed by Stephanie Lynn Blackman
Whitman, Massachusetts

Cover Picture © bingokid

Prologue

The third part of the *Slip of the Hand* series continues with *Deep in the Shadows*.

After two years on the run, Jack stretched out in a lounge chair while sipping a cold beer, watching Sampson playfully chase a rabbit around the large backyard. He had finally found refuge in a small quaint town in Canada, although his mind constantly replayed the darkness that had followed him throughout his life.

His guilt at not saving his little brother when they were kids – the memory of his hand slipping, losing grip as the current carried his little brother under the ice – had propelled him to become a decorated Navy SEAL. Jack didn't consider himself fearless; he just didn't have anything else to lose.

But when his sister was kidnapped, raped, and murdered, and the legal system failed to punish the two frat boys responsible, Jack became a vigilante, killing those who had taken his sister's life. This set in motion a chain of events that he couldn't control and even more carnage.

Jack took another sip of beer and stared at the cloud formations, the flowers that swayed in the breeze, and even the bees that pollenated the flowers. Sampson returned, wagging his tail, guarding him like secret service. As the months had gone by in this new life, Jack hoped his tormentors might move on, but these were ruthless people who would never leave him alone. It was the people deep in the shadows that he feared most though: the ones no one ever saw or expected, the ones dressed in suits who smiled to your face and then stabbed you in the back.

He thought about all of the enemies he'd made. The fathers of the two boys he'd killed: Frank Gallo, mafia kingpin of the Gallo crime family, and Sam Atkins, the former senator and now President of the United States with his seemingly endless government henchmen. Then there was the Moreno Cartel.

Jack considered who he had left to turn to. There was the uneasy alliance with James Mattison – the powerful industrialist and influential political player with his own agenda. And then there was Art Glover, who had his own score to settle with Jack but had also been useful in the past. These thoughts lurked in the shadows of his mind. And the knowledge of the covert Phoenix Project, stored on a flashdrive in his possession, kept Jack awake at night.

Jack shook his head and admitted to himself that he only had one person he could truly confide in. The woman he loved – Kelly.

He patted Sampson on the head as a tear slowly rolled down his cheek. He'd seen too much death, experienced too much loss.

Too many people were now involved. Too many had been hurt. Too many had a stake in the game. The cast of characters seemed endless:

- **Eric Steele**, a member of the cabal pushing the new world order and one of many searching for Bolton;

- **Art Glover**, one of Mattison's hitman for hire who blamed Jack for the death of Glover's brother, who was one of the bank robbers in Seattle;

- **James Mattison**, a rich industrialist who had formulated the rescue mission for Laura Weston, placing him in the crosshairs of Atkins and his cohorts, all in an effort to convince Jack to relinquish the Phoenix Project files;
- **FBI Director Shone Williams**, a close friend of the president now finds himself in a more precarious position since the death of Gus Banner. President Atkins had stepped up the pressure to find Jack Bolton and it's Shone's job to make it happen;
- **Mike Weldon**, a CIA spook originally brought in by former CIA Director Gus Banner to play the role of an FBI agent and unofficially take out Bolton in Seattle. It was supposed to be a short-term job, but here he was still on assignment and now he was the lead FBI agent to get the job done any way possible;
- **Frank Gallo** swore he would avenge his son's death. He came close to snuffing Jack out only to be interrupted by the dealmaker, a CIA Operative, aka Robert Tripp. Jack escaped Gallo's clutches with the help of an outside force, Mattison. When FBI Agent Ryland suggested to Gallo that he wanted to take out Tripp after he'd threatened his family, a secret allegiance was formed between the two. Gallo order the execution in broad daylight in a small dinner;
- **Paul Ryland**, a disgraced FBI agent convicted of aiding and abetting Jack Bolton. Ryland's real crime was getting too close to uncovering the truth behind the president's malfeasance. Disillusioned by the corruption in the Bureau and Atkins's administration, Ryland conspired with Gallo, which – if revealed – could threaten his own existence or

expose him to a life prison sentence;

• **President Sam Atkins** is still reeling from the death of his son and, more recently, CIA Director Gus Banner. Now that he's in charge of the country, he finds that his past mistakes – including his affair with Laura Weston – have consequences;

• **Laura Weston** was rescued by Jack Bolton, Art Glover, and a crew of former SEALs from the hands of the Mexican Moreno Cartel where then Senator Sam Atkins had her held captive. Returned safely to Washington D.C., she's intent to expose those who faked her death and framed her former fiancé, Jeff Keller, for the crime;

• **Jeff Keller** is a broken man, caught in an increasingly dangerous love triangle. Believing Laura dead and after escaping from prison for a crime that didn't exist, he began a relationship with Jennifer Atkins, the president's estranged black-sheep daughter. Now he has to choose between the two women and soon finds out that the hangover from Laura's previous indiscretion is far from over;

• **Jennifer Atkins** can't forgive her father for all of his infidelities. His behavior destroyed their family, and she also blames him for her brother's actions which led to his death. She now finds herself in love with a man her father wronged, and she doesn't know if Jeff loves her or if he will return to Laura.

Chapter 1

Vibrant foliage dotted the landscape as the Pearl 75 luxury yacht cruised the open waterway on Lake Champlain near Burlington, Vermont. A few smaller boats paced at a distance.

An anchor dropped, and the boat sat in calm water, fishing rods leaning forward on the stern of the boat. President Sam Atkins sat with a cup of coffee, enjoying the view while his right hand tugged at a fishing rod. He was accompanied by FBI Director Shone Williams and a few other men dressed in casual clothes.

The conversation was lighthearted, and the men laughed and smiled from time to time.

Eric Steele, wearing a black polo sweater and white shorts, emerged from below deck looking as if he was getting ready for golf. The sun glistened off his gray hair.

He smiled, looking beyond the water. "What a beautiful fall morning. It doesn't get any better than this. But, Sam, we have some unfinished business to discuss."

"We're all friends here with the same goals, so your concerns are my concerns," Sam said, looking at Steele.

Eric sat down in front of the president and FBI director. "The Sanderlin group has been very impressed with your presidency."

"Well, your group was very generous with your campaign contributions."

"Identifying the ideal candidate who has the same ideology as us and who can win is a very extensive process."

"I'm glad you're pleased."

"You've done a great job, Sam." Eric smiled again. "The right has been neutralized. The organization of protesters and agitators railing against every policy the conservatives favor, along with the liberal media hammering home the liberal narrative every day, have done an excellent job of keeping the right off balance. But these activist federal judges are where the real power lies. Former President Farley understood the singular importance of the lower court, which is why he was so vigorous in appointing judges with a greater commitment to the liberal political agenda than to the Constitution. It has worked out pretty well without gaining the House and Senate."

"But it would be a great advantage if we could get control of the House and Senate," Sam stated.

"That will come in due time," Eric said with confidence. "But we must start looking ahead toward the next election in two years. If we can get you elected for four more years, the other party will never recover, and we can finalize our global agenda."

"Is there really going to be any competition?" Sam asked with a chuckle. "The other side of the aisle doesn't seem to have anyone."

"Senator Ethan White from New Hampshire could be a problem."

Sam smirked. "Ethan White? Come on."

"Mattison has begun courting this guy; he might give you trouble." Eric added, "The guy has no baggage, he's a great talker and debater, and he speaks from the heart. And being a former vet doesn't hurt either. But he's a subject for another day. We have some issues that we need to clean up before your next election run."

"There's nothing we can't handle."

Eric ignored the president's snappishness. "We know all about Bolton and the potential information he might have. Then again, he's had this information for a couple of years without releasing it."

"It doesn't matter. If it comes to bear, my brother could be implicated; Banner certainly, but he's dead. It would all blow over."

Eric shook his head. "We need to clean up your loose baggage. We can't take any chances. We're so close to grabbing power in three continents. Sanderlin made it clear: do whatever is necessary."

"You know, Eric, I got here because I know the pulse of America, not from all that campaign money you threw at me and the media machine."

Eric frowned. "Not exactly, Sam. Farley was the one who pushed for you. It certainly wasn't your womanizing ways, which the Sanderlin Group overlooked based on the recommendations we received from highly respected people."

"It's funny you mention Farley, Eric. He funded basically all of your left-wing global socialist agendas. You didn't come all the way out here to talk about how I like women."

Eric called over to Oz who took a seat. Smiling, he patted the man's knee. "My man Oz here has found Bolton for us. You look surprised, Sam."

"Well, it's about time someone found him. Don't expect any medals. He's done enough damage. I hate the bastard. So finish what Banner failed to do."

"Oz is going to take care of our little problem. I know Banner was a close friend of yours, Sam, but I don't think his heart was in it. It ended up costing him his life. We won't make the same mistake."

Oz sat stone-faced, staring at President Atkins who noted that beneath his bald head he had crazy eyes.

Sam glanced at Eric. "Where the hell you find this guy, huh?"

"He's very effective at what he does," Steele shot back.

"Just get it done," Sam said, shaking his head. "I don't want to keep talking about this guy. He's a big distraction."

A wide smile formed on Eric's face. "Look, he's living a nice life in a small town in Canada. He has a girlfriend. He won't see it coming. That's what happens to these guys when they go soft. They forget. They think their past has been forgotten." He closed his eyes and mused, "The look on their faces when the past catches up with them."

"Do you really have to take care of the girl? I just want Bolton."

Oz chimed in with a slight German accent. "Mr. President, it's better that anybody associated with Bolton be dealt with. It sends a strong message to others."

"He talks," Sam smirked then stared intently at Oz. "Let me tell you something: just get the job done. I'm tired of all the excuses."

"Mr. President, I won't fail."

"Let me change the subject a little bit, Sam," Eric said. "I didn't know you were going to bring another player into our little inner circle."

Sam didn't like being questioned. "Shone is a good friend. You can trust him."

"I'm sure we can." Eric's smile twisted into a smirk. "Shone, we know all about you: Army Ranger, received a Medal of Valor, a nice family of four, worked your way up the ladder, and here you are an FBI director. Bravo."

"I don't need a review, Steele. To tell you the truth, I don't give a shit what you think."

Eric snickered. "A man who's not afraid to say what's on his mind. I like that. We're all friends here.

Look, we're about to get rid of all Sam's problems; you could show a little more appreciation. But let me remind you, Shone, just in case you forgot: you put an innocent FBI agent behind bars. Maybe he wasn't that innocent. That poor guy Tripp, getting gunned down like that a few years ago. I never liked the guy anyway. But since Sam here is vouching for you, then, it's all good."

"Wait a minute." Sam eyed Eric. "How would you know that?"

"It's my business to know things. Did Tripp ever talk to Ryland?"

"Yeah, he met with him," Shone said.

"So maybe he had a reason to want him dead," Eric suggested.

"Ryland wouldn't do that," Shone said with some heat.

"Tripp could be pretty blunt at times, and some people took it the wrong way. You got to think a little bigger, Shone. How many times did Ryland meet with Gallo?"

"I don't know. I'm sure quite a few. Gallo was under investigation."

Eric sneered. "You signed off on giving Gallo's right-hand man – What's that guy's name, Russo? – a damn get out of jail card, right?"

"He was going to give up Gallo."

"How do you think Gallo's men were coincidently in Seattle?" he asked. "Did Banner ever confide in you that

6

Russo was going to have a convenient heart attack because we wanted Gallo's men to take care of Bolton? Who do you think arranged that?"

Williams looked confused. "Tripp?"

Eric said to Sam, "I'm surprised that Shone here has been kept in the dark."

"Banner did whatever he had to do. He didn't need to get Shone involved – or me for that matter. He worked in the shadows."

"Without Banner and Tripp, who the hell is going to get rid of your problems, Sam? It sure isn't going to be Shone here. He looks like he's in a state of shock."

"I'm fine," Shone said, sounding anything but.

"Well, do you have any leads on who took out Tripp? It's been almost two years."

"No," Shone replied quietly.

"What about Banner?"

"Well, there was someone there that night; it was most likely Bolton, but the video can't prove it, and there're no prints or DNA."

"Which basically means you have nothing," Eric concluded.

"Without any material evidence, it makes it pretty hard to prove either case," Shone asserted.

"Well, Tripp's death had the earmarks of a frigging execution," Eric said. "But we can't just let it go. So dig into the connection between Ryland and Gallo. If Gallo did this, he couldn't have done it alone."

"Ryland wouldn't be part of this," Shone insisted. "He was a good agent."

"He was so good you put him behind bars. This is what you are going to do…"

"So now you're an expert on how to run the FBI?" Shone snapped.

"Look; you tell Gallo that Ryland has made a deal with the feds. This should set off Gallo."

"I can't do something like that. It could get him – or worse, his family killed."

"I don't give a damn about Ryland," Eric barked. "He's expendable."

"I don't give a shit about Ryland either," Sam Atkins said. "If he had just made a call to the college, maybe my son would still be alive today. But lay off of Shone, Eric; he's just doing his job."

"You're right. I'm sorry, Shone. It's just business. You need to learn you don't get attached to anyone. And if, as you say, Ryland would never be part of something like this, then Gallo will not care about Ryland. But if Ryland did have something to do with this, then there are consequences."

"Sam, Ryland is a former agent for God's sake," Shone pleaded.

"Shone, if he was part of this, then he should be serving a life sentence or, better yet, a death sentence."

Shone shook his head. "I can't believe this."

"You don't understand, Shone," Eric said. "Tripp

was a vital asset under Banner. He was fluent in five languages, was a hell of a negotiator, did things around the world that I'm not going to discuss here. So it's important for us to find out who killed him. Was it based on vengeance, a foreign power, or just plain stupidity on someone's part? And I don't have that answer yet."

"Let's move on," Sam said. "The past is done. Shone will initiate a conversation with Gallo that Ryland has something on him and we'll see where it takes us."

"Could I talk to you alone, Sam?" Eric asked, standing up.

"Why not? Let's take a walk."

They stopped on the starboard side of the boat and leaned on the railing.

"Sam, I don't think it was a good idea bringing Shone here. How much can he be trusted?"

"Look, we have been friends for over twenty years. He can be trusted."

"I hope you're right, for Shone's sake."

"So that's what you wanted to tell me privately?"

"No. Our next little problem is Mattison. He took sides when he decided to help Bolton get Laura Weston home, which is unfortunate for him. I gave him a chance to give us Bolton, but now we have to take care of him."

"How do you propose to do that?"

"You don't have to worry about it. Sanderlin wants me to start with his good-hearted brother, Tyler. That should send a message."

"That might make him do something crazy."

"That's what we want. He'll make a mistake, or maybe he'll come out of his fortress. Anyway, what are you going to do about Laura Weston and the book she's writing?"

"She won't say anything about me."

"Do you know that for sure?"

"She won't."

"I don't think we can take that chance."

Sam shook his head. "Damn it. I will deal with it."

"Well, there's always her fiancé, Jeff Keller. You can play with his emotions and get the results you want."

Sam stared at the horizon. "You really want to go there?"

"Maybe I should ask: do you want to run again? If it gets out that you had something to do with Weston being held in Mexico, whether real or imagined, your presidency is history. So think about it carefully."

"What? You want to get rid of her too? Is that what you want?"

"Sometimes we have to do things we don't like. You should've gotten rid of her in Mexico."

Sam's rage boiled. "Don't tell me about tough decisions. You know that this whole global utopia that Sanderlin and Farley envision is a stretch."

"It's the only chance the world has of moving forward; otherwise, eventually the world will self-destruct."

10

"The world in harmony is never going to happen; read history, Eric."

He put his arm around the president. "Sam, trust me; when most of the world is on the same page, it will be able to do amazing things. So just do your part, and the pieces will all fall into place. We have the European Union, NATFA, a group of powerful, rich industrialists, and we're on the verge of the Trans-Pacific Partnership with your help. And add in the UN doing our bidding around the world, and we're very close."

"I'm with you. The world together makes my job so much easier, but it's just this thing with Bolton and what he did to my son and his knowledge of the Phoenix Project."

"I'm here to ensure you that your little problem is as good as gone. Don't worry; we'll take care of this and any other issues that come up."

Disagreements mended, the men shook hands and reiterated their alliance.

***

A miniature spider-like drone maneuvered over the open water then gently touched down on a rocky ledge. A man wearing a baseball cap and shades nonchalantly reached down to pick it up then slid it carefully into a backpack. He got on a mountain bike and rode along the Colchester Causeway as if he was a tourist enjoying the beautiful views of Lake Champlain.

Chapter 2

The sun broke through in the eastern sky. The Cape Cod-style house was surrounded by a few acres of flat land. Jack Bolton leaned back in a chair on the small deck with his special brew. He had found refuge in a small town called Maple Creek in British Columbia, Canada, 739 miles from Vancouver.

Jack watched his dog Sampson as he ran across the frost-covered grass, loving his leash-free early morning run. Despite the serenity of the moment, Jack was on constant guard, his past always lurking in the back of his mind.

Looking out from the kitchen window, Kelly stood in a bathrobe with her brunette hair pulled back in a ponytail. She made a cup of coffee, hesitant to interrupt Jack's deep thoughts. Another sleepless night and dark dreams continued to haunt Jack's soul.

She slowly, quietly opened the sliding door. He wouldn't even notice until she pounced. Her hands gently massaged his shoulders and, before he could say a word, she planted a kiss on his lips.

"Good morning, Kelly. Why did you stop?"

"I don't want to spoil you," she said with a chuckle. "What are you doing up so early again?"

"I couldn't sleep, and Sampson wanted to run. Now,

where were we?"

Kelly smiled. "I was by the window for a few minutes making some coffee and couldn't help but notice that you weren't here. What's on your mind?"

"I worry about something happening to you."

"I don't want you to worry about me. Anyway, you showed me how to use a gun. I can take care of myself."

"I haven't been able to sleep for a week. I can sense it, Kelly; they're coming."

"It's been almost two years; why now?"

"I don't know."

"Jack, worrying is going to kill you; forget about the bad guys. You need to let it go."

"I can sense it. Like an animal sensing a storm."

"Okay, what am I thinking?" she joked while standing up with her hands folded. "Come on, what am I thinking?"

He hesitated then smiled. "You're thinking that I don't have a clue."

She paused then bellowed out a laugh, "Okay, that was too easy."

Jack just grinned then his expression turned serious. "Just remember; nobody knows I'm here. Anybody looking for me is not my friend. So don't…"

"I know: don't be afraid to use the gun," she said with a sly smile.

"This is serious, Kelly. I love you too much."

"I'm just teasing." She wrapped her arms around him

from behind and leaned in.

"Now that's more like it," he said, his hands clutching her arms.

"If it makes you feel any better, why don't we do a little target practice later today?"

"That's a good idea."

"Okay. My shift at the hospital is over at three," Kelly said. "Let's do it then."

"Sounds good, honey."

***

The afternoon sun had warmed the air. Jack ran errands and came home with a bundle of firewood, a pound of salmon, a bottle of wine, and a bouquet of flowers. He stepped onto the patio to be greeted by Sampson wagging his tail.

"What're you doing, fellow?" Jack patted him on the head. "I didn't forget you." He held out a large bone; Sampson gladly took it and went under the table to whittle it down.

Jack placed the cord of wood by the stove and put the flowers in a tall vase. He took out two Glock 17s, placed them on the table, sat in his lounge chair watching a hawk glide overhead, and waited for Kelly's return.

A while later Kelly pushed the sliding door open and stood on the deck. "Are those mine?" she giggled and picked up the vase of flowers. "You're so sweet, Jack."

He stood. "You sure look good in your blue scrubs." When he reached in for a hug, she pulled back. "You have no idea where these scrubs have been."

"I don't care."

"I do." She turned to go back inside. "I'm going to take a quick shower and change into something more comfortable for target practice."

Jack sat drinking a beer while waiting for Kelly. Sampson was by his side, working on the bone.

When Kelly returned, Jack eyed her appreciatively. "You sure look good in jeans."

"Just how many beers have you had?" she said with a laugh. "You didn't mention the sweatshirt."

"This is my first one. I just call it the way I see it, but the sweatshirt is cute too."

Kelly rolled her eyes. "Well, let's go."

They grabbed their guns and walked about a hundred yards to the far end of the yard. Jack had set up an array of targets; Kelly fired shot after shot knocking them off their placeholders.

"How's that, Jack?"

"You're the sexiest gunslinger I've ever seen. Good job!"

Jack took a turn. He fired away, hitting every target with bullets to spare.

"That's pretty good, Jack."

"Just *pretty good*?"

They spent another twenty minutes shooting targets. "How about we head back and fire up the grill," Jack suggested.

"You getting tired?"

"No. I'd just rather be cuddling with you and having a glass of wine while sitting by the fire."

"You win."

As they strolled back, Jack took in their surroundings. "It's so nice here, especially the rolling hills against the sunset. And look at us holding hands and carrying guns with the other."

"Quite romantic," she joked.

"Just remember: don't hesitate to fire the gun. The people looking for me have no souls."

"Don't worry, Jack. I'll dazzle them with my gunslinging," she smiled.

"That's what I'm afraid of."

***

Jack got the fire going, uncorked the wine cork, and threw the salmon on the grill. The daylight turned to darkness. A full moon emerged accompanied by a vast array of stars that brightened the night sky.

Kelly joined Jack out on the patio. "What's with the big smile?" he asked.

"Oh, nothing."

"You look like the happiest person on the planet," he said softly. "What's going on?"

"I'm pregnant!" she blurted, waving the pregnancy test as if it was a flag.

"We're going to have a baby?" he asked with excitement. "I can't believe it." His eyes glistened.

"Are those tears, Jack?"

"I'm just so happy. We're going to start a family. I can't wait to play catch with the little guy."

She made a face. "Wait a minute; it could be a girl."

"A girl would be great too. I could do the same things with her. I mean I'm happy if it's a girl or boy."

"I'm just giving you a hard time, Jack," she chuckled. "You'll be a great dad."

Jack rubbed his eyes and they embraced. "I guess you won't be drinking wine with me tonight."

"Nope, I've got to watch what I eat and drink now."

Jack tended to the grill, made a salad, and served the meal.

"You sure know how to cook salmon," Kelly complimented.

"What about the salad?" he teased.

She smiled, eyes soft. "You're such a good guy, Jack. You cooked, and you brought me flowers for no reason. And you look so cute in your jeans. I'm so lucky to have found someone like you."

"No, I'm the lucky one."

***

The temperature dropped into the low forties, and they cuddled under a blanket on an oversized chair next to the open fire. They took in the maze of stars overhead while chatting about life. Sampson took his usual spot in front of them, barking when he was ignored.

"I never thought I would ever feel like this, Kelly.

I'm just so afraid it won't last. Since the day my brother slipped from my hand, I've felt I didn't deserve a good life."

"Come on, Jack; you're too hard on yourself. You were just a boy; you dismissed your father's warning – parents tend to be overprotective. You thought you were being a good brother by taking him to play hockey with a group of your friends. The ice cracked and Tommy fell in. It wasn't your fault."

"Killing those two frat guys really weighs on my conscience."

"Look, you've seen more tragedy than anybody I know. You deserve to have a good life. With me. With our child. What those frat guys did – gang-raping and murdering your sister – was despicable. They got what they had coming to them. You know there'd never have been justice for Nicole if you hadn't done what you did.

"You had lost your sister and were in a bad state of mind," Kelly said. "But those guys brought it on themselves by what they did to her."

"That's one of the things I love about you, Kelly: you try to make me feel better even though you know in your heart what I did was wrong."

"Jack, what *they* did was wrong. You just reacted to that. They paid the ultimate price and deservingly so."

He sighed. "I'm better than that, though."

"You know, back in the Wild West they would have put together a posse and caught up with those guys and hung them from a tree, and nobody would have thought twice."

He raised an eyebrow. "I didn't know you had a dark side."

"Well, when you see your sister die of an overdose and your mother fail to be a parent, you view things in a different light."

"I like your tough side."

She leaned her head against his chest. "You learn a lot from your past. Probably why I became a nurse. I like helping people in their most difficult times. It was hard watching my mother pass away from liver cancer, but she was never there for us. Partying, different men, the drugs…it wasn't a good environment. I wanted a better life, but my sister just carried on my mother's legacy. Maybe genetics played a role – who knows?"

Jack listened while stroking her hair.

"I've told you this before; I blamed my mother for my sister's overdose. I held that grudge until her final days. On her deathbed she told me how much she loved me. She admitted she was a lousy mom, and she thanked God that I had a strong will and was stubborn. It was a tough conversation with a lot of tears for both of us."

"I see her point on the stubbornness."

She playfully swatted at Jack's shoulder.

He smiled. "Well, it's true."

"I'll never understand why people withhold expressing their love." Kelly sat up and looked at Jack.

"Tell me that will never happen to us. That you'll always express whatever you're feeling. It's so important in a relationship that we talk things out, never go to bed mad, and never forget or be afraid to say I love you."

"I feel the same way."

"Even when I'm fat, old, and ugly."

"You'll still be you, and you will always be beautiful to me. Besides, I'll probably be the one fat, old, and ugly."

She laughed and held him tighter. "I'll never forget the day my mother announced we were moving. I was so excited. I really thought that all the boyfriends and the parties would go away. We would be one happy family in this new place. Except the happy place didn't last long, and when the same clowns showed up again it just broke me. It took me a long time to get through it. But when I met you, I saw someone who had love in his heart and a soul that carried a heavy burden. I saw myself when I looked at you. I knew then that we belonged together. Of course, I never expected the burden you were carrying."

"I love you so much, Kelly. You mean the world to me." He held her tightly. "I'm sorry I get these crazy thoughts of doom, but it's hard not to worry about my past. When you feel like the luckiest guy in the world, you're so afraid it's going to end."

"Jack, we have to live our life. Nobody knows we're

here. And just maybe they don't care anymore. It's been almost two years."

Jack knew better. He hadn't told Kelly everything, like about the flash drive that could have major ramifications for President Atkins. "You don't know these people; they don't forget. Look, they found me in a Vancouver hospital of all places."

"This is our home, and we've made friends here, and you play on a softball team," she said, stroking the back of his head.

"That was your idea."

"And how much fun did you have with those guys last summer?"

"You're right again," he said. But knowing the dangers that lurked in the shadows, he just could only hope that an assassin would never be sent. "Hey, if it's a girl, I get to name her. And if it's a boy, you get to name him, okay?"

She narrowed her eyes. "I don't know. Can I trust you with a girl's name?"

"You can; I already have it."

"You do? What is it?"

"Holly."

"Holly Walsh. I like it."

"Kelly Walsh sounds pretty good too."

"Jack," she smiled wide, "our bigger problem might be keeping our last name."

Chapter 3

Jeff Keller sat at the bar in a tailored gray suit and purple tie sipping a beer while waiting for his guest. During his darkest days, he discovered a cozy bar called the Willow Tavern on 19th Street NW in the heart of Washington, D.C. It was 7:30 p.m. He listened to a man playing the piano; the music was mellow, just the way he liked it. The crowd was mixed, young and old.

He had survived seven years in prison, a prison escape, his character thrown under the bus, the woman he loved turning up alive, only to be tortured with the thoughts of another woman. He had been exonerated for the murder of Laura Weston then, just as his defense team prepared to fight another battle for his freedom, the government had dropped all charges in the murder case of Aaron Greenberg. There was never a reason given. He was a free man with plenty of scars from these past ordeals that had not completely healed.

He was reinstated as a lawyer. He got his old job back at Bain, Strong, and Crosby – the top law firm in DC – with a little help from his father. But as with any good story, there was something that continued to play at Jeff's soul, and the harder he tried to resolve it, the tougher it got.

Jeff held up his empty bottle. "Drake, I'll have

another one."

The bartender placed a fresh beer in front of Jeff as a beautiful young woman, the type who was hard not to notice, walked toward the bar. She wore a short red dress that hugged every curve. She strutted her way through a few patrons then slid onto the stool next to Jeff.

Jeff sprang up, like a dog waiting for its owner. "You look great," he said, devouring her with a big hug. "Wearing a dress like that, people can't help but notice."

"I'll have a glass of merlot," she told the bartender then turned her attention to Jeff. "Are you afraid someone might notice us?"

"No! I'm sorry. I just love the dress, okay?" She looked absolutely stunning in it. He tried to look away from her gorgeous legs and make conversation. "So how was your day?"

She focused her attention on Jeff. She knew how to play on his emotions. It was a battle for his heart against an arch-rival who had the same vested interest and the looks to match.

"I did some shopping with my mother today, and you came up in the conversation."

"You told your mother about me?"

"What, I can't talk about you to my mother? What are you afraid of?"

"Nothing. Jennifer. I mean, I guess it's okay. I'm just surprised."

"Why? Because she's an expert on being the other woman?"

"I didn't mean it that way."

"You know, we meet like this, and then you come up with an excuse why you need to stay with Laura. The last time we met, what about all that passion and saying *I love you*. Did you mean it or was that just your way of getting me into bed?"

"No! No. There's a lot going on. I'm trying the best I can. It's not easy."

She frowned. "What's not easy, Jeff? Tell me. When you love someone, it's actually very easy. But I get it now: you're in love with both of us, and you can't make up your mind."

"No. I'm going to leave Laura, but it's not that easy. Just give me some slack, okay?"

"I've been waiting around for two years. You need to decide. I can't live like this anymore. I just can't. It was a real shock when you renewed your engagement to Laura. Then you start texting me, followed by walks and talks. Am I Plan B or something?"

"This is difficult," Jeff said, trying to comfort Jennifer. "Laura's been working on her book, and we're scheduled to go on Mandy Clark's show next week. After the show, I'm going to tell her about us."

"So let me get this right: you're going on the *Mandy Clark Show* and tell the world how much you're in love, and then after the show you're going to tell Laura it's over. Did I get that right?"

"You're making this extremely difficult, Jennifer."

"You know, Jeff, love is only difficult if someone makes it that way."

"Can you just give me some time to work this out?"

"I'm not going to be the other woman, that's for damn sure. I saw what my father's affairs did to us."

"I don't want you to be the other woman. Look, this isn't easy; Laura is planning a wedding. The wedding is four months away now."

She chuckled sarcastically. "You're part of it, Jeff."

"I know I am. I'm going to break it off. All I ask is that you give me some time."

"Maybe it would be better if we stop seeing each other until you break it off."

"But…"

"You're a great guy, Jeff, but I can't wait for you. Or wait for when you have an argument with Laura and call me up for some comfort."

"I think of you all the time, Jennifer. I can't get you out of my head."

"Well, I'm here. Just tell Laura the truth. If you can't do that, then the answer is simple."

Jeff leaned back and exhaled. "I do love you, Jennifer."

"Do you love Laura?"

Jack's mind went blank. He was confused and hesitated.

"Just what I thought."

"It's not like that. This is hard. There's so much history between her and me. And, on top of that, you have no idea what she endured while held captive all those years in Mexico. Abandoning her wouldn't be right."

"You're either in love with her or you're not," she stung back at him. "You know, when you figure it out, give me a call; otherwise, it might be better that we both move on." She got up from the stool.

"Jennifer, just wait; come on," he pleaded, grabbing her hand.

She frowned and pulled away, leaving in a huff.

Jeff hunched over the bar, dejected. "I need a shot of something, Drake."

Drake placed a shot of whiskey in front of him. "What happened?"

"It's complicated."

"Two women, huh?"

A patron next to Jack said, "I couldn't help but overhear. Tough dilemma."

"Yeah," Jeff said, turning away.

"Hey, you're that guy who was framed for killing your girlfriend. And she was being held by some cartel."

"I really don't want to talk about it."

"I mean, seven years in prison," the man continued. "And now you're seeing two women. You dog, making up for lost time. You don't get those years back. So, who do you think did it?"

"I don't know."

"Oh, come on, you must have an opinion."

"I really don't."

"I guess I'm going to have to watch the *Mandy Clark Show* next week to find out, right?"

"I don't want to talk, okay? I'm sorry."

"I understand. I got to be going anyway. But before I leave, Jeff, I have a message."

"Who the hell are you?" he asked, his blood pressure rising and his heart getting tight.

The stranger got off his stool. "You're a smart guy, Jeff. Just make sure you say nothing political or about any politician on the *Mandy Clark Show*. You know what I mean."

Jeff's face went pale and his heart pounded faster.

"Now, your fiancée, Laura Weston, has a book coming out. Just make sure she says nothing to implicate anyone. You know what I mean, Jeff. Oh, let me show you something." He pulled out his phone. "I got to tell you; this is a great picture of you and your girlfriend. Don't you think?"

Jeff could feel his insides rising and downed the shot. "What do you want?"

"You just keep your mouth shut. You don't want to see me again. You understand what I'm saying to you?"

"Yeah, I do," he said with a lump in his throat.

The stranger's eyes were piercing. "Good. I think you

need another drink. It's on me. Remember, don't screw this up." He patted Jeff on the back and threw a twenty-dollar bill on the counter. After signaling the bartender to get Jeff another shot, the man walked out.

"Here's your whiskey," Drake said. "Who the hell was that?"

Jeff gulped the shot down. "A hitman."

Drake laughed, but Jeff didn't crack a smile.

***

Jeff's car pulled into the Blue Sky condominiums in McLean, Virginia, at 10:30 that night. He spent an extra fifteen minutes driving around the complex looking in the rearview window. Laura was already under the covers when he finally got into their condo. He was late and didn't want to argue. Trying to juggle two women was getting to him. He knew he was drinking more than he should.

It had been a long day, but the idea that the past had been left behind was a false premise. Those people weren't done with them. He was still on their radar, and so was Laura. Jeff sat in the living room staring at the ceiling, tired, and afraid to face Laura. He couldn't help but think how people were watching them, analyzing their every move, reading every keystroke, and hearing every conversation. Nothing was safe.

He went around the condo, nervously looking out the windows for any strange cars or sinister objects in the sky. After a trip to the bathroom, he tiptoed into the bedroom, slid under the covers, and rolled onto his side, facing away from Laura.

After a few moments she asked, "Where've you been? Why are you so late?"

He exhaled. "I went over to the Willow for a few drinks."

"You don't need to be drinking during the week. Who were you with?"

"Just myself," he lied, turning to face her. "I forgot how much fun it is to burn the midnight oil at the firm. My heart doesn't seem to be quite into it. I wonder why?"

"Don't put this on me," she said. "Don't blame me for all that happened. You were never there when we were engaged – like now."

"I don't want to argue, Laura. I had a busy day. I just needed to blow off steam, okay? That's it."

"You know, I wouldn't be mad, but lately you seem like you're not really here. Tonight you came home, and you don't even roll over and cuddle me."

"I didn't want to wake you up."

"Most guys would be all over me, sleeping or not. Not you. Is it that you don't find me attractive or something? You getting cold feet? Talk to me. What's going on?"

"I have a lot of work on my plate. We're getting married. There's just a lot of stuff to digest. We have that stupid show next week."

"I feel like you're checking out on me. Nobody said you had to marry me. Hell, I survived seven years in the damn jungle. If you don't want to marry me, I think I'll survive. You don't owe me anything, Jeff. Please, don't do me any favors."

"Laura, I love you, but it's taken a lot of work to get us here."

"What are you looking for from me? What?"

"I don't want to argue anymore. I'm tired."

"You were once the sweetest guy," she said, shaking her head. "I remember when we would talk all night and watch the sunrise and then fall asleep in each other's arms. I felt so much in love, and now I just don't know. Maybe we have been through so much that it's impossible to forget the past."

Jeff felt a shadow of sadness cast over him, and his eyes watered. Laura always had a way of putting things into perspective. Even when they were apart, they were in some strange way together. "I'm sorry, Laura."

"If you are going to continue to rehash the past, and blame me for the seven years you lost, we can never move forward. This has been a problem for a while."

"Laura, I'm sorry," he repeated, his voice soft. "You're right. I have to get past this. I know that. I need to tell you something though."

"What?"

"I think we're being watched."

"You do?"

"Yeah. I was sitting at the bar and this stranger came up to me tonight. He kind of threatened my life in a roundabout way."

Laura eyes widened "Who was he?"

"I've never seen the guy in my life, but he knew me. He told me to keep my mouth shut and to make sure the book didn't incriminate any political figures. He was a scary bastard."

Laura sighed. "After what we've been through, why would we think it would all go away? So, we go on the show and just talk about general stuff."

"Yeah, I get that. But what about the book?"

She chuckled. "I hate these people; they think they can just control you. Jeff, these people took seven years of our lives. It's not all about money, but if I add President Atkins in the book, that's the difference between a best seller or a book collecting dust."

"These people are capable of killing us, and they are never going to let you publish that book if you mention President Atkins. They killed Aaron Greenburg because he knew you were alive. They kidnapped you and brought you to Mexico, and they framed me. These people can get to anyone they want."

She exhaled and covered her face. "Why is this so difficult? I have a blank chapter all about President Atkins, but I have yet to write it."

"Maybe you can spin it another way to leave him out."

31

"I hate that man."

"I hate him too."

She exhaled slowly. "I never told you this, but he visited me when I was in Mexico at Moreno's ocean villa."

"He did?" Jeff's disbelief quickly turned suspicious. "You didn't have sex with him. Did you?"

She didn't answer.

Her silence was a gut punch. "Oh my God."

"I didn't enjoy it. I did it to survive. That's all."

"I can't believe you had sex with him," his voice quivered.

"I had to do it to survive," she repeated in frustration. "It meant nothing. I love you. I know I've made a lot of mistakes and hurt a lot of people, but I'm a better person now."

"Are there any other secrets I don't know about?"

"No, and don't turn this around like I'm the bad guy. You're the one whose mind seems to be in other places."

Jeff moved to the other side of the bed. "I have to get some sleep," he said, ending the discussion. But he was tormented by thoughts of what the future had in store.

Chapter 4

Jennifer woke with a pain in her gut and a pervasive uneasiness. She put it off to the previous night's seafood or nerves from her troubling relationship with Jeff.

She went into the bathroom and stared in the mirror. She wasn't going to be the other woman anymore. It was tearing her apart from the inside out. He consumed her thoughts night and day. She couldn't live like this and every time she saw him it was like throwing kerosene on a fire. She was better than this. He had to make a decision. It was either Laura or her. No more excuses.

She wanted to be loved and not constantly fighting for it. She didn't need to wear a sexy dress to be loved. That wasn't how love worked. Love was two people just caring about each other no matter what, not competing for their affection. She was tired of always feeling like she needed to look her best to win him over. If they had a small disagreement, it wasn't the end of the world. She just wanted to do the simple things and enjoy each other's company. She dreamed of being like a normal couple, staying up all night and chatting about life and laughing at the stupidest stuff.

And then it hit her: love should be simple, not exhausting.

Her stomach erupted like an earthquake, and she

leaned over the toilet, heaving her insides. When she finished, she flushed and sat on the cover, hoping it was over. Then a thought popped into her head: her period was late. She got up and rummaged through the vanity drawer and found a pregnancy test kit. After following the directions, she wandered to the kitchen for some water while waiting for the results. The three minutes seemed like hours. She returned to the bathroom and picked up the stick.

Jennifer stared at the results, her mind numb. She was pregnant.

***

The sky was overcast later that morning when Jennifer requested permission to enter the White House grounds.

"Name?" asked the security guard.

"Jennifer Atkins."

After a few phone calls, the president's daughter was greeted by one of her mother's aides and escorted inside the White House to a room between the East and West Wing. When Jennifer's mother entered, they embraced.

"How's my girl doing?" her mom asked.

"I'm okay. What a place you've got here." Jennifer couldn't quite believe she was there; she'd sworn she would never step foot in the White House.

"It's nice, but I prefer the quietness of Washington State. It's like walking into Grand Central Station sometimes around here." She sat on the couch and pulled her daughter down beside her. "So, what's wrong? I can always tell when there's something on your mind. Is it that guy, Jeff?"

"Kind of."

"Okay; so what's going on?"

"Mom, I don't know what to do? Love shouldn't be this hard."

"I'm obviously not the expert on love, Jennifer. Your father and I just play roles now; love went out the window a long time ago."

"That's why I want to get it right the first time."

Her mother's expression was melancholy. "Not everyone finds love. Oh, you think you're in love with the passion and all, but it's a marathon, not a sprint. Those still holding hands in their old age are the winners. Sometimes the charmers aren't so charming."

"I see your point, Mom."

"At least you're smiling."

"I need to get closure one way or the other, but this just got a little more complicated."

Her mother's expression was pained. "Jennifer, you're not pregnant, are you?"

"Yeah, I am."

"How is he going to feel about this?"

"I really don't know. I mean if he loves me, maybe this will bring us closer."

"I wouldn't count on that. Men have a way of running away when they feel cornered."

Jennifer sat back, frustrated. "Why can't I just find a normal guy who just loves me for me? Why do I get myself into these things?"

"Maybe because you're an Atkins. I don't know."

"I'm nothing like Dad. I actually want to be loved. I'm just tired."

"Are you going to tell him?"

"Oh, yeah. I'm meeting him for lunch today."

"Well, good luck, but I'm here for you, Jennifer, no matter how it turns out. You'll find your Prince Charming, whoever it might be."

The door opened and Jennifer's father appeared.

Jennifer stood. "I'm sorry, Mr. President; I was just leaving."

"You must want something, otherwise, why would you be here?" Sam said with a smirk. "Since you're living off Grandma's trust, it can't be money."

"Something you can't control, right, Dad?"

"So why are you here?"

"You really want to know? I needed to talk to Mom about being pregnant."

That wiped the arrogant smile off his face. "You're pregnant? Who's the father?"

"Like you really care."

"I'm just curious what deadbeat you hooked up with."

"Nice, Dad. You've always been so comforting. The father is the guy who spent seven years in prison because you framed him. Ring any bells?"

Sam's jaw clenched. "Get the hell out of here before I have security throw you out."

Jennifer's mom jumped to her feet. "Stop it, Sam!"

"Thanks for the advice, Mom," Jennifer said softly, giving her a hug. As she walked past her father, she said: "It's always such a pleasure to see you."

***

The small café on 14th Street was filled with politicians feasting on their power lunches. The post-and-beam rafters and large windows gave the place a quaint, cozy ambiance. Keeping a low profile, Jeff found a corner table. He looked around at the other patrons and focused on the couples, watching them banter back and forth. They all seemed happy; he wondered if they were in love.

Trying to balance two women was tearing him apart. It was affecting his work. Laura was getting suspicious. He wondered if Jennifer was going to finally put her foot down; he wasn't ready for that.

When Jennifer walked in, he waved her over. "Wow, you look good."

She fluffed her hair. "You never lack for compliments," she said with a hint of sarcasm.

He frowned.

She took a seat. "My mother told me to watch out for the charmers; they end up not being so charming. And she should know."

"What does that mean?"

"I don't know yet what category you fall in."

Jeff apologized for their last argument. "I don't know what I'm doing anymore. Sometimes I just want to run away and forget it all. I don't like who I've become."

Jennifer nodded slowly and sighed. "I can't do this anymore. I want to find love before I miss it. Love is not a sprint, Jeff; it's a marathon. I don't know if you are really ready to commit to anyone."

"Look, I'm trying; it's hard. I know what you want, and I'm working to do that."

"I need more; I need a commitment. I don't know if you can do that. And maybe I'm not fair by pressuring you. But I've given this a lot of thought, and you need to figure it out." She stood up. "I'm done with the excuses."

"Where you going?"

"To the ladies' room."

Jeff couldn't keep his eyes off her tight jeans as she maneuvered in between the tables. A few minutes later, she came back with a smile.

Jeff wasn't in the mood for food and sipped on a cup of coffee. The waitress said she'd be right back.

"I wanted to talk to you about a few things," she said. "First, I'm not angry. I don't think I've been fair to myself."

"I understand."

"No, I don't think you really do, Jeff."

"Hey, we have fun together. You're on my mind so much. We have good chats, and the sex is great, right?"

She shook her head. "Do you look at me like the fun girl or something more? What are your plans for the future? Is it a normal life with a family or do you see yourself sitting under a beach umbrella on some exotic island, sipping on gin cocktails?"

"Well, I lost basically nine years of my life. I want to have a little fun, make up for lost time. I didn't know you had a problem with that. You talked about traveling and all. What's changed?"

She ignored the question. "From what you told me about Laura's frustration with you, I can now see why. You're stuck."

"What do you mean?"

"You're not growing as a person."

"Where is all this coming from? You've never talked about this stuff before. I thought you wanted to travel and see the world."

"I guess I was just thinking in the moment."

"Whatever. Instead of just considering yourself, have you thought about what I've been through? Nobody knows how it feels to rot in prison for something you never did then have to defend yourself in court again. It affects you, okay?"

"Okay. You've never talked about this before."

"For a long time it's felt like I've been living in a fish bowl, trying to make everybody happy except myself. I was supposed to just get back on the horse like nothing happened, resume the old work rut. When I saw you, I felt alive again. You weren't telling me what I needed to do, asking what time I had to be home, asking where I was?"

"So I'm basically the other woman who's giving you temporary relief from your own deeper issues?"

"Women are so complicated."

"It looks like I'm the good cop, and Laura's the bad cop."

Jeff exhaled. "No. I'm just trying to sort it out."

"Jeff, I'm trying to understand, but let's say you leave Laura; how long will it be before you want out from me?"

Jeff paused, his expression sulky. "You never cared about this stuff before. There's a lot going on, and I'm pretty confused. I can't guarantee anybody anything. I'm sorry."

"That's my fear."

He held his hands out, palms up, and leaned back. "I am who I am."

"Fair enough."

The waitress came back, and Jennifer ordered a bowl of chicken soup, even though she didn't feel like eating. After the server walked away, Jennifer took a deep breath.

"There's something else I needed to talk to you about."

"What?"

"I'm pregnant."

Jeff's mind went momentarily blank as he struggled to comprehend. Finally he said, "Wow; I didn't see this coming."

"We're going to have a baby, Jeff. What are you feeling? Love? Anger? Does it make you want to run away? You told me you loved me, or was that just in the moment?"

"I have to go the bathroom."

Jeff bolted from the table. Once in the bathroom he ran to a stall and heaved. When there was nothing left, he leaned against the stall door. His body was covered in sweat and tears formed in his eyes. Time was up. He had to come clean with Laura. He wasn't sure what to do. He needed to go somewhere and clear his mind.

There was no way he could focus on work right now. He took out his phone and called his boss to say he felt sick – not a lie – and was going home. Then he went to the sink and splashed water on his face. He looked in the mirror and stood straight as he gathered his composure. He organized his tie and then walked out.

"I wasn't sure you were coming back," Jennifer said.

"I need some time to digest this."

"I understand. How do you think I feel? But things happen for a reason."

He smiled, but his mind was in another place. He felt cornered. He imagined Laura's ire, the hitman who was watching his every move, and how his parents would react to him canceling the wedding. He even resented the pressure of meeting his job deadlines. All he wanted was to find happiness, but he was more miserable than ever. He wanted to run away.

"Did you hear a word I just said, Jeff?"

He looked up, momentarily confused because Jennifer had sounded just like Laura. "I did. You said your mother was cool about it. Does your father know?"

"Yeah, he knows." She paused. "And he knows you're the father."

"Great," Jeff muttered, closing his eyes. "He'll probably have me killed now, Jennifer."

"That's not funny."

"I'm not joking."

***

A two-headed monster was chasing them. Jeff held both Laura's and Jennifer's hands as they ran for their lives, only to come to an edge of a cliff.

He woke abruptly from the nightmare, his T-shirt soaked with sweat. He looked over at Laura; she didn't stir.

It was 6:00 a.m. He got up and went into the bathroom to throw cold water on his face, wondering how he was going to hold it all together. He wasn't ready to be picking up his clothes out in the parking lot. He hopped into the shower and let the water bounce off his back while staring, deep in thought, at the wall.

Hearing the shower, Laura turned to her side and grabbed Jeff's phone off the nightstand. It was unlocked. She browsed through his texts and came across a series of exchanges that clearly confirmed an affair. She grabbed a pen and scribbled down the number. When the shower water stopped, she locked the phone and replaced it then rolled back over, feigning sleep.

When Jeff entered the bedroom and saw his phone, he panicked. But Laura was still asleep, and he was relieved to see he had remembered to lock the phone. The last thing he needed was Laura ransacking through his phone before he figured out his next moves.

Chapter 5

The light from the rising sun brightened the room and Jack's eyes opened. He looked over at Kelly, grateful his world was still in place.

Kelly stirred and draped her arm across Jack's chest, snuggling up against him.

"Okay, what are you thinking about?" she asked.

He smiled. "You always know when I'm thinking."

"That's pretty easy, Jack. You're always thinking."

"Well, I was just thinking about my mom. A few years after my brother's death, I was sitting down talking with my mom, and I began sobbing uncontrollably. I just couldn't stop. My father had left us emotionally, but my mom was the rock. I remembered her comforting smile, assuring me it would all work out. She told me to stop blaming myself, that things happen for a reason. *You take this experience, and you turn it into something positive, or you'll just wallow in depression, which will eventually lead to a broken life.*"

His eyes tearing, Jack turned his head toward Kelly. "Just that little talk made me want to do something bigger, so I joined the Navy. I'll admit I was still consumed by the aftereffects of my brother's death. But I took all that negative energy and turned it into something positive."

"Your mother was right. Look at all the lives you saved. That would have never happened if you hadn't become a SEAL."

"True. But of those six guys I saved, only one is still alive today. You begin to wonder what's it all about."

"Jack, you have to let go of the past if you want to move forward. That's what your mother was trying to tell you."

He smiled. "I love you."

"I love you too, Jack," she said with a slight chuckle.

"What's funny?"

"You. They all think you're this psycho killer and they need an army to stop you. Little do they know you're really a sensitive guy with feelings. Maybe even a little wimpy."

He laughed. "I'll show you a little wimpy."

He started tickling her all over, and she surrendered quickly.

"Okay, okay...I'll take back the wimpy," she pleaded.

They embraced each other, and when their laughed faded, she brushed his hair back. "I'm going to make you forget your past, Jack."

"You've already started." He rubbed her stomach and gazed into her kind eyes. "How's the little guy doing?"

She just smiled and nodded.

He kissed her. "I need to get up and head over to the

45

hardware store. I think it's time we build Sampson a doghouse. Clay said he'd give me a good deal."

"How is Clay?"

"The guy is always happy."

"Well, tell him I said hi."

"I will."

"While you're taking a shower, I'll cook you up a nice breakfast."

"You don't have to do that."

"I want to. You're always cooking dinner and bringing me home flowers."

"That's my sensitive side."

"I know, and I like it."

***

After breakfast, Jack and Kelly embraced at the front door, then he got into his black Acura TL. As the car rolled out of the driveway, Kelly waved with Sampson by her side, and Jack smiled back.

A mile away from Jack's home, two cars were parked off to the side of the road along a line of tall hemlocks. Two men standing out of sight observed Jack's car pass. They walked over to the second car where four men sat waiting.

"Bolton just drove by. So I guess we can now drive to his home and wait for Oz."

"There's been a little change in plans," Keith, the driver, said. "We're tracking Bolton's vehicle, so we know where he's going. But I don't want to be part of killing the girl. That's not what I signed up for."

"Oz said we have to wait at the house."

"I want you to get something straight. I don't take orders from Oz. I'm not sure why the hell you guys are here. I'll take out Bolton, and I don't like doing that. But if that's what they want, that's what I'll do, but on my terms. You got that? I'll let you know how it goes."

Keith pulled the car out onto the roadway and sped off. The other two men drove to within a hundred yards of the house and pulled to the side of the road. A few minutes later Oz drove up and parked behind them. He walked slowly to the waiting car with two additional men in tow.

"Where's the rest of them?" he asked, his voice menacing.

"They followed Bolton's car. They said they would take care of him in town."

Oz slammed his fist on the hood. *Americans, they always marched to their own frigging drummer*. "I shouldn't be surprised by this, I guess."

"Keith said they didn't want to be part of killing the girl."

Oz showed little emotion as he focused on the house.

"What do we do?" the associate asked. "The girl is the only one in the house."

"We wait," Oz said.

Jack's car pulled into the parking lot at Bobwick's Hardware. The sky was a crystal-clear blue, perfect sweatshirt weather, and he felt at peace for the first time in a long time. Kelly expecting a baby was a gift. He had settled into a normal life; the people here were so nice. He was almost two years removed from the madness, and his mind was slowly recovering from the past atrocities. He was in love. He deserved it after all those years of heartache. His mother had always been right to forget the past, and Kelly was sure to enforce it going forward. But he still heard a faint echo of his commanding officer warning him: *There's a bullet behind every corner*.

He walked into the store, and as usual good old Clay was manning the cash register. The guy never missed a day and always wore a smile. The hardware store had been passed from generation to generation.

"Hey, Jack, how've you been?"

"Great. Kelly's pregnant."

"Congrats!"

"Thanks."

"Hey, are you interested in playing hockey in a men's league? It'll be a lot of the same guys that play softball."

Jack smiled. "I haven't played hockey since I was a little kid, but that sounds like fun. I think I'd like to play. It'd be good for me."

"That would be great. So, what brings you in today?"

"Well, before I get working on fixing up a room for the nursery, I figured I should finally get around to building that dog house I've been talking about."

Clay chuckled and leaned against the counter. "About time. I have everything you need for the dog house over in aisle four."

Jack grab a cart, did his shopping for Sampson, then checked out.

Clay rang up the items and handed Jack his receipt. "The guys are all getting together on Friday night and going out to the Silver Tavern. Why don't you join us?"

Jack thought about it. Kelly would like him being more social and putting down roots. He nodded. "Thanks. I think I will."

"Good. I'll see you then. Around seven."

Jack walked out of the store. His mind was at ease, thinking his life was finally all coming together.

From down the street the assassins watched Jack as he crossed the parking lot.

Keith made a call. "We got him."

***

Oz and his crew were waiting by Jack's house when Keith called. One of the team answered, listened, then hung up.

"They got him."

Oz shook his head in frustration; this wasn't how he had planned for the operation to go down. "Last I work with these guys," he muttered, then told his men, "Let's finish this. The big, bad Jack Bolton…not so much."

He instructed one of his men, Markus, to go around the back. Two of the team went with him, and Adel stayed back at the car. Oz marched up the steps with an air of overconfidence and knocked on the door.

"Hey Jack; it's your buddy, Oz," he said with gusto, his men smiled in the background.

Kelly heard the knock and digested the voice. Her body shook. Her heart pumped faster. Her senses elevated, which caused a wave of adrenaline to kick in. As much as she wanted to believe it was just a few of Jack's friends, she remembered Jack's words: *Nobody knows I'm here.*

Kelly had always assured Jack she was never worried about his past, but that was just a ruse to calm his nerves. She grabbed the Glock 17 from the drawer. She was now comfortable with a gun and not afraid to use it. She was accustomed to the life of hard knocks; it was part of her DNA. She was a fighter, not the type to run the other way at the first sign of trouble. She was going to confront the threat head-on. She would let them in and assess the threat. Her decision making would be the difference between life and death – for both her and her baby.

"The door is unlocked; come on in," she yelled in a friendly voice.

Oz turned the knob, smiled slyly back at his cohorts, and walked in followed by his two wingmen. They stood in the foyer as Kelly looked down from halfway up the stairs. Oz scanned the inside of the house, getting ready to pounce. He thought a little small talk wouldn't hurt before reality struck.

"Where's Jack?" he asked with a fake smile, already knowing the answer.

Kelly immediately picked up on the men's body language, which gave away their true intentions. Sirens sounded in her head as her instinct made the decision easy. Without warning, Kelly calmly raised her gun and started firing, catching the assassins flat-footed. While they dove for cover, Kelly ran upstairs.

Hearing the shots, the gunman from the car ran to the house. He found one of the team dead, one standing looking dazed, and Oz bleeding from a leg wound, swearing angrily.

Oz ripped off his sweatshirt and used it as a makeshift tourniquet then yelled at his two cohorts, "Go find her!"

The men cautiously climbed the stairs, firing shots as they went. Oz slowly followed them, dragging his injured leg. The lead gunmen searched the second floor while Oz wobbled at the top of stairs. There was no sign of Kelly. Then Oz spotted an open window in the bathroom.

A gunshot came from outside, followed by a dog yelping. He limped over to the bathroom window and saw their target running.

He yelled, "Go get me the sniper rifle now!"

Adel sprinted to the car, grabbed the sniper rifle from the trunk, and sprinted back. Before going back in he saw Markus staggering around the side of the house, soaked in blood. But there was no time to stop and help him. Adel ran up the stairs and handed the rifle to Oz, who set the rifle on the bathroom sill.

Kelly ran steadily, not looking back. She estimated she was maybe just ten yards away from safety.

Taking several deep breaths to calm himself, he looked through the scope, lining up the shot. Ignoring the throbbing pain in his leg, Oz exhaled then squeezed the trigger.

Kelly felt a piercing pain rip through her body. She staggered forward a few more strides then dropped to the ground.

Oz watched as his shot hit the target. "How about that? Now that was one hell of a shot from more than a hundred yards away."

"Should we make sure she's dead?" Adel asked.

Oz smiled at his two associates. "Adel, you ever shoot a deer?"

"No."

"Well, a deer hears the shot and runs. The deer doesn't realize it's been hit. Its instincts are to run, and it does, but it doesn't get too far. It eventually drops from the shot. It just bleeds out. So, my point is, if she's still alive, she'll just bleed out. I need to get medical attention. We don't have time to observe our work. Let's go."

On their way out, they picked up their dead partner lying at the base of the stairs and placed him in the trunk.

Markus sat by the car holding a large blood-soaked bandage against his neck. He looked weak and pale.

"You don't look good," Oz said, stating the obvious. "Adel, you drive Markus. Berg will drive me in the other car. Get me back to the nearest hospital, and we'll meet you there."

"What about the other guys?" Adel asked.

"I'm not worried about the other guys unless they screwed up. You told me they got Bolton."

"That's what Keith said."

"I'll call him to confirm, but I need to get this wound treated."

The two cars sped off, leaving the destruction behind. Oz pressed a few buttons on the phone, but Keith didn't answer. He slammed his fist down on the dashboard.

"This is the last time I work with those guys."

Oz pressed a few more buttons.

When Eric Steele answered, he asked, "Is Bolton dead?"

Oz wasn't sure. He always wanted to see a body, but this time he had to wing it. "Yeah, we got him."

"This is good news. Sanderlin and the president will be very happy." Eric didn't care how it was done, just that the problem had been eliminated. "You'll be paid very well for your efforts, Oz. Do you need anything?"

"A couple of us need medical attention immediately. We're heading to Maple Community Hospital. The police will start asking questions; we need some cover as to who we are, or they might hold us."

Eric leaned back in his chair. "I'll take care of it. Get the medical care you need. I'll have people up there as soon as possible."

***

Jack had been ambushed as he crossed the parking lot. Bullets were fired. Pedestrians took cover. Eyewitnesses watched the firefight in disbelief, shocked this could happen in their quaint little town. Jack had crawled to his car, miraculously suffering only a flesh wound. He opened the passenger door in a crouched position, reached underneath the driver's seat, and pulled out a loaded Glock 17. He pulled the trigger just in time as one of the henchmen rushed in to finish the job. The assassin dropped by his feet as another rushed him, firing away. Using the door as cover, Jack exchanged fire. The second assassin slumped against the door. He pointed the gun at a third man and pulled the trigger. The gun just clicked, out of ammunition.

The third hitman smiled. "You can do better than that, Jack."

He grabbed Jack and started bashing his head against the side of the car, stopping when Keith walked up. Jack sat propped up against the car – groggy, beaten, and with no way to escape.

When the shooting started, Clay had grabbed the shotgun he kept behind the counter and made his way out of the store. His adrenaline kicking in, he advanced as if he was hunting big game, crouching down and moving forward from car to car until he was two cars away from Jack's. He could hear his heart pumping, and his throat was parched. He heard someone walking up and lifted his head to see who.

Keith pointed his semiautomatic at Jack's head. "Looks like you've run out of luck. I wasn't a big fan of this assignment. I'm just doing what they tell me. I'm sorry, but orders are orders. This is what we do. If it wasn't me, it would have been someone else. Goodbye, Jack."

Before Keith could pull the trigger, Clay sprung up and fired, hitting Keith square in the back. When the other assassin started to lift his weapon, Clay fired again, striking him in the chest.

He rushed over to Jack. "Are you okay?"

"I'm fine."

The adrenaline wearing off and shock setting in, Clay reached to help Jack up with trembling hands. "Who the hell are these guys?"

Jack ignored the question. "Listen to me. When the police get here, can you do me a favor and just stall them a little bit by not giving them my name right away?"

Clay frowned. "Who are you really?"

"It's a long story, but I have to get home."

"The police will be here any minute. I think it would be wise to stay."

"I'm sorry, Clay, but Kelly could be in danger. I've

got to go." He gripped Clay's hand then hugged him. "Thanks for saving my life."

Jack picked up his gun from the pavement, got in the car, and roared out of the parking lot while dialing Kelly's phone. It just rang,

"Come on, Kelly; pick up, damn it."

He floored the accelerator, but the minutes felt like hours. He couldn't get home soon enough.

Chapter 6

Jack's car came to a screeching halt in the driveway. He pushed a fresh seventeen-round magazine clip into the Glock and hopped out of the car. He opened the front door, saw the pool of blood on the floor and yelled Kelly's name over and over as he went room to room. Tears flowed down his cheeks, and it felt like his heart would explode.

His shirt sleeve was soaked with blood, and he had several lumps on his head, but his fear and anguish over Kelly made him oblivious to any physical pain. When he got to the second floor, he peered out the bathroom window and, in the distance, saw what looked like a body. His bowels turning to ice, he galloped down the stairs and out the door. His heart clenched when he saw Sampson's still body, but he didn't stop running until he found Kelly on the ground.

Choking on tears, he screamed her name in a voice he didn't recognize, the pain in his chest excruciating. He knelt down and checked her pulse; she was still alive. Blood was oozing from her wound; he had to get her to hospital. He dialed 911.

"Please, I need help at 6 Conway Drive. My girlfriend has a weak pulse. She's been shot."

Her eyes opened, and he dropped the phone, cradling

her in his arms.

Her voice was low and weak. "Jack, I knew you would come back. I prayed that I could hang on until you got here."

"I'm so sorry, Kelly. This is all my fault. I love you so much." He choked out the words, his anguish making it hard to breathe. His tears dripped on her face, mingling with her own.

"I'm not going to make it, Jack," she wheezed, her breathing getting heavier. "Just know I love you. I always will."

"Kelly, just hold on. The ambulance will be here any minute. Please, hang on."

"I got them, just like you told me. I'm a pretty good shot, you know."

"I know you are. I know."

"We would have been a really good team."

"The best."

"Sampson got one of them." She coughed, spattering blood on her lips. "I'm so cold. Hold me. Don't let go of me, Jack. I love you so much."

"I love you so much. I'm here. I'm never letting go. You hold on, Kelly. You have to hold on. Please. Please."

He watched as she took one last labored breath, then went limp and silent. She was gone, and something broke deep inside him. He looked up into the pure blue sky and wailed. He continued to hold her tightly while rocking back and forth.

They had taken everything from him. There was nothing left. His last chance of finding true love and a normal life was gone forever. He didn't know what to do. Where to go. A thought formed to just end it. Make all the pain go away. There had to be a better world. But like the times before, he couldn't give in to these monsters. He had to make them feel his pain. And he was in hell.

He gently laid Kelly on the ground and closed her eyes. She looked peaceful. He stood up, still unable to stop crying, and took a deep breath. He knew he had to go; there was no time to stay and grieve. He knelt back down and softly kissed her cheek. As he walked away, his anguish turned to fury. He ran to the house and went down to the cellar. He opened an old trunk he had hoped to never need again.

He took out guns, money, and documents, then hurriedly tossed the items into a duffle bag. He raced upstairs to the bedroom and added some clothes. On his way out he stopped in the kitchen and used the rest of the space for food. He was tossing the duffle into the backseat when the ambulance arrived. The police had yet to show.

Two paramedics got out of the vehicle with black bags. "We got a call that someone has been shot."

Jack look at them with no emotion. "You're too late. She's dead."

"Where is she?"

He pointed. "About a hundred yards that way."

One EMT rushed off while the other hesitated and asked Jack to accompany him to the body.

"I can't. She's about a hundred yards from the house."

The EMT was getting suspicious. "It would be a big help if you went with us."

"There's no point."

"Well, she might be still alive."

"She's not. You go ahead and do what you do."

"Well, the police will be here any moment, so don't go anywhere. They'll want to ask you some questions." The paramedic then turned and quickly ran to join his partner.

Jack watched then got into his car and sped off, not sure where to go. He headed north and drove for fifteen minutes then pulled off to the side of the road. The sun was beaming into the car, but all he saw was darkness. He jumped out of the car, walked about ten feet, and leaped over a low railing, then heaved out his guts. His last breakfast with Kelly was now on the side of the road.

He went back to the car and just sat there staring at an endless road in front of him as dark clouds gathered in the horizon. Tears started to flow again. He was full of rage, yet a sense of calm came over him. He noticed Kelly's ID dangling from the mirror. He took it off and stared at it. Kelly said she had shot them. He grabbed his phone and called the hospital.

"Hi, I'm looking for Adam Fink; he works in the emergency room," he explained to the operator. She connector him.

"Hey, Adam, it's Jack."

"Hey, Jack. You looking for Kelly?"

"No. I was just wondering if it's busy there. I'm thinking of coming in. I'm not feeling well."

"Yeah, you don't sound good. But actually it's kind of crazy here at the moment."

"Yeah? What's going on?"

"Some guy came in with a gunshot wound in his leg. Says it was a hunting accident. But he and his friends sure don't look like hunters."

"What do you mean?"

"They look like military types. Something's sketchy."

"Really. How many?"

"There's three of them. But the one with the serious leg wound is going into surgery now, so maybe it won't be too bad coming over now. Hey, did you hear the news about that shootout down at Bobwick's Hardware Store?"

"No."

"I would have bet these guys had something to do with it, but the EMTs told us there were no survivors. But my gut still tells me these guys could be involved somehow."

"Crazy morning here in Maple Creek. I thought this was a quiet town."

"I did too."

"Okay; I'll see you in a bit."

Looking straight ahead, Jack punched the gas pedal making the car jump. The tires squealed, and pebbles kicked up; he turned around and headed back into the fire. He had done this for most of his life on the battlefield. Rage pulsed through his veins. They were going to pay the ultimate price.

He banged a right into the Maple Community Hospital parking lot and maneuvered the car next to a side exit. He knew the layout of the hospital from Kelly giving him an unauthorized tour. They had talked about what she would do if a criminal ever entered the building with bad intentions. He knew the plan, except it was for Kelly, not him.

He made a final check of his gun and hustled out of the car. He walked briskly into the emergency room and saw Adam at the desk. He paused and scanned the area of people in the waiting room

"Hey, Jack, you need to sign in over here," Adam said with a smile.

"I'll be right there," Jack said, zeroing in on the enemy. "I see someone I know."

As Jack walked toward two men in the waiting area, he calmly pulled out his Glock 17. When they saw him coming, they reached inside their jackets. Jack's instincts kicked in, and he fired with precision, double tapping the first squarely in the chest. The second man stood up and got off a few wild shots that missed before Jack killed him with one accurate shot to the head.

People were screaming as they scrambled to get out of harm's way. Adam stared in shock and disbelief then ducked behind the counter. A security guard came running down the corridor with his gun drawn and shouted for Jack to put the gun down.

In Jack's mind he was back on the battlefield, and the mission wasn't complete. He shot the guard in the leg, dropping him to the floor writhing in pain. Jack walked up and stood over him.

"Put your gun on the floor if you want to live."

The guard set his weapon down, and Jack kicked the gun away. He handcuffed the guard to a railing. "I'm sorry," he said. "They'll be a surgery room available shortly."

Adam got up the courage and blurted out from behind the desk. "What are you doing, Jack?"

Jack faced Adam. "I'm sorry about this; these men were assassins. They killed Kelly. They got what they deserved."

"Kelly's dead?" Adam tried to comprehend the situation but couldn't.

Jack turned and strode down the corridor toward the surgery area, swiping Kelly's security card, which swung the electronic doors open. He walked briskly down the corridor, peeking into each operating room as he went. He came to the last one, looked through the door window, then barged in.

The surgeon barked, "What are you doing here?"

Jack raised his gun. "Surgery is over; step away."

The nurses and surgeon backed off. Oz was under a spinal block, preventing him from moving. He could only watch as Jack walked over to him.

"You know who I am," Jack said.

Oz stared back with intense eyes. "So they didn't kill you."

"No, but they're all dead. Are you the one who pulled the trigger that killed my girlfriend?"

Oz's steel-cold eyes lacked any empathy. "I enjoyed it, Bolton," he said, flashing a wide smile. "It was an awesome shot from over a hundred yards away."

Jacks veins bulged along his neck. "Who sent you?"

"You can go to hell, Bolton."

Jack regarded him calmly even though an alarm had sounded. "It's ironic that you can't move, and I'm about to send *you* to hell. It's a shitty feeling, huh? Enjoy your trip."

He raised his gun and fired two shots into Oz's chest. Some of the nurses screamed; the surgeon just stared at his now dead patient.

Jack looked at the surgery team cowering against the wall. "I'm sorry you had to see this, but he killed my fiancée and our unborn baby today. I'm not a monster, but he was. He took everything from me that I loved."

He left the operating room and sprinted to the nearest exit where his car was parked. In seconds he was speeding away. Jack glanced in his rearview mirror and saw two police cars pulling into the parking lot, lights flashing.

Chapter 7

Wearing a tan suit and combing what was left of his gray hair, Tyler Mattison stepped out of his modest ranch house into the fresh air. He was a creature of habit. Frugal was his middle name, even though he was a multibillionaire. He lived by a discipline of punctuality, the first guy at work and the last guy to leave.

He was CEO of Mattison Chemical and the company workhorse. His younger brother, James, was the money man of the Mattison empire. Tyler got his hands dirty, knew everybody in the company, and found a way to pay bonuses during the good years even if it meant he got less.

He had started at the bottom when he was sixteen, working for their father, who laid down the law to him: "If you want people to respect you, you have to know what you're talking about and walk in their shoes."

Tyler never forgot those words. He could often be found working the floor and taking in the concerns of his employees. Safety was a top priority, and he was proud of the company's clean OSHA record. He fought the board and his brother when it came to spending money that ensured their workers had the latest and safest equipment technology. He wasn't just their boss; he cared.

When one of his employees was given a dire cancer diagnosis, without a second thought Tyler sent the private plane to fly them to a Boston hospital that specialized in that type of cancer. Amazingly, the employee survived the ordeal and was now in remission.

Tyler kissed his wife goodbye and stepped into his fifteen-year-old Chevy pickup. He was old school; if it worked, he drove it. It was a quick eleven-minute ride from Bedford, New Hampshire, to Mattison Chemical in Merrimack.

The early sun had broken through the clouds reflecting off an array of colorful trees lining the road. Tyler rolled up to the intersection when a jarring bang came from the rear of his pick-up. He got out of his car to access the damage.

The other driver came out of his car, apologizing profusely.

"Don't worry about it," Tyler said. "It's really okay. It's nothing that can't be fixed easily, and nobody was hurt." He didn't want to take the time to exchange papers or the insurance aggravation that would surely follow.

Tyler started to get into his truck when the other driver called out. "Hey, this was your fault. I got a small dent in my bumper."

"Are you kidding me?" Tyler muttered before walked up to the man. "Excuse me, but you rear-ended me. I was giving you a break, and now you're saying it's my fault? I don't have time for this."

"You stopped short."

"I rolled to a stop for a stop sign."

"Well, are we going to exchange papers? I need your insurance company to pay for my damage."

"I'm the one with the damage, and it was your fault," Tyler said, his voice loud and his tone annoyed.

Other drivers were giving them dirty looks as they maneuvered their cars to pass.

Tyler looked at the other driver. "It's your damn fault. There's nothing wrong with your car. So just feel lucky we're not swapping papers."

The man started swearing at Tyler. The situation was getting out of hand, and when a good Samaritan tried to intervene, Tyler pointed to the bumper. "Do you see any damage? And he rear-ended me."

"I have to agree with him," the good Samaritan said.

"Suit yourself, but you're both wrong," the other driver said.

He reached into his side pocket, pulled out a gun, and without hesitation fired two shots at Tyler who staggered and then collapsed. The man jumped into his vehicle and sped off in the opposite direction.

The good Samaritan called 911 as he tended to Tyler.

***

James Mattison was sitting in his office, watching the wild horses roam his land. He took a swig of coffee as Luke stepped into his office. "James, they found Bolton

68

in Maple Creek, British Columbia. It's just coming over the wire now.

"Is he dead?"

"I think he escaped. It's not entirely clear what actually happened."

"What do you mean? Isn't he in custody?"

"I don't think so."

"So who found him?"

"That's not clear either. They're not giving out much information. I've called a few sources up there. They're telling me there were shots fired at his house, a parking lot, and a hospital."

"That doesn't make any sense, especially when you're telling me they didn't get him. They sent a hit squad, and he killed them all? Is that what I'm supposed to believe?"

"I don't know. Let me see what I can find out."

Mattison's phone buzzed. He picked it up, listened intently, then hung up.

"What's wrong?" Luke asked.

"They've killed Tyler."

"What?"

"They killed my brother. The authorities are saying it was some sort of road rage incident. I'm not buying it. I warned him that he should be using security, but my brother's a stubborn bastard. Was a stubborn bastard. He told me the day he needs security is the day that America is no longer America. Well, maybe he's right about that."

James stared out the window thinking about his brother, the nicest guy he knew. No way he died in some random road rage incident. He turned around and faced Luke.

"The meeting that Atkins and Steele had on Lake Champlain is what's playing out today."

"I'm so sorry about your brother, James. What do you want me to do?"

James put his face into his hands. It took him a moment to regain his composure. "I have to plan a funeral. I will need tight security. I mean tight."

"I'll work on that."

"I need to know exactly what transpired in Canada, but I think we have a good idea who's behind this. Let's confirm that. Also, find the man who killed my bother and bring him here. I want to know who was behind Tyler's death."

"Okay."

"If Bolton's out there, we need to find him before they do. Put Glover on it. He knows those guys who were part of getting Laura Weston back. Bolton is running out of places to hide. He'll need a place to go. And I'm thinking I'm his only friend."

"Will he give us the flash drive?"

"He's out of choices now."

Chapter 8

After driving south five hours at top speed on BC-97, Jack finally eased off the gas. He had no idea where to go even though he was automatically heading toward Vancouver. He imagined that Kelly was waiting for him at Wood's Grill. That was what his mind wanted to believe. He fought back tears as reality swept back in on a fresh wave of grief that crashed through the barrier his mind had tried to erect.

His eyes were bloodshot and not focusing. The lump on his head throbbed, and the blood on his shirt and skin had hardened dry. He found an area where he could pull over and disappear for a while. He maneuvered the car into the breakdown lane and then pulled further off into a secluded area that was invisible from the main highway.

He killed the engine and sat in the car, trying to come to grips with his life being in complete shambles once again. Just when he had started to believe the past might just melt away and a new life would take its place, it was gone. Just like that he was alone again.

This loss was even worse than the emptiness he felt after his brother's hand had slipped from his grasp. Like now, he had tried to be stoic. He remembered walking home through the woods with the other boys after the accident.

Nobody said a word. The only sounds were from their shuffling footsteps on the ground below and crow caws in the sky above. He didn't cry until later when the reality of the experience hit him so hard he fell to his knees and asked God why over and over. He had crawled into a ball and wanted the world to go away. He didn't say anything to anyone for days. He went to the wake and funeral never saying a word. People tried talking to him, but he never heard a word. When it was over, everybody else went on with their lives, but he was left behind.

Jack got out of the car and heard running water nearby. He grabbed his duffle bag and strolled through the woods, the sunlight beaming through spaces in the trees. He soon came to a stream and found a dry area under a ledge then sat staring at the water bouncing off the rocks, swirling and flowing at a frantic pace. All he could think about was that the best thing in his life was gone, and he no longer belonged anywhere. He had nowhere to go…

He woke up thirty minutes later, his head leaning against a rock. Almost immediately the reality of what had happened hit him again like a full-body punch. It wasn't a dream. He glanced up to see an injured bear staring at him from the other side of the stream. Jack stood and they stared at each other with pride, both wounded and suffering in their different worlds.

When the bear disappeared, Jack took out his gun, a weapon he had hated all his life, yet, it was glued to him like a sword in a knight's armor. He opened his duffle bag and placed it under some clothing. From a side pocket he pulled out a small piece of paper with the address and phone number of Brian's uncle, Chip Butler, on it.

Brian had often said, "If you ever need a place to go, my crazy uncle is an option."

Jack wasn't too far from where he lived. He took out his phone and called the number. He didn't give it a thought that someone might be able to trace it.

***

Downtown Maple Creek looked more like a war zone than a peaceful village as dozens of investigators fanned out collecting forensic evidence.

Mike Weldon had arrived in the late afternoon with a contingent of agents carrying black bags. The group wore long overcoats and short haircuts. Weldon introduced himself to the lead investigator from the Royal Canadian Mounted Police in front of Bobwick's where the initial attack took place.

"I'm Special Agent Mike Weldon."

"I'm Inspector Sid Mack."

The men shook hands.

"Looks like you have quite the mess here," Weldon said.

"From what I've been told, it's your mess."

"You got me there."

"They told me once you got here we'd be working the case jointly," Mack said amiably. "We're happy for any assistance you can offer."

"Can you give a little more detail of what actually happened here?"

Using eyewitness accounts, Mack recounted the events of that morning. Weldon listened in disbelief; somehow Bolton had survived another close call. The guy's luck had to run out at some point.

"I want to talk to the guy from Bobwick's," Weldon said. "Is he still around?"

"Yeah."

They walked into the store and found Clay in the back room.

"Hello, Mr. Bobwick," Mack said. "This is Special Agent Weldon. He would like to ask you a few questions."

"What do you want to know?"

"Did you know Jack Walsh?"

"Yeah. He was a friend and a really nice guy."

"Well, Mr. Bobwick, he's not as nice as you think. He's a wanted man. He's on the FBI's Most Wanted List. His real name is Jack Bolton. Hell, had you done your civic duty, you could have received a nice reward. I think it's now $2 million. I admire you for stepping in the way you did, but I'm not sure where it fits in under Canadian law, which I'm going to have to discuss with

Officer Mack."

"Maybe I should get a lawyer before I answer any questions. In fact, I'm done talking to you."

Weldon's jaw twitched. "Well, don't go too far. In fact, is your gun registered?"

"Yeah."

Inspector Mack intervened. "It's legal to own a shotgun up here. It's non-restrictive. He has all the appropriate paperwork."

"Will be in touch, Mr. Bobwick," Weldon said, agitated. "We're going to confiscate your shotgun."

"We already have it," Mack said. He turned to Clay. "We'll get it back to you when we're done."

As Weldon and Mack started to walk away, Clay said. "Hey, Special Agent. I saw what happened out there. Those men were animals. They weren't your average thugs. They were on a mission. I did what I had to do. And I knew Jack; he would do anything for anyone. He's a good guy. And his girlfriend was pregnant. Did you know that? You probably don't give a shit, but I hear these guys shot her in cold blood. Maybe that's what you should be investigating, eh?"

Weldon stared at Clay. "My job is to bring people in who break the law. I can't have sympathy. Did you know Jack was sentenced to life in prison for murder? He broke out and continued his killing ways. He made a lot of enemies in the process. Unfortunately his girlfriend was collateral damage. If you play with guns, it doesn't always work out the way you want. Maybe you should learn something from that, Mr. Bobwick. So, if anything jogs your memory that's relative to this investigation, it would be in your best interest to notify us."

Outside the store Mack said, "The media is waiting for a comment."

"I don't give a damn about the media. I'm not prepared to tell them anything."

Mack met Weldon's eyes. "You know who these men are."

"This is a matter of United States National Security, so I'm not at liberty to say." Weldon wasn't about to admit a US agency had sent a bunch of assassins. "You just worry about the evidence gathering, and we'll get along just fine. Now, explain what happened back at Bolton's house."

Weldon listened as Mack explained how Bolton's girlfriend had done a number on a group of experienced military men. "So Bolton prepared his girlfriend for the day somebody came knocking?"

"Looks that way," Mack agreed. "Even the dog played a role. We found one of these guys dead in their car with his carotid artery shredded. The guy bled to death."

Weldon just shook his head. "What else?"

When Mack finished detailing the events with the paramedics and at the hospital, Weldon smiled. "Thanks for the morbid summary. You know, I've been on this case for three years – since the carnage in Seattle – and here I am again cleaning up Bolton's mess. I've got to get this guy. Can you drive me over to the hospital? I'd like to see the crime scene."

"Sure."

Alex came over. "We've got something, Mike. These guys were using a laptop to track Bolton's car."

"Are you telling me they have a tracking device on his car."

"Yeah, and the program is still open. We're playing around with it now."

"Is it real time?"

"I don't know yet, but I think we'll know soon."

"You work on that. Let me know when you get the location. I'm going over to the hospital. We might be leaving sooner than expected."

Chapter 9

Jack drove another two hours and got off Highway 97 at Cache Creek and traveled north through the Bonaparte valley and Loon Creek. He followed the directions he had jotted down and eventually turned onto a dirt road that led to a lakeside cabin as the sun was slowly setting.

When he turned the car off, Chip Butler stepped out of the cabin in overalls and a baseball cap to greet him. Jack walked over, not knowing what to expect.

Chip smiled. "I finally get a chance to meet Jack Bolton. Come on in; we have a lot to talk about. Anybody who's a friend of Brian's is a friend of mine." He could see the strain of the day on Jack's face. "How you holding up?"

"I'm trying to block it out. I might cry at a whim."

"I'm so sorry to hear about what happened to your girlfriend; it's all over the news. Of course they haven't given out that much information, except that you're armed and dangerous. You hungry?"

"I'll take a strong drink. I don't have an appetite."

"I'll pour you a little Jack Daniels to get you started. Why don't you take a shower? You look like death. And that arm looks nasty. I got some antibiotic cream in the medicine cabinet."

"I'm okay. It looks worse than it feels. But I would like to clean up."

Fifteen minutes later, Jack eased into a comfortable leather chair with a view of Loon Lake.

"Here's your whiskey." Chip handed him a glass and patted his good shoulder before settling into a chair opposite Jack. "You look better."

"Looks can be deceiving."

"I understand. I can't imagine."

"I'm trying to block it out. That's what a good soldier does to move forward, right? If I think about it, I'll cry like a baby. I don't think I'll ever be okay again."

"Do you need to talk about it."

"No. Not today anyway."

"Okay. Then you just sit back and relax as best you can."

"Look, I don't want to drag you into my world. I'll be out of here in the morning. I appreciate you giving me a place to sleep for the night."

"It's fine. And I've been in that world since Brian was killed." Chip broke out a pipe and packed it. "You mind?"

Jack shook his head. "You have a nice place here."

"It's not mine exactly. Long story. But it's a great place where I can think and be away from people. You know, Jack, after I got divorced, I met another woman then realized I just wasn't the marrying type. So I left my job, and I've been here ever since."

"You don't miss anything back in the States?"

"I got a place there. But, when the world implodes, I'm all set here. I got well water; I can live off the land. I'll survive. The masses won't be so lucky. In case you can't tell, I'm probably a little nuts."

"I wouldn't say that." But with his gray hair, gray beard, glasses, and pipe, Jack thought he looked like a mad scientist and told Chip so.

Brian's uncle grinned. "I like to fool people. I'm actually a black belt in karate. Anyway, up here nobody cares how you look." He watched Jack finish off his drink. "You sucked that down pretty fast."

"I'll take another if that's okay. I'm not a big drinker, but I'm in a lot of pain."

"I see that."

When Chip stepped away, Jack stood and peered out the large windows, taking in the amazing view of the lake as the sun was making its final descent.

"It's an awesome view, huh?" Chip said, handing him another shot of whiskey.

"It puts life in perspective."

He nodded. "War, hardship, losing a loved one, cancer, will do that to you. Maybe in a way it's a gift, which we take for granted."

"It doesn't feel like a gift."

"I'll give you a wild theory of mine while we're on the subject. Let's sit down." They sat back in the leather chairs. "I sometimes believe that the world is an amusement park, and people's lives are the rides."

"I think you've been out here too long."

Chip laughed. "I know. I don't get much company. What I mean is that we might be part of some higher being's community. Maybe they're just so intelligent that emotions like love, hate, whatever are absent. So they created this world. I know; it's crazy. It's just a theory."

"Your theory is safe with me."

"I got a slight smile out of you, so it was worth something."

Jack finished the second shot and set the glass down on the coffee table. He glanced up to see Chip staring at him.

"What?"

"Do you know what your brain just did?"

"No."

"It calculated the distance of how far you had to reach to grab your drink and put it up to your mouth and then recalculate the distance you needed to place the glass back down. Isn't that amazing?"

"I've never thought about it."

"Of course not. The mind makes those calculations in microseconds every day. My theory is that life is based on mathematical algorithms. For example, two hundred people board a plane from all walks of life. The plane crashes, no survivors. Basically all those people crossed paths based on a mathematical algorithm. Did you know that there are about forty people in the world with acquired savant syndrome?"

"What's that?"

"Some people are born savants. Others get hit in the head or suffer some physical trauma like getting struck by lightning, and when they recover they have acquired some extraordinary talent. Some start playing classical piano. Others start to draw. Many acquire genius math skills and become like Rain Man, able to draw approximations of fractals, the repeating geometric patterns that are building blocks of everything in the known universe."

"So their brain sees the lines behind the images?"

"Exactly." Chip excitedly puffed out a few rings of smoke.

Jack needed another drink. "Why are you telling me this?"

"I don't know. I don't have many visitors, so I get a chance to think a lot, and this is what I think about. But what I'm trying to tell you is that everything you've been through, maybe you have no control over; it's just based on a damn algorithm created by a higher being or something else we can't understand."

Jack shrugged. "It's way over my head, Chip. Brian mentioned you fought in Vietnam. Maybe you were exposed to Agent Orange. Or too many drugs." He considered his host and said, "I'm just kidding."

"Yeah, I know it's crazy stuff. But I want to show

you something. You stay there. I'll get you another drink." Chip opened the side door off the kitchen to let his dog in, who immediately went to check out the stranger.

"Your beagle is really friendly," Jack said.

Then his thoughts turned to Sampson. He was trying so hard to blank out the day and hold back the tears, but the dam might break anytime. Chip had done a good mind trick to keep him off his dark thoughts. He pretended as if nothing had happened today, but it was all a defense mechanism his body had learned to use.

This time Chip returned with a tray of shots.

"What's the dog's name?" Jack asked.

"I call it AI."

"Strange name. One friendly dog though."

"It should be."

Jack brushed his hand against the dog's fur, but it didn't move. At all. He looked at Chip. "The dog is weird."

"I know. It ran out of juice."

"What do you mean?"

"It's not real, Jack."

"What are you saying?"

"I'm saying it's robotic, as in artificial intelligence. Hence, AI."

"You're kidding."

"No. I work for the Department of Defense. I create artificial intelligence. The pay is good. They let me use their place here. They come up here a few times a year to see how I'm progressing. They're very impressed with my dog, but that's just skimming the surface of what I'm working on."

Jack didn't know what to say.

"I know," Chip said. "Shocking when you see stuff like this. Who could have ever imagined this twenty years ago? I programmed the dog to be friendly through algorithms. Whatever this dog does is based on what I've programmed into it. I control its destiny, the same way a higher being would control us."

"This is incredible."

"It's just the beginning. I'm working with human replicas that will act and feel just like humans, except I program their actions. It's all top secret. I do it because I want to understand everything about these things. I want to be able to dismantle them as well. My fear is AI will eventually get out of control. Those that understand math will control the world. For all the good that these things will do, they'll be used for plenty of bad."

"Thanks for the math lesson."

"If we're controlling AI, then who's controlling us."

"It does make you think. You always this entertaining?"

"Only when I have good company and someone to drink with who I can trust."

Jack just nodded. The alcohol was dulling his senses while Chip's stories helped block the horrific events of the day.

"I once worked with this guy who runs an aerospace company. Have you heard of Area 51 in Nevada?"

Jack nodded. "Who hasn't. It's some top-secret site."

"Yeah. Now he had clearance to just this particular site, and he was able to get me clearance as well. Before I left he showed me something that I'll never forget. It was a UFO that crashed. The aliens didn't survive. Now, what do you do with an alien craft when you don't understand it? It took him years, but he eventually cracked the code. He figured out how to program and use the ship. One problem: it can go the speed of light; no human could survive that. So they're working on a couple of AIs to fly it. I'm one of the people working on the AI piece. Amazing, huh? Probably more than you wanted to know. Again, all top secret."

"Doesn't matter to me. I'm on a mission, and my days are short."

Chip changed the subject. "You know, Brian was one of a kind. He wanted to live life to the fullest. He was a little wild as a kid, but he always wanted to do the right thing. He was a good athlete. When he told me he was joining the Navy, I thought it would be good for him. Give him some discipline. And when he told me he made it as a SEAL, he was really proud of himself. I was pretty impressed. I wondered how he was going to do with authority."

"I loved him like a brother. If you were in a firefight,

he was the guy you wanted next to you."

"He broke you out of prison."

"I didn't ask him to," Jack said

"That was Brian. Loyalty meant something to him."

"I know." Tears began to form at the edge of Jack's eyes.

"Hey, I'm sorry. I didn't want to rehash the past."

"It's not that. It's everything. I'm just barely holding it together. The drinks are just numbing my pain for now."

"Maybe it would be better if we didn't talk about this stuff."

"No, I want to. On this particular mission, Brian wasn't going to stand down. He was going to save a village from the barbarians. Outnumbered, we managed to hold the village. I was just doing my job. Amazingly, we all made it back safely. I took a bullet, but we weren't supposed to do what we did. The commanding officer, Armstrong, was pissed. It caused him to use firepower that put other soldiers in harm's way. He let it go after an earful of rage. He emphasized, in not kind words, that he was responsible for every man under his command and anybody going home in a body bag because of stupidity would be dealt with severely. Surprisingly he put me in for a Purple Heart and told me sometimes you survive stupidity, but eventually stupidity will kill you. Then he added: *Don't confuse stupidity with bravery*. He hated being in Afghanistan.

He hated the politicians who sent us into that hell hole. He said it was a waste of good men. Thinking back, he was right. The war accomplished absolutely nothing for all the loss of life and life-long disabilities."

Chip nodded. "They learned nothing from the Vietnam War. The politicians don't care." He set down his pipe. "Brian dropped by a couple of years ago. It was a good reunion. We went out fishing. Did a little hunting. He told me everything. Then he handed me a flash drive and asked if I could safeguard it. I put it away, didn't think much about it. Then when Brian got killed, I took a look at it. I hacked into the Cayman Islands bank account; it wasn't that hard. I had the full run of their computer system without them even aware. I spent six months studying the account, following the money flow. And what I found was pretty amazing."

"So you saw the Phoenix Project where Atkins and Banner stole $18 billion earmarked to rebuild Iraq?"

Chip chuckled and took a sip of whiskey. "Yeah, that's bad, but you have something here that people only read about in conspiracy novels."

Jack frowned. "I'm confused."

"I'll try to explain it without getting too complicated. This account has been funding third world dictators, liberal activists, political campaigns, super PACs, NSA, European elites, media propaganda, and CIA activities."

"So they are spying on everyone?"

"It gets better. From what I gather, this account is

funding Sanderlin Group initiatives. Do you know about the Sanderlin Group?"

"Only what James Mattison told me."

"You know James Mattison?"

"Well, I met him under bizarre circumstances. I probably wouldn't be here without him, but I don't trust the bastard. He wants the flash drive."

Chip slowly nodded. "That all makes sense. He has his own agenda from what I've been told. You're right about not trusting him. I don't know what he told you about Sanderlin, but it's a group of rich and powerful kingmakers seeking to impose a one-world government. I'm not going to get into the politics of it except to say that this account connects what's going on under the surface."

"What does all that mean?"

"Besides that you've stumbled into the biggest conspiracy of our time? This drive exposes a deep state."

Jack didn't understand. "Explain."

"It means influential members of government agencies who are involved in the secret manipulation or control of government policy."

"So, Atkins is part of this?"

"No. I believe he's just a puppet they're manipulating."

"So there's a puppet master?"

Chip nodded. "I'm going out on a limb here and say

the former president, Ed Farley, is the puppet master, with assistance from powerful globalists like the Sanderlin Group. It's all about money and power and changing America from within."

"Farley?"

"It's like he never left. I didn't believe it at first, but the more I dug, the more it made me sick."

"So what does it all mean?"

"What it means for you is that you're a dead man walking as is anybody associated with you. These people will stop at nothing to run their agenda as you already know."

"I've been a dead man walking for a long time, Chip." Jack frowned. "Maybe I should be on my way. You've done enough."

Chip gestured for Jack to stay put. "When Brian got killed, I became part of this. My guess? They're not aware that this flash drive leads right to the inner workings of the deep state. They're more concerned about Atkins being exposed and causing them to lose the next election. They need more time to finish their global agenda."

"They should be. I've come too far to stop now. Too many people have lost their lives because of me."

"Well, I'm on board to take on the people responsible for Brian's death and to expose this deep state. I've never been one to get involved in politics, but this is beyond the American system. These types of people won't stop until they've achieved their objective. And nobody is aware of what's going on except you and me."

"I know what I have to do."

Chip leaned forward. "Let me ask you something. Who killed Brian?"

"I'm really not sure. I don't know what Brian told you or what you gathered from the flash drive."

"He told me everything."

"Then you know Banner and Atkins both wanted me dead."

"Yes."

"After Brian was shot, I confronted Banner at his house before he jumped."

Chip's brow lifted in surprise. "So you didn't kill him?"

"No. He told me he had nothing to do with it and that I was there because they wanted me to be there. Then he leaped off the side of the deck."

"If it wasn't Banner, then who?"

Jack shrugged. "I have a lot of enemies, Chip. It could have been a bad shot for all I know, but I do think about it. The one person who knew I was there was James Mattison."

"How'd you get tied in with him?"

"He wasn't a fan of Atkins and Banner. To make a long story short, he saved my ass from the Gallo crime family and expected something in return. He gave me Banner's address. But I sometimes think he had something to do with Brian's death. As I said, he has a big interest in the flash drive. You said earlier I shouldn't trust him. You know him?"

"I know a guy who did some work for him. It didn't go so well. They tried to kill him. Actually, they thought they did kill him, but he's very much alive. He just disappeared. Maybe we should talk to him."

"I can't get you any more involved."

"Jack, I'm already involved. The moment I shook your hand I was a dead man. We can't stay here. I'm guessing the guys you killed were tracking you somehow. However they found you, the authorities – or whoever else – will soon figure it out."

Jack closed his eyes. "The car."

Chip nodded. "Probably. Try to get some sleep; we're leaving first thing in the morning."

"Where are we going?"

"Back to the States."

"Won't the authorities be waiting at the border."

"I know a few security guards at the border. I flash my DoD badge and they let me right through. We're heading for Wyoming. There's someone I want you to meet. So, come on; try to get some sleep."

Chapter 10

A motorcade of four black SUVs rolled down Highway 97. Special Agent Weldon sat in the lead vehicle. Bolton's car had been pinpointed on Loon Lake Road. The SUVs came to a halt next to the car, and the agents fanned out with high powered rifles, surrounding the cabin. They moved with caution, like a pack of wolves ready to pounce. They had the advantage of surprise. On Weldon's signal, they kicked in the doors and flooded into the home with guns drawn.

They found nothing.

There was no sign of Bolton or anyone else. The agents checked for any evidence, but the place was cleaner than a five-star hotel.

Alex reported that the car was indeed Bolton's, and there were blood stains in it.

Weldon shook his head in disgust. "What good does it do us? Bolton is still out there. The question is why did he come here? Who does he know? The car is parked here to throw us off. He could be anywhere by now."

Alex nodded. "I guess we're back to square one."

Weldon wanted to break something. "We need a list of people who live out here to see if Bolton has a connection to someone. But yeah, for now he's gone, and we have no idea where."

***

Jack and Chip were on Highway 99 heading toward the Peace Arch crossing at the Canadian-United States border.

"Do you think they've shown up yet?"

"Probably. And I'm sure they're a little frustrated right now because they have no idea where you've gone."

Jack looked at Chip, concerned. "What if they find out about you? They'll put two and two together."

"Don't worry about it. I'll take care of it when and if it comes to that."

Jack stared out the window lost in thought.

"You okay?" Chip asked.

"Not really. I loved her so much. All I wanted was a nice simple life and to raise a family with the woman I loved. And they took it all way. Just like that."

"That's why you have to finish this. Just blow-up the system. I'll help you. For Brian."

"I'm going to bring them all down or die trying."

"Do you have a plan? I think you should find Mattison while the heat is on and give him the flash drive."

"I'm not giving him the flash drive. I have other plans for it."

"Okay, but you might have a different opinion after you talk to my friend in Wyoming. We served in Nam together."

"I have a media guy who interviewed me in prison. I think I can trust him to expose this whole deep state thing. As far as Mattison, I think he'll give me the means to go after the people responsible for Kelly and then I'll deal with Mattison in due time. If I get that far."

"Sounds like a plan. I think it's time to hide you in the back; we're almost at the border."

Chapter 11

Federal Medical Center Devens, a minimum-security prison located in Ayer, Massachusetts, and operated by the Federal Bureau of Prisons, a division of the United States Department of Justice, housed a variety of inmates, including white-collar criminals, mobsters, and sex offenders.

Paul Ryland sat in his bright yellow cement cell rubbing his beard, pondering yet again how he ended up there. He now knew exactly what Jeff Keller had gone through.

His trial was high-profile, and in the end Paul never had a chance. The feds had thrown enough at the jury to prove that he had aided and abetted Jack Bolton and had obstructed bringing Bolton to justice. After the tears, the broken dreams, and a family torn apart, Paul was led away to serve thirty months in a federal penitentiary, essentially in solitary; he had been kept from the main population of the prison for safety precautions. He now only had five months left in his sentence, and he counted the days until he'd be freed.

But a dark cloud hung over him regarding his collaboration with Frank Gallo to take out Tripp, the Deal Maker. He'd acted to protect his family, but that decision weighed on his mind daily. After two years nobody had figured out who had shot the Deal Maker dead in broad daylight as he ate breakfast in a popular diner outside of Washington, D.C. The media had covered it as a mafia hit that led right to Frank Gallo, except there was no evidence; it was a big dead end. Yet the Feds kept circling like sharks.

That wasn't his only worry; he had noticed a subtle change in his wife. She missed a visit here or there, and the kids didn't come as frequently. Donna had also become quiet, preoccupied. He tried not to get alarmed, but the homemade baked goodies were now store-bought, as if she no longer had time to make something special, like she was just going through the motions. She also used to always leave a love note in the goodies, but no more. Those love notes had given him the uplift he so needed in this dreary place of tattoos, psychiatrists, rules, misfits, social deviates, and the constant movement of people – a world he thought he knew but now realized he never had a clue.

He threw water on his face, wiped it away, and made his bed according to prison protocol by 7:30 a.m. Paul had gotten used to the rules. In bed by 9:30 p.m., up by 7:00 a.m. He put on his green trousers and short-sleeved green shirt. The one great thing about the attire, there was no thinking, just the same look day after day. Suits and ties had become a distant memory.

He felt like a janitor, mopping and sweeping the floors, cleaning windows, vents, and trash cans daily.

He didn't know what had happened to the players in Jack Bolton's saga. It was ironic that so much of his past life was no longer relevant. He had his own life to deal with. His main concern now was making it through five more months and repairing the damage to his family. After that he'd figure out where to go from there. For now, he was just looking forward to a visit from Donna and the kids; that's what kept him going.

***

Paul got up as Donna walked in. She smiled, he smiled, and they hugged. Any observer would assume they were two people still in love. But love was fragile. Like a high-performance car, the smallest problem can cause it to break down.

A guard watched their exchange; appropriate physical contact was permitted. Other than the three of them, the room was empty.

When Donna pulled back from the hug, Paul asked, "Where are the kids?"

"It was just too much for them today."

Paul frowned. "What do you mean?"

"It's not always easy getting them over here."

"Donna, I'm their damn father."

"I know that, but most fathers come home at night."

Paul winced, and Donna immediately apologized. "I didn't get much sleep last night. Matt wasn't feeling well."

"Is he okay?"

"Oh, yeah. It was a little stomach bug, but he's fine."

"I'll be out of here in just a few more months. I'm going to make this all up to you and the boys."

"I'm sure you will."

Paul leaned back; his FBI instincts told him something was going on. Donna was distant, but she looked better than ever. He swatted his suspicion away and tried to make small talk. "So, no baked cake? You afraid they would find the hammer and chisel inside?" he joked.

She just smiled. The conversation went dead.

Paul was consumed with thoughts of another man.

So was Donna.

"I'm going to make this right when I get out."

"I don't know how you're going to do that with a criminal record. Have you thought about that? How are you going to get a decent job? All you know is law enforcement. You have three boys to support."

He was lost for words; it was the way Donna was talking, like she wasn't part of it.

"You seem to be having time for the gym."

"What do you mean by that? A woman can't look good?"

"I just was making conversation."

Donna stood, her body stiff. "I think I should be going. I have to pick up the boys from my mom's."

"Why do you have an attitude today? I'm the one in here."

"This whole ordeal hasn't been easy for me either."

"Well, it sure hasn't been easy on me."

"You did this to yourself. You were going to be the big superhero, but the only thing you got was a prison sentence. All I wanted was for you to get out of the whole business."

"There you go again. You blame me for all this. The last time I checked, money doesn't grow on trees. Someone had to work."

"I don't want to argue here. It's done. "

Paul nodded, irritated. "You're right; what's the point now?"

He waived the white flag in his mind. He wasn't in a place to fight; now was time to retreat. Regardless of what he said, she was either disinterested or ready to jump down his throat. It was better for them to part ways before something was said to put a further wedge between them.

He got up and hugged her. Donna seemed like she couldn't get out of there fast enough.

"When will I see you next," he asked, afraid of the answer.

"Probably in a few days. I'll let you know."

He just nodded and watched her go.

***

By 2:00 p.m., after Paul had finished cleaning the windows and had moved on to sweeping the floor, a guard tapped his shoulder. "You have a visitor."

"I don't have a scheduled visit."

"It's someone important I think; just follow me."

Paul followed the guard down the hall and through a checkpoint. The guard opened a door to a rear room. Standing there was his former boss, FBI Director Shone Williams. He hadn't changed: same gray hair, same gray suit. They awkwardly shook hands with half smiles.

As they sat, Paul wondered what Williams was doing there. Closure on the Bolton case was his initial thought, then a spike of fear went through him. Had they figured out who killed Robert Tripp?

"How you doing, Paul?"

He shrugged. "Maybe I should ask how you're doing."

"I'm doing fine. You're probably counting the days to when you get out of here."

"It's felt like a long time. I miss my family. I haven't followed the Bolton case; with me out of the way, I would think Bolton would be behind bars by now."

"Paul, I didn't like what happened to you."

"Well, it's almost over, and then I'll get on with life, and this will be just a bad memory."

Shone shook his head. He knew they had set Ryland up. Now Atkins and Steele pushing the theory that Ryland had taken part in the murder of Tripp was bizarre, but he had to push it forward. "Jack Bolton is still a fugitive."

"So he just disappeared?"

"Not exactly. You didn't hear what happened?"

"No. The one good thing about this place, you can forget about the outside world."

"He was found the other day in a small town in British Columbia. A special unit went up there to take him in, and it ended with seven body bags."

"How does that happen?"

"I don't know. Somebody screwed up. I don't want to get into the details, but I'm sure he has revenge in his veins."

"Why do you say that?"

"Let's just say when you kill his pregnant girlfriend, the dossier on Jack Bolton pretty much tells you he's coming for you. So the answer to your question, he's very much alive and very much not in jail."

Ryland took the news hard but didn't let Shone see it. It had to be the girl he met in Vancouver. Kelly. They had killed her.

"I'd like to know what happened."

"Forget about it, Paul. What if I told you I could get you out of here now?"

Paul's quiet laugh was bitter. "I was just thinking today how I offered deals to criminals, and now you're throwing me a bone. Ironic, huh?"

"Yeah, I get your point."

Paul met Shone's gaze. Nothing was ever offered without a price or consequence.

"Where's the catch?"

"This is a no-brainer. I just need to know the truth, okay? Your record will be expunged. I'll give you a recommendation for any job application."

"The truth about what?"

Shone tried to find the best words. "I just need you to admit that Frank Gallo's people put a hit on Tripp."

"How would I know that, Shone?"

"I don't like this any more than you do, but if you admit that Gallo had something to do with this, you're a free man. No funny business. We'll get you an official document signed by all the parties involved. You can have your lawyer review it to your satisfaction. I'll make sure you have a clean record. Nobody will ever know you served time."

Paul leaned back, confused by the proposal. They had probably figured out there was some connection but couldn't prove it. They had no legal evidence to pursue Gallo, but they wanted to know for sure who had put down Tripp. Maybe it had to do with some international connection, or maybe it was payback for Gallo's involvement.

"So I can get out here by saying that Gallo and I concocted some scheme to get rid of Tripp. Is that where you're going with this?"

"Look, you don't have to admit to anything. Just testify that you gave information to Gallo for him to kill Tripp."

He shook his head. "This is unbelievable."

"Paul, you met with Gallo a bunch of times. You met with Tripp."

"Yeah, I did. I was trying to solve a case."

"Were you, Paul?" Shone asked.

"Really, Shone? You've got to be kidding."

"We'll put you and your family in witness protection."

"I can't believe what I'm hearing," Paul said, his voice rising with the indignation of an innocent man being falsely accused, even though in reality he was the mastermind, the man behind the curtain. But they had nothing. He wondered if Shone was there to read his facial expressions.

Shone tried another tack. "I could suggest a lie detector test. If your answers are non-deceptive, I'll make a motion to get you out. If you confess that Gallo was the hit-man, then I'll make sure you get out right away."

"What the hell is this all about, Shone?" Paul asked again.

"It's all in your court because tomorrow afternoon somebody in the agency is going to visit Gallo and say you're turning over evidence against him. If you had nothing to do with it, then Gallo will laugh at it. But if you conspired with him, I can't protect you or your family."

"I can't believe this."

"That's the deal, Paul. I'm sorry. So you sleep on it. Let me know tomorrow morning what you've decided."

"You know, you people are frigging crazy. You can go to hell, Shone. That's my frigging answer."

"I'll give you until tomorrow; you might change your mind after a good night's sleep."

Shone got up and left.

Paul rubbed his face, his mind racing. They were playing a game of chicken; who would blink first? Going to Gallo and telling him that Paul was going to sing would be a death sentence.

Chapter 12

Frank Gallo sat in the back of a late model Cadillac with his longtime friend, Aldo Mariani. In the front Marty drove, and Johnny sat in the passenger seat.

Aldo was from the old neighborhood. He still managed the family package store at the age of eighty-eight. He looked out the window as they turned onto the Albany exit.

"So, Frank, why the long drive? I'm still feeling the effects of the gunshot wound around my shoulder, and I'm no spring chicken here. Unless you're thinking of getting rid of me."

Frank smiled. "I wanted you to see the foliage."

"I'm sure."

"We're almost there."

"Just don't hand me a shovel."

"The shovels are lighter now," he said, making Aldo laugh. "Remember when I was a teenager and a bunch of us stole a case of beer from your store?"

"I still got my memory, Frank."

"We thought we were so smart. Of course, we pushed our luck and went back."

"I knew you kids stole the beer. I let it go. But most people, if they get away with something once, they try a second time. So when you pulled the same crap again, I kicked your asses in the back alley. It was all about teaching you guys a lesson. If you were going to be thugs, you better be smart about it. Or you don't last long out in the streets."

"Your cousin Marco kicked our asses."

"Except for you, Frank. You knew enough not to wise off. You were smarter than the rest of them; you just followed a stupid idea."

"Sometimes you got to know when to fold," Gallo said with a sly smile.

"I could've gone to your old man, but it was a better lesson to get your asses kicked by someone your own age. The only way you weren't going to rip me off again was if you respected me. And the funny thing, you were all very polite after that. Funny how that works. Russo, he had those sick eyes, not worried about consequences. But Marco hit him with one punch and he dropped like a dead weight."

"I don't want to talk about Russo; he turned out to be a rat. He was the last person I thought would break omerta."

"You find out a lot about a man's character when they break the Mafia code of silence. Loyalty and respect and knowing when to keep your mouth shut, as you know Frank, it's the difference between being alive or dead in our business."

"Aldo, the young guys don't respect the old ways."

"Back in the day, Frank, I might have been small, but

I was quick and didn't back down from nobody. Today, these young thugs don't understand respect or loyalty, and they react without thinking. And most of them don't understand when to keep their mouths shut. You know what I mean?"

"I usually have to teach them the hard way," Frank sighed.

"Look at all your old friends. They're either dead, alcoholics, or in prison. Like I said, I always knew you were the smart one."

"A little luck doesn't hurt. Hey, whatever happened to your cousin?"

"Marco, it's been, I don't know, fifteen years ago. He hung around with stupid friends who liked to get in trouble. He was minding his own business in a bar and tried to break up a fight. He got stabbed in the back. And that was it."

"That's sad."

"Yup. So, why you bringing me out here?"

"Well, we're almost there. You know, I look at you like a father figure, Aldo. I can't let what happened to you go. You understand that? Just like the lesson you taught me many years ago."

"I'm glad you still hold onto the old-school ways."

Frank smiled wide. "I've done a lot of bad things, but if I didn't do them, I wouldn't be here. And today is just another chapter in the book."

The Cadillac rumbled along a dirt road and slowed

down as it came to a small grassy field surrounded by tall trees. The car rolled to a stop. The men got out. A van and two other cars were parked off to the side. A group of men stood nearby.

The men straightened up as Frank emerged from the car. He was dressed in dark slacks and a gray shirt, his large, menacing frame and bald head drew respect from the soldiers who jumped at his every command.

He walked slowly up to three young men who stood blindfolded with their legs and hands tied.

"Take off their blindfolds," he ordered in a booming voice. "What do we have here?"

Not comprehending their fate, the three men stood silently, surrounded by Frank's soldiers and lieutenants.

"Aldo," Frank barked. Aldo walked slowly to Frank's side, grimacing. "Are these the scum that robbed and shot you?"

Aldo stared at them. "Yes," he said in a quiet voice. "I'm too old for this shit, Frank. I have enough on my soul. You understand?"

"Yeah," he said, then shouted at the three gang members in front of him, their bodies littered with tattoos. "Do you remember him? You thought you could do whatever you pleased in this country. Do any of you speak frigging English?"

He was greeted with blank looks.

"You're wasting your time, Frank," Aldo said. "They have no idea what you're talking about."

"I'll get a response. Look at all these frigging tattoos. These people have no frigging souls." Frank stepped back and looked at Marty, who pulled out a handgun. "Give the gun to Jimmy."

Jimmy took the gun, and Frank put his arm around him like a son. "What do you see here?"

"A problem that needs to be taken care of."

"That's a good start, Jimmy. You see the guy at the end? You can see it in his eyes that he hates us. He puffs out his chest as if he's a wild animal, but the problem for him is that we're the bigger predator. He also thinks that this is a land of sheep, that you can do whatever you want without consequences. They didn't understand a thing I said. So, Jimmy what's the next step?"

Without hesitation Jimmy shot the man on the left in the head, blood splattering everywhere. The man dropped to the ground.

"I like this kid," Frank said out loud, impressed. "He could be my son."

The crew smiled.

The man on the far right blurted, "Fuck you!"

"So you do speak frigging English," Frank said. "You come to this country and think it's a land of opportunity for your crime sprees. Well, you screwed with the wrong person. You come into my neighborhood and try to kill a man of character, who worked hard all his life and deserves respect?" Frank stared him down. "The least you could do is tell Aldo here you're sorry."

The man spat in his face. "Fuck you!"

Frank wiped his face and broke a smile. "You're going to have to do better than that. Dom, drive Aldo back."

Frank nodded to Jimmy, who again, without hesitation, shot the second man in the head. The last man standing swore in a foreign language, screaming words that no one could understand.

"That's right," Frank said calmly. "You didn't think. Nobody comes into my neighbor and thinks they can steal money and shoot someone like a wild dog. Not you or anybody else."

Frank stared down at the man covered with tattoos and filled with hatred. He'd been there many times before; some had begged for their lives, others mouthed off, cursing their last words. There were two types of crazy: the silent types who were more methodical, and then there were the ones who didn't think; they just reacted. He could always pick them out and used their weaknesses against them. The crazy guy had played his hand. It was over for him, and Frank was finally done playing. He pulled out his gun and shot the last man standing in the head.

He had no remorse; he never did. In his mind they all deserved their fate. He never thought twice when he shot Gino, the hitman; he had disrespected Frank, and that was his mistake, and he didn't care who he pissed off.

"Jimmy, you see how easy this was done? This is a learning experience. And being stupid can cost people their lives. Always think before you act."

Marty asked, "What do we do with the bodies?"

"Bury those two bodies, but take the one with the loud mouth and all the tattoos and toss him in front of his gang's hang-out for all to see. You kill the crazy one, the others think twice about screwing with you."

Marty nodded.

Frank looked at Jimmy. "You have a girlfriend?"

"Yes."

"Bring her over to the restaurant for dinner tonight. It's on me. After dinner, you join me down in the cellar. We'll talk. Okay?"

Jimmy smiled. "Thanks, Frank."

After Frank ambled back to his car, Marty patted Jimmy on the back. "Frank likes you kid."

Chapter 13

By late morning the breakfast crowd had dispersed and Frank roamed his restaurant making sure everything was in order for the lunch rush. Special Agent Mike Weldon walked in and waited by the front counter. He appeared more like a businessman looking for a bite to eat than a man with an evil plan to expose Gallo and Ryland.

A maître d' greeted him with a wide smile. "Are you here for lunch?" she asked in a pleasant voice.

"I'm going to pass on the lunch. I need to talk to Frank Gallo. I'm Special Agent Weldon." He showed his badge. "If you could let him know I'm here."

"I'll see if he's available. Could you wait here a minute?"

"Sure." As he waited, Weldon studied the famed gangsters in photos on the wall.

Gallo walked up behind him. "Special Agent Weldon. I've kind of missed you guys ever since you locked up Ryland. I liked him, but you guys like to eat your own."

"I'd like to talk to you."

"About what?"

"Do you have somewhere we can go?"

"We'll grab a table."

The two men sat down.

"Do I need a lawyer?" Gallo asked.

"You might. I'm not here to arrest you. I'm just here to give you a message."

Frank shrugged. "What type of message?"

"Ryland is willing to testify that you two conspired in the killing of Robert Tripp in Washington, D.C. two years ago."

Frank barked out a nervous laugh. "That's really funny. I worked with Ryland to take out who? What has it come to? Now every time you find a body you're going to knock on my door?"

"Ryland wants out of prison. A new life, a clean record. He misses his family. So we offered him all that if he testifies against you."

Frank knew in his own mind this might always be a possibility, but he was confident that Ryland would take it to his grave.

"You know, Special Agent Weldon, I know people really well. And I look at you with the badge and fancy suit of an FBI Agent. But you're so much more than that, aren't you?"

"I'm not here to be analyzed, Mr. Gallo. I'm just here to give you a message that the next time I show up, it won't be for lunch."

Frank chuckled. "How you guys doing tracking down Bolton? I heard all about that debacle in Canada. Don't you have better things to do, *Special Agent*?"

Weldon stood. "I think we're done here." He pushed his chair in with force. "Sometimes stuff happens, Mr. Gallo."

"Well, thanks for the concern." Leaning back in his chair Gallo stared at the Fed intensely. "But being a thug with a badge and a fancy suit doesn't protect you either."

"Are you threatening me?"

Gallo grinned. "Nah, I just run a restaurant."

***

The next day Gallo's private jet landed at Fort Devens Moore Army Air Field in Massachusetts. He was accompanied by Marty and two loyal soldiers. He was picked up by a limo and was driven to FMC Devens. He left his men in the parking lot as he sauntered through security. He joked with the guards as he cleaned out his pockets.

"Can I trust you guys with this?" he said with a chuckle, getting no answer.

He accompanied the guard down the corridor through two electronic gates to a visitor's room where two guards sat at each end. Ryland sat a table in the center.

Paul got up as Frank approached and shook his hand. "I was expecting you," Paul said with a wry smile.

"I bet you were," Frank said gleefully. "How do you like the place?"

"I don't know; they keep me out of the main population so, based on that, it's a place to sleep."

"I can't help but find the irony in all this. I'm on the outside, and you're in here. And you were so close to putting me behind bars. Life has a sick sense of humor."

Paul shook his head. "Yeah, tell me about it. Anyway, I have a good idea why you're here."

"You do? Can't a guy visit a former agent who tried to take him down?"

"I know why you're here."

"Okay. Then let me ask you something. Are we good?"

Paul knew his body language was all Frank needed to assess if there was a problem. "We're good, Frank."

Frank paused; the less said, the better. "That's what I thought. I have this uncanny ability to see through people. I don't know if it's from experience or I was just born with it. I always liked you, Ryland. Your problem? You're an honest guy in a dishonest business. In my business, I make the rules."

"Yeah, my wife wanted me to get out of the FBI, and I just didn't listen."

"Well, you got caught in something that's bigger than both of us. I know how to handle thugs, but we're well beyond that now. So if you hear that something happened to me, it won't be from some Mafia hit. You'll have to think a little more creative, like the people who put you behind bars."

Paul frowned; he knew what Frank was talking about. "Why do you say that?"

"I got a visit from Special Agent Weldon. Where did they find that guy? Do you know him?"

"Yeah. I never liked him."

"You shouldn't; he's not an FBI agent."

"How do you know that?"

"It's just a hunch, but, like I said, I know people. You can tell by the eyes; he's a killer."

"You mean like a hitman?"

Frank smiled. "How long have you known the guy?"

"A little over a year before I ended up here. Matter of fact, he came to the department from overseas right around the Seattle shootout."

"Coincidence? I don't think so. I don't want to say too much here. I don't know who's listening. But hopefully they don't have time to screw around with me as long as Bolton is out there."

"Did you hear about Bolton? Looks like they screwed up again."

"Oh yeah. When you send seven guys to kill him, and he walks away, and in the process you kill his girlfriend, it's just a matter of time before that guy finds you."

"And he is that type of guy."

"He's a guy with nothing to lose; he's already lost everything."

Paul smiled. "Is he still on your watch list?"

"He'll always be on that list. He's just not a priority right now. I got other problems. But when you think about it, ever since Bolton walked into our lives, it's

116

been a chaotic shit show that took on a life of its own."

"Yeah. I'm what you call collateral damage."

"Well, there's been a lot of that."

"Hey, I need a favor."

Frank looked at him then laughed. "What type of favor?"

"It's simple."

"Nothing is simple."

"I need you to check on my wife and find out who she's seeing."

Frank's eyes opened. He had not seen that coming. "You think your wife is cheating on you?"

"Yeah."

"Women. Well, if she's cheating on you, it's someone close."

"Why do you say that?"

"Trust me on that one. It's my instincts. And that's why I'm out there and you're in here. Favors don't come free; you know that."

"I get out in a few months. I'll pay you something."

"I don't need your money. Don't worry about it."

"Now I am worried," he said with a nervous laugh.

"I'll take care of it. I'm going to enjoy this, Ryland. And you know what? It's on me because I'm a good guy."

"Thanks, but where's the catch?"

"No catch. Seriously. A good woman stays by your side through thick or thin, and the smart ones throw you out if you cheat on them."

Paul chuckled, feeling more at ease. "Is that the book on women according to Gallo?"

"You could say I've been around the block." Gallo shrugged. "I'm a survivor in this crazy world we live in. You know, when you remove the bullshit, it's easy to see where you're going. You should try it sometime, Ryland, and stop worrying about hurting people's feelings."

"I can't argue with you about that; look where I am."

Gallo smiled and nodded, Ryland had stayed disciplined and loyal to the cause. Two people on opposite ends of the spectrum, knowing the consequences of their past actions would undoubtedly cause both of their demises.

Chapter 14

Art Glover took the call on a secure line. He was back in the game. Mattison gave him orders to find Bolton no matter what it took. Another opportunity to pay back Bolton for the death of his brother in downtown Seattle. Brian was gone; there was nothing holding him back now.

He had gotten to know Bolton's buddies, and the guy that he might turn to was Chris Baron, who lived in Spokane, Washington. It would be the most logical and closest place to go while on the run. Jack was running out of friends and places to hide.

Art packed his bags and took a flight to Seattle. He rented a car and headed for Spokane. He remembered that Chris was a regular at a bar there called O'Malley's on the outskirts of town. He arrived at 8:30 that evening and pulled into a nearby parking lot.

Art pushed through the front door and surveyed the bar. His eyes settled on a man sitting at the counter wearing blue jeans, a plaid shirt, and a baseball cap. There he was: good old Chris, trying to forget his past with alcohol. Art smirked, thinking how people were such creatures of habit, unable to break out of their chains. Maybe it was just easier to accept their circumstances. Bolton had at least tried to escape his fate, yet his path continued toward the same destination.

Art adjusted the brim of his baseball cap down and slid his six-foot frame onto the empty stool next to Chris.

"Surprised to see me?"

Chris looked over at the last person in the world he wanted to see. His instincts were immediately on red alert. Art couldn't be trusted.

"What the hell do you want?"

"I'm not feeling the love, Chris. Last I remember, you guys left me in Mexico all alone. I have no hard feelings. You did the right thing. I screwed up. I just wanted to apologize."

"Right. We both know the real reason why you're here."

"You do, huh? Couldn't I be here just to have a drink with an old friend and apologize?"

"You think I know where Bolton is. Well, you're wasting your time. I haven't seen him since Mexico."

"Okay, I believe you. Let me buy you drink, and we can talk old times. Bolton is amazing, huh? They find him up in Canada, and he shoots his way out. Quite the warrior. But anyway, I really just wanted to say I was sorry about Mexico."

"Forget about it. I don't care. No harm, no foul."

"Hey, that was a crazy ride in Mexico, huh?"

Chris said, expressionless, "We all got back safely, and we got the girl home."

"You're a serious guy, Chris. Hard to break the ice with you."

"Maybe it's the company."

The bartender dropped two whiskey shots in front of Art. He pushed one over to Chris. He pushed it back.

"I'm okay. I can buy my own drinks."

"I'm sure you can." He downed his shot. "Mattison pays pretty good, huh?"

"Yeah."

"If you're not going to drink this, I'll take it." Art gulped down the second whiskey and slammed the glass on the counter. "Now that's what I needed. You know, I still can't believe that Brian's gone. I really liked the guy. I had some good times with him in Antigua, a lot of laughs. I miss him."

Looking straight ahead, Chris motioned the bartender for another beer. "Who do you think shot him?"

Art shrugged. "Maybe they were trying to put down Bolton."

"If that was the case, they hired the world's worst sniper. I think Brian was the target."

"What makes you say that?"

He turned and looked Art straight in the eye. "Maybe that's why you're here. Sorry, Art, but I don't trust you or anyone, for what it matters."

Art laughed. "Come on; why would I be part of something like that?"

Chris looked away. "I think it's time you left. I just

want to drink my beer and be left alone."

"Those demons are hard to get rid of, huh? They just consume you. Well, I'll be on my way. I understand. I deserve the cold shoulder." Art dropped a couple of twenty-dollar bills on the bar. "The drinks are on me. I'll see you around."

After Art left, Chris continued to drink, like he always did. He didn't have to worry about driving home. He lived a half a mile down the road. He knew the routine, but Art being here wasn't a coincidence. He was looking for Bolton. But maybe he was considered a loose end in the big picture.

When the clock struck midnight, it was time for Chris to take his nightly walk home. He took no chances; instead of leaving through the front exit, he quietly took a side door out of O'Malley's. He walked fast and stayed in the shadows, paranoid that Art was waiting around a corner. He got to his Victorian-style house and scoped out the old-fashioned porch and cone-shaped roof lines and surveyed it like a detective at a crime scene.

Once inside he quietly went up the stairs and checked in the first bedroom to see his mother sound asleep, the wine glass on the nightstand empty. He then went to his room at the end of the hall, a nightlight radiating all the light he needed. All he wanted to do was sleep.

"You got a nice place here."

Chris jumped and turned toward the voice to find Art

sitting in the corner chair.

"What the hell are you doing in my house?" He eyed the nightstand where his Glock 17 was hidden under a hand towel.

"I'm sorry; I forgot to ask you to do something for me."

"God dammit, I told you: I don't know where Bolton is."

"Yeah, I know. But Mattison wants to talk to him, and he's probably the only one that can help him."

"Hey, if I see him, I'll tell him. Now get the hell out of my house." Chris sat on his bed then quickly grabbed the Glock 17. He pointed it at Art with both hands. "I said, get the hell out of my house."

Art shook his head. "Technically it's your mother's house. And I don't think you want to wake her up."

"I'm warning you."

Art sat there calmly. "Did you ever read *The Prince* by Machiavelli?"

"What the hell are you talking about? Leave or I'll kill you."

"I believe you, but let me make my point. And I promise I will leave without you firing a shot. So *The Prince* is basically about being unscrupulous, cunning, and deceptive – how people grab power through manipulation. To stay alive in this game that we're in, the same rules apply."

Art dropped the bullets from Chris's gun on the

hardwood floor.

His survival instinct kicking in, Chris lunged at Art, who stopped him with two shots fired from his gun fitted with a silencer.

"I'm sorry, Chris," he muttered. "I liked you. But I need for Bolton to run out of places to go, and I like him to feel the pain of guilt over losing friends. It was nothing personal."

Art stepped over Chris's body. He calmly grabbed the towel to wipe the blood off his shoes then left.

***

Two days later Art arrived in Dover, New Hampshire, a small town not too far from the Massachusetts border. He drove around an attractive neighborhood of homes surrounded by manicured loans. Art pulled the car in front of a row of trees and killed the engine. He watched Charlie Anthony Costa's house from a distance.

When Charlie arrived, two little kids greeted him. He was living the American dream and receiving a good chunk of blood money from Mattison didn't hurt. No sign of Jack Bolton.

Art had sold his soul to Mattison a long time ago. He quietly took care of loose ends for him. He was the silent soldier, the one who didn't question the job. He got paid well and did a few jobs a year, which had supplemented the bank robbing business. After the debacle in Seattle, robbing banks was no longer one of his pastimes.

As the evening turned to night, it was time to finish the job. Family, no family, people made choices. Once you got involved in the dark side, you were fair game. Art had learned that empathy was an enemy that could get you killed. He repeated to himself, *Just do the job and go home*. He had become a cold, calculated killer; the one Brian saw in action in Antigua.

He pushed the suppressor over the barrel of the Glock 17 and got out of the car then walked slowly down the road. The neighborhood was quiet. Houses were set some distance from the street. The moon was bright and full. Nobody would see him as a threat if they even noticed him at all. He wasn't sure how he wanted to do this though. A knock on the door and then the curdling screams after the shots were fired would draw attention. He hated that, not to mention the commotion afterwards and the quick sprint back to his car. These hits were a lot harder to stage.

He positioned himself by a tree near the base of the driveway to formulate his plan, then he heard voices as the garage door opened.

"Honey, I'm taking out the garbage; you have anything you need thrown out?"

Art waited in the shadows until Charlie rolled the barrels to the end of the driveway. He stepped out, startling Charlie.

"What the hell?"

"It's me, Art. You surely remember me."

"What the hell are you doing here?"

"I'm looking for Bolton. Mattison wants to help him."

"Hey, I don't like you coming around here. I have a family. And I haven't seen or heard from Bolton since Mexico. Now, I would like you to get off my property."

"Okay, fair enough. Hey, maybe you can answer this. I'm a little confused. Why do some people call you Tony when your name is Charlie Costa?"

He shrugged. "My legal name is Charlie Anthony Costa. My SEAL buddies started calling me Tony because Brian said I looked like a Mafia kingpin."

"That's Brian."

"You didn't come all the way up here to find that out."

"You testified against Jack for the murder of Gallo's son. You see the irony there?" Art smiled. "You looking like a Mafia kingpin and all."

"I don't see the humor."

Art's smile disappeared. "I want to apologize about Mexico; you should have shot me then and there. I'm sorry; don't take this personally."

Art raised the gun and pulled the trigger twice. Charlie staggered and fell over the barrels. Art walked back to his car and made a quick call.

All he said was, "It's done."

As he started the car he heard Tony's wife screaming. He rolled up the window and drove off.

Chapter 15

Jack had found refuge at Chip's home in Gillette, Wyoming. He was still awake when the sun broke the eastern horizon. The harder he tried to sleep, the more he tossed and turned. He stared up at the fan, watching each revolution. His mind was in total conflict. Thoughts of Kelly triggered bouts of sorrow. He tried focusing on the good times – the laughs, the hugs, the walks, the love – but then those final moments of her life crept into his head and the fury bubbled up. *They* had once again taken everything that mattered to him.

He rolled out of bed and made his way to the kitchen, which was open to the rest of the home. Jack fired up the Keurig and, after filling his coffee cup, he sat at the table and gazed out the row of windows. The dry, barren land seemed a fitting metaphor for how he felt.

The house was a two-level trailer built on a foundation that had a cellar, which was like a house of horrors. Chip was a mad scientist, showing off how artificial intelligence worked. It was amazing, but Jack really didn't care.

Chip walked into the kitchen in his bright red flannel pajamas. "Don't you sleep, Jack?"

"I haven't slept since I've been here."

"I have something that will knock you out."

"I'm good," Jack said, distracted. After five days of living in Chip's hideout, it was time to go. "Hey, I think I've put you out long enough. I need to move on."

"You do? Well, what's the plan? Where you going? You know everybody is out there looking for you. You're not going to get far without a plan."

"I know that."

"Then let me hear your plan."

"I don't really have one."

Chip nodded, understanding. "You've been consumed with the past. You need to forget about the past; you can't change it. It's gone. You can't bring Brian back or your girlfriend. So the question is where we go from here."

"I have some ideas."

"Being down in the dumps and feeling sorry for yourself isn't going to change anything," Chip said with a kind smile. "I'm going to help you. Brian didn't lose his life for nothing; your girlfriend didn't get killed for nothing; and I didn't fight in Vietnam for nothing. What we have here is a deep state running this country. That's not the way the United States was founded. So, we're going to take the fight to them. Just remember: we're the good guys."

Jack smiled. "Brian always said that." He looked at Chip, concerned. "I didn't want to get you involved. Anybody associated with me usually ends up dead. But if everything is based on an algorithm like you say, it's already predetermined."

"Jack, it's just a frigging theory. I might be totally wrong about it."

"The more I think about it, maybe you're right. Death has followed me throughout my life. I watched it play out in the Navy, except I never died. I was invincible. And even today, everybody around me gets killed, but somehow I'm still standing when I shouldn't be. So maybe your theory is pretty damn accurate."

"Just forget about that theory of mine, okay? I'm a little out there. And as far as getting me involved, when they killed Brian that got me involved. Brian told me you got the flash drive from Joe Cap who got it from his brother who worked in the CIA, right?"

"Yeah."

"Well, I don't think you want their lives to go to waste, do you?"

"No, of course not."

"Then it's time to bring these bastards all down. Every frigging one of them. So what's the plan to get the flash drive information out there?"

"I know an investigative reporter who interviewed me in prison. He's a straight shooter."

"What's his name?"

"Greg Wilson."

"I've heard the name. Has he been on the *Charlie Thompson Show*."

"Yeah. I can trust him."

"If you give him this information, he's a dead man. These people are not going to sit idly by and just let this guy tell the nation that President Atkins is a crook and that our former president, Farley, is running the country from his vacation home in Martha's Vineyard. Oh, and by the way, he's working with world elitists like the Sanderlin Group."

Jack exhaled. "The last thing I want is someone else to lose their life because of me."

"This guy Mattison is probably the person you want to see, but don't hand him the information."

"He wants it."

"The hell with him. It's time you met my old service buddy. I think you'll find his story interesting."

"Where is he?"

"He's about forty miles south."

"Let's go."

***

Jack looked around as they drove through the town of Wright. "Not too much to the town."

"Yeah, it's not a tourist attraction," Chip grinned. "It's an old mining town with maybe two thousand residents. A place where you can disappear."

The minivan rolled through a cluster of trailers separated by a large tract of land. Chip found the space he was looking for and parked.

"We're here."

They got out and Jack stretched, taking in a crystal-clear sky. He followed Chip, who knocked on the door.

A tall, lean man with gray hair and a hard face, wearing blue jeans and a T-shirt, answered, holding a gun pointed at them.

"Hey, Connor," Chip said. "Do you greet everyone this way?"

"Chip, sorry man." The two men embraced.

"Hey, this is Jack Bolton. Jack, this is Connor Harris."

Connor reached over and shook Jack's hand with a tight grip. "A friend of Chip's is a friend of mine. Come on in."

There wasn't much to see inside: a small living room, cramped kitchen, tiny bedroom, and a bathroom.

Connor asked, "I know it's early, but you want something to drink?"

Jack sat on the couch. "Whatever you got."

Connor pulled the refrigerator door open and pulled out three Bud Lights. After handing them out, he took a seat. "So, Chip, what brings you and your friend here?"

"Jack's a former SEAL. He was good friends with Brian."

Connor slowly nodded. "You're the guy who shot up Seattle, right?"

"It's not something I'm proud of, and it was supposed to be an easy arrest and it just got out of control."

Connor took a long drink of beer. "I can't believe the FBI's Most Wanted is sitting in my living room. Quite

131

an honor, I must say."

"Not the life I envisioned."

Connor smiled. "I don't give a shit what you've done in your past. You always have a place to stay with me."

"That's awfully kind of you, but I'll pass on that offer for now."

"I understand. In a way, I'm much like you, Jack. A dead man walking. I get through by reading the *Book of Revelations*. You should try it. It gives you a true perspective on life and beyond."

"I need to try something. I have few people I can trust."

"You can trust us," Connor said flatly.

"Jack knows Mattison," Chip said.

Connor didn't look surprised. He explained, "Chip is the only one who knows I'm alive."

"What happened?"

"I worked for Mattison for quite a few years, doing mostly security. Nothing too difficult and it paid well. I was working a business function at a Florida resort quite a few years back, and I picked up on a guy who just gave me a strange vibe, you know what I mean?"

Jack nodded. "I do."

"So I watched him closely, and as Mattison moved closer, I noticed the guy reach into his pocket and slowly pull out a gun. But he never fired. I shot him dead. I don't have to tell you, Mattison was impressed. He loved loyalty. He thanked me personally and mentioned that if I ever wanted to make more money to just let him know. I wasn't sure what that meant. I had gone through a divorce a few years earlier and was getting closer to retirement. So I figured I'd take him up on the offer.

"The first couple of jobs were easy. I was just a driver, making sure the perimeter was cleared. Again, nothing too tough, and it was great money. I had no idea what the others did, and I never asked or wanted to know. I was more interested in the money and retiring. But that all came crashing down. On this one job in Cambridge, Massachusetts, I wasn't going to be the driver; I was going to be a player. I swore to myself that would be my last gig; I had saved enough. I knew deep down that whatever they were doing was probably illegal.

"Nobody explained the job, and I never asked. There were three of us, and we broke into a very nice house. The guy never had a chance. We gagged him and gave him a shot in the neck, killing him. Then I realized the guy was a federal judge, a liberal one at that. I complained that I didn't want to be part of it. They told me I was now an accessory to a murder, so to keep my mouth shut.

"On the way back, I was in the front passenger seat, not feeling too good about what had happened. The guy in the back fired a shot right through the seat, then they stopped the car on a bridge and threw me into the Charles River like I was a bag of shit. The bullet somehow missed my vitals, and I survived the plunge into the icy water. When I made it to shore, I decided to disappear and never be heard from again. I found this trailer park, where nobody would look. I've been here ever since."

"What happened with that federal judge?"

"It was reported that he died of a heart attack. But he didn't. He was murdered. I'm sure there were others."

"Why did Mattison want the judge dead?"

"I really don't know. We weren't paid to think. I suspect he wanted to get his own federal judges in place, but who knows the real reason? Nobody explained anything, so even if you got caught, you knew nothing. This is my little world now, quiet and simple. Just the way I like it. And I found God, which is something you should do for yourself, Jack."

"Let me ask you a question."

"Fire away."

"Did you ever bump into an Art Glover?"

Connor paused. "He was one of the men on that job that night. He's the worst type of psychopath."

"What do you mean?"

"He has no empathy, but his outgoing personality can fool you. I'm afraid to ask your connection."

"I killed his brother in Seattle in the mayhem."

"So he's looking for you."

"I don't know. Brian met him in Antigua – I guess Art saved Brian's life. The Moreno Cartel had sent a hit squad to kill him, and Glover killed five of them. After that they became good buddies."

"That's what psychos do," Connor said. "I'm pretty sure it was Glover that put that bullet in me. I would be careful, Jack."

"He's just one of many. I can take care of myself, Connor."

Connor held up his beer. "I'm sure you can. Why was a Mexican Cartel sending a hit squad to kill Brian?"

Chip explained, "Brian thought it was a good idea to steal money from the Moreno Cartel."

"You guys are frigging crazy. I hope it was worth it."

"It was millions."

"I don't understand why there is so much hate in the world," Jack said. "It would be a much better world with a lot more love."

"It's not about hate, Jack, "Connor said. "It's all about power and control, manipulating the masses into thinking they're getting something when in reality it's all about the people in power. This is one thing Mattison has right: the politicians on both sides of the aisle want bigger and bigger government, which eventually leads to more dependency, more debt, less advancement, less freedom, and eventually a dictatorship to control the masses when the money runs out."

Chip added, "History tells the story, and it never changes; it always ends the same way. Our forefathers had great foresight. They put together the greatest document the world has ever seen. It was the first time in history that the little guy had freedom from the oligarchs, the ability to empower oneself. But as time evolved, the people in power keep chipping away at the great document, through the liberal judges, the media's constant barrage of a false narrative, and the people in power accumulating mass wealth. And we have proof, Jack, in that little flash drive, of a true dark pool funded by dark money."

"Thanks for the overview," Jack said. "I'm going to blow up that narrative, starting today."

"One man can't change the world," Connor said. "If you're successful, you might put it off for a while, but at the end of the day, history always seems to repeat itself."

"Mankind has been doing this for quite a long time," Chip agreed. "Now we're in an age where the oligarchs think this time will be different, and as the masses get more and more dependent on them, the more control they take. Now they have social media and the use of the Internet to spread propaganda, but that's only the first phase of this utopian society that they foresee. The second phase is using artificial intelligence and a global blockchain technology to do their bidding since man is flawed. As they make these foundational technologies and machines more and more powerful, these systems will eventually turn on their makers."

"You don't paint a very nice future," Jack said.

"Me and Connor are patriots. We joined the military because we understood what the American flag represents, which a larger majority of the younger generation today sadly doesn't. If they only knew the flag is a symbol of defending against tyranny, but the only way you understand that, I guess, is to experience tyranny, which our forefathers knew all too well."

Chapter 16

The next day Jack and Chip drove five hours to Livingston, Montana, with a population of seven thousand people. They parked downtown by a small collection of shops with an array of mountains in the background, the sun barely visible between thick white cumulus clouds.

They found a cozy restaurant called Sneakers. A waitress greeted them with a warm smile then directed them to a quiet corner table by a large window. She poured two cups of coffee and handed them each a menu before walking away.

"You ready for the next chapter?" Chip asked.

Jack shook his head. "There's no Brian this time."

"You want me to drive you farther?"

"The less they know, the better. I'll call them. They'll be more than happy to come and pick me up, I'm sure."

Chip took a phone out of his pocket and slid it across the table. "It's secure. You call me if you get in trouble."

"It's a crime to help a fugitive."

"You know I'm well beyond that," he smiled. "I'm not too worried."

"Maybe you should be. There's an FBI agent I know who's sitting behind bars. He got two and half years because they thought he was helping me evade the law."

The waitress came back, took their order, and left with the menus.

"Do you think it was a good idea to send the package to the reporter?"

"He won't do anything with it until I give him the okay, but if something happens to me, he'll announce it."

"I'm just going to have to go along with it, huh?"

"I'm meeting him in DC next week. Brian had a good friend whose an expert at forging papers. He'll set me up with a new identity."

"So you do have a plan."

Jack nodded. "I'm hoping that Mattison knows the people responsible for Kelly's death, and I'm going to kill them all."

After breakfast they walked outside and hugged each other goodbye.

"I wish you good luck," Chip said.

Tears welled in Jack's eyes. "Thanks for helping me out. I'm so sorry about Brian. He was like a brother to me."

Chip almost teared up; he couldn't remember the last time that happened. "Keep your eye on the ball and trust no one. Just go with your instincts and you'll be fine. I'm not sure where that's going to take you, and I'm not sure you are going to like where you end up, but it will be what it will be. So long, Jack."

They shook hands then Chip got in his van and, with

a final wave, drove off.

***

A black SUV rolled up in front of Sneakers. Jack watched from a bench as three large men in suits emerged from the vehicle. The first leg of the journey had begun.

He walked over and introduced himself. "I would like a meeting with Mr. Mattison."

One of the men stepped forward. "My name's Luke. I work with Mr. Mattison. He's looking forward to seeing you again, Mr. Bolton. I think the two of you have a lot to talk about. Before we can go, we need to pat you down. You understand."

Jack put his hands up half-way as one of the men patted him down and pulled the Glock 17 from a back holster. Jack shrugged with a smirk then got into the back of the SUV accompanied by Luke, and they headed west. Twenty-five minutes later the SUV came to a large gate at the entrance to Mattison's compound. Security men inspected the vehicle then allowed it to pass through and continue on. Small rustic cabins dotted the premises. Eventually the SUV reached an oversized colonial and parked in the circular, brick driveway. Jack followed Luke inside the house and up a large stairway. When they reached the second floor, Luke told him to wait for Mr. Mattison out on the terrace.

He sat down in a large recliner under a trellis and gazed at the rolling hills. The view was breathtaking. He was in God's country, and yet the devil was among them.

A woman came up and asked him if he wanted anything to drink.

"Yeah, I'll take a Sam Adams."

A few minutes later a cold beer was served. *Quite the life*, he thought. He finished that beer and ordered another. A short time later he could hear the distinctive thump of a helicopter approaching and watched it touch down a hundred yards out. Within a few minutes, James Mattison walked out to the terrace.

"Jack, it's good to see you," Mattison said in a booming voice, shaking Jack's hand energetically. "We have a lot to talk about. What has it been, about two years? A lot has happened since then."

"Yes, it has. The last time I was here I was in rough shape. I hardly remember the beauty of this place."

"The world is complicated, so being here lets you get close to nature and realize how lucky you are." Mattison sat. "I was sorry to hear about your girlfriend."

Jack's face hardened. "I had a pretty nice life for a while. I was in love. She was pregnant. I should've known I could never lead a normal life. My mistake. And it cost Kelly her life. But that's the past; I can't bring it or her back. I put myself in this position, and it cost people – too many people – their lives."

"My offer still stands. We could use someone with your skills in our organization. Few people in this country realize that we're at war, not from the outside but the inside. The Trojan horse is already in Washington. We can protect you, set you up with a new identity."

"I appreciate that, Mr. Mattison. I'm here because I want to take out everyone responsible for the deaths of the people I love, especially Kelly."

"You came to the right place. We're both on the same page. I want to show you something." He turned to Luke. "Please go get the folder."

Luke returned in a few minutes and handed his boss a folder that Mattison placed on the coffee table in front of Jack. "Open it. Let me know your thoughts."

Curious, Jack opened the folder, and he peered intently at a group of photos.

"Where did you get these?"

Mattison shrugged off the question. "I have my ways. I always like to know who the opposition is meeting with. Do you know any of the players on that boat?"

"Atkins, of course, and next to him is FBI Director Shone Williams. The guy with the bald head, I remember quite well. I killed him in surgery at the local hospital. The bastard shot Kelly from about a hundred yards. But I had taught her how to use a gun, and she was pretty good. She wounded him first, which allowed me to finish him off."

"His name was Oz Wolf, a former intelligence agent for Germany's BND before going to work for the

Sanderlin Group."

Jack pointed to a man wearing a Polo shirt. "Who is that?"

"Eric Steele. He also works for the Sanderlin group. I had a conversation with him a couple years back. He wanted me to give you up. I told him to go to hell."

"I guess I should thank you."

"I'm just a patriot," Mattison smiled. "Steele is the one who set the attack on you in motion."

"Who runs the Sanderlin group?"

"Peter Sanderlin. Why?"

"After I deal with Steele, I'm going after Sanderlin."

Mattison laughed. "I applaud your tenacity. And I want Eric Steel dead as well. I'll help you on that one. But Peter Sanderlin is way out of our league. He's protected by an army. You would never get close."

"Mr. Mattison, no offense, but you just aren't thinking big enough."

Mattison leaned in, hands folded on the table. "You aren't the only one personally affected here."

"Why do you say that?"

"That meeting," he nodded toward the photos, "wasn't just about you. They conspired to kill my brother to send me a message. I begged my brother to have some security. But he told me to forget about it."

"What happened?"

"The news reported it as a road-rage incident. A fender bender gone wrong. Witness said they were arguing over the accident. But that was all a sham. The guy pulled out a gun and shot my brother dead. As I said, we're in a war that nobody will see until it spills out into the streets."

"Did they catch the guy?"

"The police? Come on; they'll never find that killer. So I'm glad you're here, but we have a lot of work to do. I need your flash drive, Jack. And this time I'm not asking."

"Nothing against you, but we're going to do this my way."

Mattison leaned back in his chair. "Don't confuse my kindness as weakness."

"I understand, but what you don't know is that Atkins isn't really in charge. He might think he is, but he's not."

"What the hell are you talking about?"

"You've heard the term *deep state*."

He nodded. "What're you getting at?"

"Ed Farley never left. He's running dark money through a dark pool that is financing all types of well-entrenched activists all over the world. He's in collusion with the media to create a narrative that benefits his agenda. I'm going to expose the whole system."

Mattison rubbed his chin, absorbing this new information. "So Farley is the puppet master. The true architect deep in the shadows. Atkins does make the perfect patsy. Okay, we'll do things your way – for now. But you're going to have a partner. People who take a hit personally usually make mistakes. I want you to work with Glover."

Jack started to protest.

"I know all about what happened in Mexico with him, but I have his assurance that it's all in the past," Mattison concluded.

"That's fair, but I'm not going to make a mistake. And you tell him to stay out of my way."

Mattison nodded then put a finger up as Luke bent down and whispered in his ear. He stood.

"I have some unfinished business, Jack. Why don't you join me?"

They descended a brick stairway then followed a dirt path to a cabin a hundred yards from the main house. Mattison pushed opened the door. Four men with their sleeves rolled up surrounded a battered and bruised man sitting in a chair, with his hands and feet tied, his face bloody, and his eyes swollen almost shut.

Jack stood off to the side while Mattison walked up to the man and spoke in a quiet voice. "What's your name?"

"Bobby-Jo Graham," he said, voice cracking. "Everyone just calls me Bobby. Do you have a smoke?"

"For you, Bobby, I think we can find one." One of Mattison's men stepped forwarded and put a cigarette in the man's mouth, and Mattison lit it. "Do you know why you're here?"

"No. I was just gambling in Vegas and these men

grabbed me. I think you have the wrong person." He nervously exhaled a puff of smoke.

Mattison paused a moment then took the cigarette out of Billy's mouth and stepped on it with his shoe.

"How was Vegas?"

"It was great. I want to go back."

"I'm sure you do." Mattison lightly patted Bobby's cheek. "Your whole life has been one excuse after another. Kids out of wedlock, never making your court-mandated child support, never being there for your kids. One job after another. A closet alcoholic. You're just a real frigging mess, am I right, Bobby?"

"I'm making my child-support payments. I see my kids."

Mattison just shook his head. "Do you know who I am?"

"No, and I don't know why I'm here." He was in tears.

"In life we make choices, and with every choice there's a consequence. You made a choice, but an unwise choice. A little over a week ago you rear-ended my brother's car. Is it all coming back to you now, Bobby?"

Jack noted that the man's growing panic was palpable.

"I don't – "

"You banged into my brother's car, and he told you to forget about it. Didn't he?" When Bobby didn't

146

answer Mattison raged: "*Didn't he?*"

"Yes, he did. I had to. They paid me to do it."

"Ah," Mattison nodded. "Who paid you?"

"I don't know who they were. Two guys."

"How much did they pay you? How much was my brother's life worth?" When he didn't get a response, he raised his voice. "I said how much damn it?"

Jack could smell the urine: Bobby had wet his pants.

"Ten thousand dollars up front and another ten thousand dollars after it was done."

"A lot of money, and yet you decided not to go back and get the rest of it. I'd like to know why?"

"I don't know. I was scared. And I always wanted to go to Vegas."

"Best decision of your life. Those men were going to kill you."

"Look, I'm so sorry. I didn't want to kill your brother. Please; I'll do anything."

"I'm sure you will. But remember what I said: there are consequences." Mattison looked around the room. "You know when I was younger and played with my brother, he was always the good cop and I was the bad guy. Everyone loved my brother because he had a pure heart. And you just snuffed him out like he was some piece of shit. But I'm a fair guy, so you know what I'm going to do? I'm going to let you go." Mattison gestured to his men. "Untie him."

Bobby stood, his legs unsteady. "I'm free to go?"

"Yes. But you only have a five-minute head start. That's the best I can do."

"What do you mean?"

"I mean that after five minutes my men are going to come hunting for you. If they catch you, they are going to kill you. So, I wish you luck, Bobby." He looked at his watch. "You'd better get going."

Bobby bolted out of the cabin, literally running for his life, with no idea where he was or where he was heading.

Mattison announced: "Whoever takes him out gets a $5,000 bonus in their next paycheck. Give him the full five minutes then go."

Jack followed Mattison back to the main house and the second-floor terrace, not saying a word. When they sat down, Mattison said, "I know that look; you didn't like what I did."

"You reminded me of Frank Gallo down there."

"That's what you think? That I'm some Mafia thug? You of all people are questioning what I did down there? If I got my facts straight, you shot Gallo's son in cold blood. Not just that, you called his father and then shot his son while he was on the other end. And I'm a thug? What you did was pretty damn cold-blooded."

"I know."

"Then after you got broken out of prison, you went after Atkins's son and shot him in broad daylight at his frat."

Jack squirmed in his chair. "I'm not proud of my past. I was an angry person."

"You sure were. So don't you dare judge me again."

Two gunshots echoed in the distance. Mattison shook his head. "Bobby made a bad choice, Jack, and the consequences were fatal. I have no remorse for people like that, and neither do you. So stop looking at me like I'm a monster. You're no different."

"I remember Gallo saying the same thing to me."

"Maybe he's got a good point. You do what you have to in this game. Otherwise you end up six feet under like my brother."

"I did what I did for love."

"That's a funny side of love."

"Mr. Mattison, do you know what real love is? I do. Everything I've done and continue to do is for the love of those I lost. Not for power or financial gain."

"That's all well and good, but you aren't going to get far without my help. I don't give a shit what you think of me. And, no, I'm not in this for people to love me. I'm in it to protect the Constitution, the greatest document ever created. The document that lets me and you make decisions and choose the way we want to live. These oligarchs or globalists, whatever you want to call them, are not interested in love either. It's about control, money, and power. They're in it for world dominance. They'll continue to chip away at our constitution, and they are doing it today by attacking the past, making our forefathers out to be evil men. The Constitution is only as good as the people who defend it. At the end of the day, it's just a piece of paper, and if you can brainwash enough people in a society to believe you have a better way, well, it's the end of America as we know it. Why do you think they leave the borders open? It's about votes. It's about people who never experienced real freedom and who come from Third-World hellholes. They'll fall right back into their old ways."

"Maybe you're right, but I'm doing this for me."

"I wish you'd trust me, Jack. I think you forget I've saved your life a couple of times now. I helped you rescue Laura. I'm more of a target than ever because of those things."

"I appreciate all you've done for me, but you're just going to have to trust me."

"Steele will be in Washington, D.C. within a week or two. Sanderlin is hosting its annual private conference for the European and North American political, industrial, financial, academic, and media elite.

"So you'll be there."

"I don't get invited anymore since I went to the dark side," Mattison said with a chuckle. "Anyway, let me show you to your room, then we should talk about putting a plan together."

Chapter 17

The sun broke through the clouds as James Mattison waited in a black SUV on a dirt road outside of Denver, Colorado. Two other black SUVs approached from the south and rolled to a stop twenty-five yards away. Mattison got out and waited until Ed Farley exited his vehicle. After exchanging greetings, they walked along a trail between rolling hills on the south and north. The tall grass swayed in the breeze.

Mattison hadn't seen the former president in a couple of years; he'd aged and lost more of his hair. "You're getting old, Ed."

"It's from all my battle scars dealing with people like you."

"How's that government-funded, free-perk-for-life of Secret Service protection working out for you."

"Pretty good. Every former president needs it in this sick world."

"Maybe some need it more than others."

"What does that mean?"

"Nothing."

Farley changed the subject. "Sorry about Tyler. He was a good guy. I met him a couple of times. The world is full of crazy people."

Mattison eyed Farley. "It wasn't road rage. He was

executed."

"That's why you wanted this meeting? You're looking at me like I had something to do with it. You really think I would do that?"

"I think you might know more than you're willing to tell me, Ed."

"I'm retired, James. You know my big hobby now is a flower garden. I'm out of politics."

"Politicians can never let go. Especially you."

"Well, I'm out."

"Do you think I'm an idiot? Maybe you had nothing to do with Tyler, but you are far from *out*."

"I served two terms; there's nothing else. I'm sorry to disappoint you. Why did you want to meet me in such a secluded place?"

"I like my conversations not to be heard by the wrong people. I know what you're doing."

"You do? Let me in on the little secret."

"You're running the country."

Ed laughed. "Really? I don't know where you get your information. Obviously you're still bitter about the election."

"No. I want to make a deal with you."

"What could I possibly do for you or what could you do for me?"

"Play dumb all you want. But let's get down to business."

"Okay, I'm listening."

"I want Eric Steele dead. He's the one responsible for Tyler's death."

"How do you know that?"

"I do. I'm not going to explain it to you either."

"Okay. Let's say I believe you. What do you want from me?"

"I get Steele. You get Bolton."

Ed smiled and shook his head. "I think you've been reading too many novels. Bolton is a minnow in an ocean. What do I care about Jack Bolton? He's a murderer. A deranged man from all I've read."

"Maybe you should care about Bolton. He seems to know a lot about you, not to mention how much he knows about Atkins."

"He knows nothing. If that's why you called me out here, I want nothing to do with this."

Mattison stopped and waited until Farley made eye contact. "You always come off like some innocent bystander. You've done that your whole political career. You've always wanted to create a world with no borders – the European Union, the Asia-Pacific Union, and of course the United American Union. You seem to think politicians that stay at five-star hotels and eat at gourmet restaurants are going to solve the world's problems."

"The world is a better place if we all work together. We'll get a lot further than a world divided, that's for sure."

"It's not up to you to decide."

"Come on, James; the sheep can't get out of their own way. Somebody has to be able to guide them. And for the first time in world history, we now have the technology to control the masses through the Internet, social media, and technology."

"Maybe if you empowered them and gave people a real education they could think on their own rather than the world according to Ed Farley and the Sanderlin Group. Oh yeah, that world should work out just fine for the 99 percent."

"You need to let go of the past and look forward to the future."

"Socialism isn't the answer."

"Who said anything about Socialism?"

"You have your own agenda, Ed. You can play stupid with me all you want, but it doesn't change everything Bolton knows about you: all the off-shore accounts, dark pools, dark money, where all that money is going, and what it's funding. He also has proof about the eighteen billion that was money-laundered back into the States from Iraq that Banner and Atkins orchestrated. How's that for clarity?"

Ed displayed his best poker face. As a good politician he never admitted the truth. "I heard rumors about that but never believed it. And I have nothing to do with any of it. But I gather you have this information and will expose it if I don't make a few phone calls. Is that what you're looking for?"

"Now that I've finally got your attention, all I want is Steele dead. Bolton will kill him, and then you can have Bolton. It's that simple."

They started walking again. "I don't think Sanderlin will like his righthand man being killed. I really just want to water my flowers and watch them bloom. I don't think you appreciate the beauty of flowers, James. You like to hunt and kill things. I like to watch things grow. You like to watch things die."

"Do we have a deal?"

"I'll call you and let you know."

Chapter 18

On a crisp autumn morning, President Atkins stood in front of his son's grave while crows squawked on the tree limb above. Secret Service agents toured the perimeter while Sam said a few prayers. Jennifer's harsh words had hit home; she blamed him for John's death. He tried to calm his emotions but became furious when the thought of Jack Bolton stirred in his mind. It had been three years since Ryland's phone call telling him his son had been fatally shot. It burned him inside that nobody notified the college that Bolton had escaped. Ryland deserved to be serving time; he was inept, and the very idea that he had helped Bolton boiled his blood.

The cemetery had become a sanctuary, a place where side business could be discussed without worrying about bureaucrats speculating on what it meant. No records were kept, so it worked well; even the media respected his right to privately visit his son's grave.

A car rolled to a stop and Eric Steele emerged wearing a long overcoat that matched his gray hair. He walked over to Sam; they shook hands.

Steele looked around. "It's quiet here – a good place to talk."

"Yeah. I used to meet Banner here all the time. It just kind of happened that way. You know, sometimes you can't fix your mistakes. You got Mattison's brother, but you damn well screwed up by not taking Bolton down. The big, bad Oz was going to take care of things. Well, he's six feet under now. What's your excuse?"

Steele was taken aback by Atkins's tone. "Bolton always seems to get lucky breaks at the right time."

"Sometimes people make their own breaks. What's the plan going forward? I'm starting to think I won't see Bolton dead in my lifetime."

"No, we'll get him. Don't worry about that, Sam."

Sam shook his head. "If I know Bolton, he's probably gunning for you."

"He has no idea about me."

"He'll figure out you were behind his girlfriend's death."

"It would be suicide to go after me."

Sam smirked at Steele's bravado. "He's resourceful. You took away the last good thing in his life. Trust me; he's running toward you, not away. And he'll find you."

"If you're right, it'll make my job a lot easier."

"Be careful what you wish for. A man with nothing to lose is a dangerous man."

"Sam, you worry too much about Bolton. If he really had something on that flash drive, he would have played it. I think he's a non-issue and a big waste of manpower."

"You know what, Eric? Every time I come out here, I'm reminded what he did to my son. I don't understand how this guy can't be taken down. I'll take care of this myself."

"You want it, you got it. Do it your way. Now that you've gotten comfortable as president, it's time we talk about your agenda; we need some legislation passed."

"Since when do you get involved with my agenda? I think you forget who's the president."

"I'm not forgetting that at all, Sam. Maybe you forget who got you elected."

"If you've got something to say, say it."

"It was all Farley's plan."

"What was?"

"You're just part of a bigger plan. We needed somebody who had a strong political bloodline, check. We needed someone with some baggage, check. Somebody who committed a crime that nobody knew about, check. And somebody who was a good bullshitter, check. You were our perfect candidate."

"You're frigging insane, you know that?"

"You've been doing this all your life to other politicians; you just don't like it when you're on the other side of it."

"I have my own agenda, and I don't need to converse with you about it."

"Our agenda *is* your agenda, so this is what we want. Propose to let in three hundred thousand refugees."

"Why?" Sam's voice was noticeably strained.

"It'll take pressure off the EU."

"I don't give a crap about the EU. We don't have the money for something like that. I mean, we could take in some, but three hundred thousand is a stretch."

"You'll find a way, Sam. Then we need a big push by you for a nice amnesty bill for twelve million illegals."

"That's crazy. It'll never get through."

"Let us worry about that. The media narrative will be on your side. We'll get twelve million potential new voters, a slam dunk for the next election. You'll be an instant hero to the left."

"I don't want it. I'll do what I feel is right. And nobody is going to tell me otherwise."

"Don't make it harder than it has to be, Sam. You remember the Phoenix Project, the whole thing behind Bolton's flash drive? I'd hate to see that come out in the headlines."

Sam stood stone-faced, his eyes burning.

"Normally something like that would have removed you from our selection process, but Farley was a strong advocate of yours and argued why you were the right candidate, and he was so right, especially in a room full of skeptics."

"Are you blackmailing me?"

"You can call it whatever you want. It's nothing against you; we just have our agenda. America's always dictating the rules to the world; with your help that's about to change to a new world where we all work together toward a common goal. So we have to spread the wealth around. Corporations make more money, America makes a little less, and the world's a happier place."

"You really believe that bullshit?"

"It's the only way the world is going to survive long-term. It's what's best for the world, not just America."

"And all I have to do is accommodate Farley's vision and his globalist buddies and his merry band of activists," Atkins stated with indignation.

"You'll go down as the greatest president, one who changed America. You'll get four more years. The Supreme Court will be totally left, and then the big one: we change the Constitution to reflect the new America."

"You think I'm going to just stand by and let Farley run the show behind the curtain?"

"You don't really have a choice, and it will be easy. The sheep can be molded any way we want. We're already doing it today. The media narrative of removing the old fabric of America is fueling activists to remove historical statues. But the sheep don't realize they're being brainwashed for the main event."

"And what's that?" Sam asked coldly.

"The disarming of America."

"You want to take the people's guns away to look like Europe?"

"Exactly."

"It won't happen here."

"Well, America is changing. You give amnesty to twelve million people and change the Supreme Court, and people will accept that the right to bear arms should be abolished. The next mass shooting will open the door to chip away at the gun lobby."

"The NRA and the Midwest states will never let it happen. A mass shooting isn't going to dissuade them. Look at how many we've had.

"I didn't say it would be easy. This won't happen overnight, but once the people demand it, then we'll be able to forward our agenda as planned. Sure, they'll be some uprising here or there, some bloodshed, but we'll put it down, and eventually the people will move on. And America will be disarmed, which will ensure our long-term success of controlling the people."

Sam shook his head. "My father would never go for this."

"You're not your father. He's not the president. You've got everything to gain and a lot to lose."

"Your smug look makes me sick. What makes you think I'm some figurehead for Farley?"

"You know how the game is played. You're a corrupt politician in the most powerful position in the world. And with your baggage, you have no choice but to follow through with our agenda. The hardest part was getting you elected. Farley was right, and now we're almost there. Bolton is a sideshow who's not going to last long."

"I don't give a damn about the Phoenix Project. I can beat that."

Eric shook his head. "You really don't get it. Farley was the master of destroying his opponents and getting legislation through. He knew weaknesses and exploited them. Sam, Laura Weston is your Achilles heel. Not only that, every conversation with us has been recorded."

Sam had no words. He looked at Steele enraged. "You frigging bastard. You're a Sanderlin shill, and Farley can go to hell. I should boot your diplomatic ass right out of the country."

"It's not going to change anything. You're sore that you got played. But, look, you got what you wanted. Nobody will ever know. You'll get credit for all of it. Look at the positive side. The world will be a better place. You'll be loved."

Sam stared straight ahead. He couldn't believe Farley had run right over him, and he never saw it coming. "I think you should go, Steele."

"It always takes a little time to understand the big picture, Sam. Oh, as a goodwill gesture to make sure Laura Weston doesn't do anything stupid, we're going to get rid of Keller. That should put the fear of God in her and ensure she keeps her mouth shut. We know how much you care about her. You don't have a problem with that, do you?"

Trying to digest his own situation, Atkins only half

heard about the imminent demise of Keller. If Banner was alive, he would have had Steele disappear. Atkins had a hard time stomaching the idea that he was owned by Farley.

Steele looked at his watch. "I have to go. We should talk again, Sam. I hope to see some major legislation has passed the next time we talk. Hey, one last thing: if Laura Weston's kidnapping ever got out, we're talking more than impeachment. Probably more like a life sentence. Have a good day, President Atkins."

As Steele was walking away, Sam called out, "When Bolton has a gun pointed at your head, do me a favor, and tell him I haven't forgotten."

Steele turned and smiled as he marched confidently back to his car.

***

Art made himself at home in a small, well-maintained ranch house in Sandy, Utah. He found a dusty whiskey bottle in a back cabinet, twisted the cap off, and placed his nose against the opening, then poured some into a short glass and took a swig. It was still good. Good old Wendell wasn't much of a drinker. This was the best he had. Art put his feet up on the coffee table and rested his head back.

It wasn't too long later that the door handle turned. Art rested in the dark shadows, waiting for the right moment to surprise the homeowner.

Wendell entered the side door to the kitchen. He was

a creature of habit. He went directly to the refrigerator, grabbing a jar of peanut butter and then opening a cabinet door for a pack of crackers. He moved to the living room where his collection of computer games, his passion, was waiting. Lost in his own little world, Wendell loaded a game into his console and didn't notice Art lurking in the shadows until he headed to the couch.

He screamed and jumped back with his hands up. "Take anything you want."

Art just smiled, still leaning back with his arms folded. "Wendell, I'm not here for your stuff. Settle down. I have some good news and some bad news."

"Who are you?" Wendell asked, his body trembling.

"It doesn't matter who I am, just what I know. Your parents live in Maryland. You work for the NSA in that black room, dark room, whatever they call it. Your job is basically to mine all sorts of data from every type of device. And I hear you're pretty good at what you do. I kill people, and I'm pretty good at that."

Wendell backed up against the back of the couch.

Art stood. "I'm not here to harm you, unless you decide not to help us."

"Who's *us*?"

"Does it really matter? Do you have a girlfriend?"

"No."

"Of course not with glasses like that. I would get some new glasses, might help you with the ladies. The good news is you're now on the payroll. Just in case the feds are watching you guys, a check will be sent to your parents' bank account. Everybody's watching everybody, am I right, Wendell? That's why they have that massive data center down the street."

"I don't want your money," Wendell said. "I don't have access to anything."

Art took a step forward. "You're on the payroll for a reason, and it's not negotiable."

"I could get in trouble."

Art laughed. "*Get* in trouble? You're already in trouble. Let me put it to you another way. You screw this up or decide to go to the authorities, two things could happen. I'll shoot you myself or maybe kill your parents. Or better yet we'll expose you for the rat you are, and you'll spend your days in jail. You're in a no-win situation, so don't fight it. You'll be paid well."

"Why me?" he whined.

"It's a compliment; we hear you're good."

"What do you want from me?"

Art handed him a piece of paper. "Here's a list. We want you to monitor these people."

Wendell looked at the list. "The former president?"

"Yes."

"I can't do that. You need court orders."

"You're starting to piss me off, Wendell."

"I can't be doing this."

"You will." Art moved menacingly toward Wendell,

whose heart was about to explode.

Cowering he said, "Okay, I got it."

"Your first payment has already been deposited. Welcome aboard." Art stuck his hand out; Wendell reluctantly shook it. "Don't screw this up."

Chapter 19

Retired Senator George Atkins puffed on his pipe while taking in the view from the screened-in porch of his home on Beaver Lake. He put down the pipe and took a sip of beer. He watched a few geese take off as the sun began its descent. His battle scars from his days in Washington, D.C. were just memories now. His reverie was interrupted by Larry, his majordomo, leading his son onto the porch.

"Sam, it's good to see you," George said, getting up to hug him. "Larry, bring him a beer, please. Sam, sit. So, did you come out here to see your dad or to clear your head?" George asked, easing back into his chair.

"How's the knee replacement?"

"I'm doing well. I'm back fishing every morning. Why don't you stay and join me tomorrow morning? I go out at sunrise. It's the best time of the day with the morning mist rising off the lake, the fish jumping. You can't beat it. It's a little lonely without your mom, but I find serenity here." He shook off the melancholy. "So how's the cesspool in Washington doing?"

"It's the same, just more people attacking you with their own agendas. The lobbyists are worse; they're like cockroaches."

Larry came out with a cold bottle of beer on a tray.

Sam grabbed it, took a swig, and nodded appreciatively. "Those micro brews hit the spot."

George changed the subject. "So, what's wrong?"

"Why can't I be out here to just visit and say hello?"

"Don't try to bullshit me. It didn't work when you were a kid, and it's not going to work now." George picked his pipe back up. "I see Bolton has continued to elude authorities. I read they killed his pregnant girlfriend up in Canada. What kind of animals do you have searching for Bolton? He sure didn't waste any time taking care of business."

"I don't know who to trust anymore since Banner is gone."

"Well, Bolton is paying the price for killing John. Karma has been a bitch for him ever since."

"What are you saying, Dad?"

"I'm saying, since you are now president, forget about him. He can only cause you headaches, and politicians have a way of using this type of dirt against you."

"It might be too late."

George stared out at Beaver Lake. "So, you have a problem. And there is no Banner to fix it. Hence, you need someone you can trust."

"Yeah."

"How big is the problem?"

"I'm being blackmailed."

"I hope this isn't one of those floozies you've been

fooling around with all your frigging life. I would've thought you'd have learned your lesson from the Laura Weston debacle."

"It's not a woman, Dad. And don't come off like you were Mr. Innocent. You slept around as well."

George drank his beer until only suds were left. He yelled, "Larry, bring us some whiskey," then looked at Sam. "Let me tell you something; I loved your mother. She was the best woman I ever met. Yeah, I had a mistress in DC for ten years or so. She knew her role. I took care of her apartment, bought her nice gifts, and in exchange she would build my ego, make me feel good after a long day of battling in the arena. She met a need; that's all she was. I sure didn't love her. I loved your mother. So don't put me in the same category as your infidelities. How many women have you slept with since you've been married? Do you have a number? Nicole's sure a good woman for putting up with all your crap over the years. Honestly, she should have taken the girls and left you a long time ago."

"I didn't come here to argue with you, Dad. It's not your life."

"Someday when you have a chance to reflect, you're not going to like what you see."

"I don't want to talk about it."

"Enough said. How are the girls?"

"The girls are good. Jennifer is another story. She's her crazy self as usual."

"What's going on with her?"

"I found out she's pregnant," he said, not mentioning the father of her child was marked for termination.

George relit his pipe and took a couple of puffs, thinking how there was nothing like the taste of tobacco. "I don't want to bring up your parenting skills, but you did a number on that girl."

"No, she did it all to herself."

"Are you kidding me? I'm not one of your aids that just smiles and nods their head yes every time you speak."

"You're a psychiatrist now?"

"I remember watching Jennifer play soccer and basketball at a very young age. She had that drive; she was going to be something. You could see it on the field. But it all changed after she saw you hugging another woman. You denied it, of course, but it affected her."

"Why are you rehashing the past?"

"The past has a direct correlation on the future. Jennifer was a sensitive kid with a good heart. She was close to your mother and told her everything. I kind of brushed it off, but your mother was so right. I should have said something. Maybe I'm at fault. I wasn't around enough when you guys were kids. I probably focused on the wrong things. I now have the time to think about that stuff. And what happened to Johnny..." His voice quivered, "I don't know."

"I don't either. I didn't raise him to be like that."

170

George cleared his throat. "So, what's your problem?"

"You know how Farley used his connections to help me get elected?"

"I told you to stay away from him, but you had all the answers and all those wonderful donations from the rich and famous."

"You were right again, Dad. Bravo."

"Farley is a calculating bastard. He acts as if he's your best friend until he doesn't need you anymore. He's really good. You cross him, you usually end up as roadkill."

"I wouldn't be president without him."

"You're president because he wanted to control you. How's that working out?"

"Not too well."

"You know, Banner kept me informed. One day we had a nice discussion about the Phoenix Project. Giving the Iraqis back their money was just a waste when Farley had a much better use. His inner circle sucked you and Banner down a black hole, and I can't forget your brother Dave. He laundered it through his bank for record earnings and a nice kickback. Banner just salted away his take, and you got the presidency. A win-win for everyone, right?"

"We made a mistake. We can't change it now."

"Has it ever crossed your mind why Bolton ended up at Banner's house?"

171

"Bolton's a sick bastard."

"No, he's just a pawn in Farley's world. They used Bolton by killing his friend, knowing how he would react. Farley's behind Banner being killed. I should have strangled that bastard myself. So, what's your problem?"

"I had a meeting with Eric Steele."

"That bastard is still running around? A diplomat my ass. You figured out he works for Peter Sanderlin, then? He should be six feet under after all the people he's double-crossed. He's another one you shouldn't trust." He puffed out a few smoke rings. "I have a good idea where you're going with all this."

"Well, I'm learning as I go." Sam waited until Larry set down the tray with the whiskey and left the porch. "Steele gave me a legislation wish list."

"I'm sure he did. And Farley is behind all this."

"Yeah."

"I could never understand why Farley pushed for you to be president. And now it's all clear. He knows all your baggage. He's blackmailing you to carry out his agenda. And I'm sure the agenda is all about changing the makeup of America."

"Yeah."

"Does he know all about the Laura Weston debacle?"

Sam nodded.

George shook his head in disgust. He grabbed the whiskey bottle and poured them each a drink. "Here you go, Sam. You're going to need it. You know, when you go fishing and catch a fish, you have two choices: you can throw the fish back or you can throw the fish in the bucket to cook later. Farley is like a fisherman; if you don't get his legislation through, he can throw you in the bucket. If you do what he wants, you get thrown back into the lake with the chance of being hooked again."

"Analogies aren't going to help me, Dad."

"Farley's got all the leverage. There's nothing I can do or say to help you. You're president because Farley wanted to have someone his group could control. The sad part is what they have on you is worse than impeachment. You could go away for a long time over a stupid woman. What the hell were you ever thinking? Never mind; you weren't thinking. I'm partially at fault because I would always take care of your problems. And you did the same for Johnny."

President Atkins poured himself another shot and downed it. "That's where we both failed."

Chapter 20

At the New York field office, Special Agent Mike Weldon sat in a room behind a long table in between a group of FBI personnel. A colleague briefed them on the rising gang violence that was seeping into the state.

Weldon's mind drifted elsewhere. He was at a loss for how he wasn't chosen to apprehend Bolton in Canada. It was an opportunity gone; he wouldn't have made the same mistakes as the clowns that were sent. He wanted to be the one to bring Bolton in; it would be a great notch to have on his belt. Without Banner around, Steele's influence on Atkins was troubling. Banner always preached: *The bigger the circle, the more holes that need to be contained*.

He thought of how Banner had recruited him for this assignment; it was supposed to be quick and easy, and now here he was, three years later, all alone on an island. Banner had created a fake dossier for a fake person – Mike Weldon was the alias he had used as a CIA operative – who had a stellar performance record. Special Agent Mike Weldon was a ruse that gave him a license to kill. He was brought in by Banner to take down Bolton and prevent a disk of damaging information on Banner and Atkins from going public.

He had been part of the Phoenix Project from the

beginning, and now he was back to cover the tracks. Banner had set up his FBI stint with Director Williams, who had reluctantly approved it. But Williams made a point to tell Banner that he was on his own if something went south. Weldon smirked at the memory. He liked playing a Special Agent. He was official, but it was much harder now without Banner or Tripp around to deflect any issues, and he worried that Williams could get cold feet at any time. But as long as Atkins was hell-bent on getting Bolton, his job was safe.

Weldon enjoyed the cat and mouse came with Gallo. He was certain that Gallo had taken out Tripp, and there was something about Ryland that stunk. He never liked Ryland – he seemed to be rooting for Bolton. He was going to get to the bottom of all this intrigue, and Gallo was going down.

Butch Sanders, the gang task-force leader, with his double chin and a belly that hung over his belt, dissected the latest video feed in front of the task force. Weldon half-listened until they plugged in the computer and showed a surveillance video on the white-board of an ongoing stakeout of a violent, intercity gang's hangout. An old Chevy Impala had pulled up at four in the morning a few days ago; a body was tossed from the back seat as if they were throwing a Frisbee, then the car sped off.

Weldon asked, "Did you guys identify the dead body?"

Butch nodded. "The guy was one of the nastier ones, so whoever killed him made our job a little bit easier. And he was an illegal to boot. He had a criminal record, but for some reason was never deported."

"To me those guys in the car looked like Mafia thugs," Weldon said. "Maybe it's the lighting."

"It's interesting you say that. A week and a half ago in the Bronx, an old-time hood by the name of Aldo Mariani, who once ran with the Colombo crime family back in his day and now runs a family convenience store, was shot by three gangbangers. The dead guy was believed to be one of them."

"Where're the other two gang members?" Weldon asked.

"No sign of them; they've apparently gone missing."

"My guess is they're in some shallow grave," Weldon said with a grin.

Butch hit a key on the laptop, and the video footage changed to the front of Frank Gallo's restaurant.

Weldon sat up and stared at the screen. "Who's the young guy that Gallo's got his arm around?"

One of the agents said, "That's Jimmy DeRosa. The kid's two-bit hood moving up the ladder. Gallo likes him like a son."

"And the girl?" Weldon asked.

"That's DeRosa's girlfriend," Butch said.

Weldon leaned back in his chair and zoned out of the discussion. An idea was forming that could take down

Gallo. It would be illegal, but it was the final score that mattered."

***

A day later, Frank Gallo invited his crew and their girlfriends and wives down to the basement of his restaurant to celebrate Marty's birthday. They laughed, they played pool, they told stories, they ate, the music blared, they danced, and the liquor flowed. Frank made a point to talk to everyone. They had become a close-knit bunch. Frank made multiple toasts to Marty and then looked at Jimmy.

"Now I want to give out a toast to Jimmy and his girlfriend, Linda. May they have many good times together." He came around and gave Jimmy a big hug. "Now this guy knows loyalty; he gets the job done. You're going to do very well, Jimmy." Feeling generous, Frank stuffed a couple hundred-dollar bills in Jimmy's shirt pocket. "Take your girlfriend out sometime and have some fun."

Jimmy basked in the attention. He wasn't quite sure why Frank had taken a liking to him, but he would run through walls for him.

"Frank, we've got to be going," Jimmy said, as the night was getting late.

"Hey, I understand; I was young once," Frank said with a wink, the booze heavy on his breath. "I'll talk to you tomorrow."

Smiling, Jimmy grabbed Linda's hand and marched

up the stairs and out the side door. They walked holding hands. Life couldn't have been better for young Jimmy DeRosa. It was all falling into place. They stopped at the corner of Broad Street to kiss, oblivious of the world around them.

A white van rolled up and four men wearing masks jumped out. Before Jimmy could reach for his revolver, he was knocked down to the ground and handcuffed as Linda watched in horror. The men threw both of them into the back of the van and sped off.

Chapter 21

Dressed in a sharp blue blazer with her hair tied back in a ponytail, Laura Weston entered James Tavern, a popular breakfast place in downtown Washington, D.C., not too far from the Capitol. She sat by a window and people-watched while she waited, nervously sipping her coffee.

Laura glanced at her phone for the time. She was getting too old for the games. Her biological clock was ticking, and closure was the answer for her to move on. She had spent seven years in hell and didn't have the energy or time to waste. Life was short.

She noticed a couple off to the side smiling, laughing, and bantering. She wondered how long they had been together. What was their story? Were they soul mates? It was always hard to watch other couples that seemed to be happy, wondering why you couldn't find that formula, what you were doing wrong. Maybe you were never compatible, or you had just grown in different ways.

Jeff seemed to be stuck, still holding onto his youth, not wanting to move forward, maybe because of the time he felt he had lost while in prison. Maybe he would never get over what she had done. Or maybe they were never really in love. Maybe cheating on him was her way of trying to get out of their engagement. But now she was trying so hard to make it work, and yet she felt miserable. Love should be simple and easy, she thought.

The moment of truth stood directly in front of Laura. There was a pause, but no words were spoken. Jennifer took a seat opposite Laura. She wore a conservative dress, her jet-black hair hung loosely above her shoulders. A stranger might mistake them for sisters.

A circle of drama had engulfed them, and the meeting today was to draw a line in the sand. A cold silence hung over the table as the two beautiful women sized each other up.

Laura broke the ice. "I didn't think you would meet with me."

"I think this is a good idea."

"It's been a long time since I last saw you."

"Let's face it, Laura; it wasn't like we were friends. You were too busy smiling at my dad."

"I really don't want to go down that road. I was young, and I made a huge mistake. And you know that's not why I asked you to meet me."

"I didn't want to come here to talk about the past either. I hate my father. I'm the black sheep of the family. I don't blame you for what happened. My father is a monster, and he runs the country."

"I'm glad you feel that way," Laura said softly.

"I kind of have a good idea why I'm here," Jennifer said, trying to determine just how much she knew. "So go ahead and ask me anything that's on your mind."

Laura hesitated. "This is hard to talk about. You know that Jeff and I are engaged and planning to get married, right?"

"Yes, I know that. Look; it just happened. The last thing I wanted was to be the other woman. I saw my mom go through so much with my father," she said, her voice strained. "I don't know if Jeff told you, but we saw each other when he escaped from prison, and it just happened. We thought you were dead. But when he found out you were alive, he wanted to be with you. Then about six months ago he starting texting me again and asked me out for a drink. I said no, but he kept trying until I finally agreed to just one drink. Which led to meeting again, and again, and then…" she shrugged. "I felt guilty at first and told him I wasn't going to be his mistress. He said he loved me, but I know he loves you too. He's conflicted for sure. I told him I couldn't do this anymore. It wasn't right."

"That's Jeff," Laura agreed. "Sometimes he's indecisive and has a really hard time making up his mind." She shook her head. "I can't keep up a façade. Maybe we were in love once, but then again, maybe we never were. It felt like love, but sometimes you can get fooled. Then end up married with a couple kids and divorced. I'd rather know now where his head is at."

"I understand."

Laura sighed. "All I was looking for today was some

sort of closure. And you've done a good job of giving me that."

"So he told you about us?"

"No. I found out when I checked his phone. When I saw your texts, I knew he was seeing you. It hurt at first, but I've been through so much the last seven years, it's better to know now than to go through a sham engagement. This is our second go around. I don't think it's meant to be."

"I'm sorry you had to find out that way," Jennifer said. "I wanted him to tell you."

"I think you were expecting too much from him. Do you love him?"

"Yeah, I do."

Laura nodded. "You know, love should be simple. I've decided to move on." Her eyes filled with tears. "It's best for everyone."

Jennifer handed her a napkin, steeling herself for the last dagger. "There's something else I should tell you."

Laura's throat burned. She saw Jennifer's expression and immediately knew. "You're pregnant."

Jennifer nodded, waiting nervously.

Laura exhaled slowly to maintain her composure. "I've wanted to start a family, and I mentioned that to Jeff a while back. I'm not getting any younger. And his response was to wait until we were married. I find it ironic that you're pregnant, considering what I did to him years earlier." She wiped away fresh tears. "Thank you for telling me. When a man doesn't want to get you pregnant and finds another woman to have a baby with, it's a sure sign he doesn't love you."

"I'm sorry," Jennifer said.

"No, don't be. Talking to you has given me the closure I needed. I wish you well. It's time for me to move on."

They looked at each other; there was no animosity. When they got up from the table, they hugged, tears rolling down their checks, then walked out the door heading in different directions.

Chapter 22

Laura poured herself a glass of red wine and waited in the kitchen. She had confided in her mother that the wedding was off; now it was time to let Jeff know the masquerade was over. It was time for both of them to move on.

Jeff walked through the door, home earlier than planned. His tie hung low, his shirt was wrinkled, and his face had a dark shadow. He looked disheveled, like a man wandering the streets looking for a buck.

"I got your message. I'm sorry I didn't get back to you. I was in meetings all day." He opened the refrigerator and grabbed a beer. "I know that look. What did I do wrong now?"

"Nothing, really. I'm not going to sugar coat it; our relationship is not working. You know it and I know it. So why torture each other going through the motions? I can't live like this anymore."

"You want to end it?" he asked, his voice filled with disbelief and accusation. "Is that what I'm hearing?"

Laura stared at him, sadness turning to anger. "You are unbelievable, you know that? You can't even admit that you don't want to marry me. You want everyone to think I'm the bad person here. Is that how you're going to sell it?"

"I don't know what you're talking about."

"You either can't forget the past and just want to hurt me or maybe we were never really in love. It's nobody's fault. This is mutual, Jeff, and you know that. I'm just making it easy for you since you can't seem to tell me yourself."

"Tell you what?"

"Try being honest for once. I had a nice conversation today with Jennifer. She didn't tell you?"

Jeff's face dropped at the realization that the game was finally over. "No. I told you I was in meetings all day. I didn't have a chance to talk to anyone." Caught in all his lies and not knowing what to say, he became defensive. "How did you get her number?"

"I looked at your phone one day," she admitted. "And it became clear why you had become so distant. I'm at peace with it. It's better to know now than to build a life based on a lie. But you know what's really sad? You knew I wanted to have a baby, but you gave me some half-assed excuse why we shouldn't, and then you got her pregnant." She started to cry.

Jeff moved closer, but Laura pushed him away. "I don't need any comfort. I guess this is karma for all the trouble I caused you."

"No, I don't want you to think that."

"It doesn't matter. We're two ships going in different directions. You know what hurts me the most? You didn't have the guts to tell me this wasn't going to work, so you just decided to sleep around with another woman."

"It just happened."

"I'm not going to let you off that easy. You contacted her; you wanted it to happen. Why can't you just be honest with me for once?"

"You want honestly, Laura? That's funny coming from you, the one who broke my heart all those years ago."

She nodded. "We were never going to work because you can't get past what happened. I think deep down you wanted to hurt me, enjoyed it. Well, you've succeeded. I hope you're happy now."

Jeff frowned. "That's not it. Jennifer was there for me when nobody else was. It's that simple."

"Okay, I accept that. I just hope you don't get bored with her too."

"Jennifer doesn't judge me the way you do. You always expect more out of me. I can't please you no matter how hard I try. It's never good enough."

"If you thought that, why didn't you just tell me? That's what couples do; they work things out. Why was that too hard?"

He looked away and just shrugged.

"Let me give you some advice: if you want it to work with Jennifer, you're going to have to communicate with her a lot better than you did in our relationship."

"See? You always have the answer."

Laura stood up. "I don't want to get into a big argument. I told my mother that the wedding is off. I'll give you thirty days to get your stuff out, but you need to find somewhere else to go immediately. I bought this place, so I think that's fair."

"That's fine," Jeff said then walked out the door, still carrying his beer.

Chapter 23

While at the Mattison complex Jack had ridden horses around the compound and reconnected with nature. He frequented a quiet hilltop overlooking a river where he would watch the sunset and dwell on Kelly. It was soothing listening to the running water and seeing the colors of dusk in the western sky. As the darkness fell, he'd sit on a hillside and stargaze, wondering what it all meant. Everybody he had ever loved was gone. He was trying to prepare himself for the next phase: more killing, more drama, and maybe the end. He was tired.

He rode back and dropped the horse off at one of the barn stalls. He walked into the main house and went to the kitchen looking for a meal. He grabbed a beer while he waited for dinner.

Mattison walked in. "Hey, can you join me in the study? We need to talk."

"Sure."

When he entered the study, Jack saw Art Glover sitting, his body language relaxed, in the corner chair. They stared at each other with cold eyes.

Mattison played the negotiator. "I want both of you to drop whatever disagreements you might have. We need to work together here."

Jack shook his head. "I don't need help, Mr.

Mattison."

"Look, I had a talk with Art. He holds no grudges, isn't that right, Art?"

"Yeah, all is forgiven," Art said. "I understand what you did out there. We have a common foe. I think we're stronger together than divided." Art got up and put out his hand.

Jack didn't move.

"Come on, Jack," Mattison snapped. "Nobody got hurt; just let bygones be bygones."

Jack shook Art's hand, not meaning it. But if that made everyone feel buddy, buddy, it was a good facade. "You want to come along, Art? Just stay out of my way. I have a few errands to run in Washington while I'm there."

Art looked at Mattison. "Sure, whatever you need to do."

"Jack, I understand that you want to do this all by yourself," Mattison said. "But Steele will be protected by a security team. So two guns are better than one."

"Whatever."

Mattison nodded. "Okay, let's get down to business. There's a Sanderlin conference in Washington next week. The world elite will be there as will Steele, so where's the best place to take him out? He'll be protected probably by a security team of four guys. He might have his guard down at the hotel, the Washington Center Hotel on Thomas Circle, where he's staying."

"Wouldn't it be easiest to take him out from a distance?" Jack said. "I can use a sniper rifle. He'll never know what hit him."

"That might work in an Afghanistan village," Art said. "But in the city, you'll never get a clear shot. And if you miss, you'll never get another chance."

Mattison added, "We have a better idea. Steele will be staying in room 416 under the name Eric Bennett. His security team will be in room 417."

"So I should knock on his door?" Jack asked.

"I can disarm his security team," Art said, "while you focus on Steele."

Mattison obviously had someone on the inside at the hotel, Jack thought. "What's the plan."

"When he orders room service, you'll dress like an employee and deliver the food," Mattison said.

"Your guy can arrange that?"

He nodded. "Might be messy, but it's your call, Jack. I don't care how it's done as long as it gets done."

"Good; then we have a plan."

"You can leave first thing tomorrow morning," Mattison said. "I'll have a car, money, and all the logistics worked out. All you'll need to do is execute the plan and then get the hell out of Dodge."

"I'm not coming back, Mr. Mattison. I'm going my own way. As long as you understand that, we'll all get along just fine."

"Where are you going? I can protect you. You're a

wanted man, and after this goes down you'll have nowhere to hide."

"I'm not stopping until I get Sanderlin."

Mattison shook his head and chuckled. "Jack, he's protected by an army. You would never get close."

"Let me worry about that."

"We want the same thing here, Jack," Mattison said, "but a little patience is needed."

"I'm done talking."

Chapter 24

At eight in the morning, Frank Gallo sat at a table in his restaurant, sipping coffee while looking over the books.

Marty walked in and stood by the table. "Frank!"

"I'm busy. Can it wait?"

"It's Jimmy."

"What's going on with Jimmy?"

"I got a call from his mother. He never came home last night, and she asked if I'd seen him."

"This is what you are bothering me with? Do I look like the kid's babysitter?"

"She said he's never done that before without calling her to let her know where he was."

"He's young; he's got a hot girlfriend. They're probably shacked up at some hotel, or maybe they eloped to Vegas. You forget what it's like to be young, Marty?"

"She sounded really concerned. I told her I would ask the guys if anyone had seen him."

"Then do that. I got things to do."

"I already checked around and nobody has."

"Marty, he's off with the girlfriend. Forget about Jimmy; he's a big boy. I got a job for you."

"What is it?"

"I told Ryland I would check on his wife; he thinks

she's having an affair." Gallo grinned. "I told him I'd find out. So I want you and Lou to take a flight to Boston, bring the high-tech camera. I want to see some beautiful pictures, and then I want to bring those photos to Ryland and see his face. It's always a priceless moment when a guy finds out his wife is seeing someone else and that someone else more times than not is their best friend."

"Yeah, I know that feeling."

"You beat that guy senseless?"

"He didn't come around anymore."

"Here's Ryland's address. Here's your airplane tickets to Boston. Angelo will meet you at the airport. Take some good pictures. You leave in three hours."

"How long do you want us to watch her?"

Frank stared. "Until you have some damn good photos."

"What if she's not cheating?"

"She's cheating; a man knows when his wife is cheating. They can feel it. You knew, right?"

"Good point."

***

Marty and Lou sat in their rented Chevy Impala in the quiet suburb of Belmont, Massachusetts, watching Ryland's house from afar. It was midnight and the street was quiet. The stars were out, and a full orange moon lit up the night sky They had spent the late afternoon trailing Donna Ryland, and at nine o'clock, after she had dropped her kids off, a man came by.

"What the hell is Angelo doing?" Marty said. "He's been gone a long time."

"I hope he's got some great pictures so we can get the hell out of here," Lou said.

Marty stared out the window. "That white van up the street parked there a half-hour ago, and nobody has gotten out."

"Maybe it's two kids having a little fun."

"Maybe. I just want to get the hell out of here and get home." Marty sensed something wasn't right. "Where the hell is Angelo?"

At that moment, Angelo was silently jumping from the roof ledge and rolling onto the grass below. He heard some noise out front and went around the house to investigate. Peeking around the corner, he saw a white van parked on the street down a bit from Ryland's house. The side door was open, and he could see a woman bound and gagged by duct tape inside the van, while two other men stood outside the vehicle, one talking, one listening, He snapped some pictures, then hustled around the opposite corner of the house, crossed into the next lawn, then tip-toed across the street into the waiting car.

"Where the hell have you been Angelo?" Marty said.

"Did you get some good pictures?" Lou asked with a leer.

He studied the camera window. "I got some great

pictures, but I got to show you something else."

Angelo reached over the front seat with the camera; Marty grabbed it and went through the pictures.

"Oh, Frank is going to like these. I don't think Ryland will, though." Then he came to the van pictures. "What the hell are these? That's Jimmy. What the hell is he doing here? There's his girlfriend tied up. And shit, it's that frigging FBI guy. What the hell is he up to?"

"Marty, look." Lou pointed. "They're giving Jimmy instructions."

"I've got to call Frank."

***

The phone vibrated on the nightstand. Still half-asleep, Frank picked it up.

"Yeah?"

"Frank, it's Marty; we got a problem. I found Jimmy."

"What do you mean you found, Jimmy? In Massachusetts?"

"I don't know what's going on, but it looks like that agent who visited us is ordering Jimmy to break into Ryland's house. And they've got Linda tied up in a van."

Frank was now wide awake. "I got a call about ten minutes ago. It was Jimmy's number, but when I answered it, there was nobody on the line."

He got out of bed and started pacing. They were trying to frame him, and that damn alleged FBI agent

195

was leading the parade.

"Shit!" Marty said.

"What?"

"I just heard two gunshots."

"Get the hell out of there," Frank ordered.

The white van sped by. Marty waited until the van was out of sight before hitting the gas and tearing out with the headlights still off.

Chapter 25

Paul Ryland had just finished his chores so now it was time to take care of his stomach. He walked into the cafeteria and filled a plate with eggs, sausage, and pancakes. He found a corner table and plopped down. He had just cleaned his plate and washed it down with a glass of juice when a guard walked over to him.

"Hey, Ryland, you have a visitor."

He made a face. "Who is it?"

"I don't know. I was just told to get you and bring you to the visitor's room."

He bussed the table and followed the prison guard, wondering if Shone Williams was back. Ryland walked through the security partition and into an empty visitor's room. He was directed to a table where he sat and waited.

Special Agent Mike Weldon walked into the room and took a seat opposite Ryland, who winced; Weldon wasn't a friend.

"What the hell do you want?"

"No time for small talk, Ryland? You know, I took over your office. It has a great view of all those pretty girls strutting around downtown. You kept that a big secret, you dog. But you have a different life now."

Ryland hated this man and was intrigued that Gallo

called him the fake agent. "Can you get to the point?"

"Last night Gallo sent one of his soldiers to your home. Does that get your attention?"

Ryland didn't react. Weldon didn't know that he'd asked Gallo to check on his wife. Maybe the feds were watching the house and picked up Gallo's soldier. "I'm not sure what you're looking for. My wife, my kids are okay, right?"

"Yeah, everybody is fine. Gallo's soldier wasn't so lucky; he's dead."

"What the hell happened?"

"I find it a little interesting actually. Around midnight last night, Jimmy DeRosa – here, I have a photo of him with Gallo's arm around him."

Ryland stared at it. "Yeah, so what?"

"He also made a call to Gallo ten minutes prior to breaking into your house."

"What do you want from me?"

"This Jimmy guy breaks into your house, and, surprisingly, your wife is in real good hands. Your buddy, Alex – I guess he must be comforting your wife while you're away – anyway, Alex must have heard him break in, and they exchanged gunfire. DeRosa went down. Alex got shot in the shoulder. He's lucky – should be fine. Now, I have no idea what Alex was doing there, that's probably a question for your wife. I'm not here to get involved in your personal life. But I think it would be in your best interest to come clean, and

Shone's offer still applies."

"I'll tell you what I told Shone. Go to hell."

"Alright. But after I talk to Gallo, he might just have a story to tell me. And then you won't be getting out in a couple of months; you'll be doing hard time the rest of your life."

"I'm done talking to you, Weldon."

Ryland got up and asked the guard to take him back.

Chapter 26

Marty walked into Gallo's upscale restaurant shortly after it opened, looking haggard. The waiters and the kitchen help were running around getting ready for the morning rush. Frank sat at his usual table, with his usual cup of coffee in front of him. Marty sat down next to him.

"I haven't slept, Frank. I think Jimmy is dead. I don't know how to tell his mother."

Frank looked at him, eyes hard. "You know the FBI will be showing up today, and it's a good possibility they'll be taking me out with handcuffs. Do you realize that, Marty?"

Marty put the camera on the table. "I think we have an out, Frank."

"I hope you're damn right because they're framing me. The cell records will show Jimmy called me before he broke into Ryland's house. I haven't seen the news today because I'm sure it's not good for me anyhow."

"Look at the photos, Frank. You might think differently."

Frank grabbed the camera and pushed the arrow button. "Ryland's instincts were right. I wish I could enjoy these pictures, but they aren't going to help me." Then, as he continued through the photos, he started to smile. "Marty, you hit the damn jackpot."

Marty grinned. "I told you: Angelo got a great photo."

Frank's mood changed. "Now I can't wait until that Agent Weldon drops in. He thinks he's one smart bastard. The idea he's going to frame Frank Gallo, well I don't think so. I'm going to turn the tables on him. But I feel bad for Jimmy and his girlfriend, who I'm sure is gone too."

"I know."

Frank stood. "I need a nice picture of Weldon with the girl duct taped in the background."

"I'll take care of it, Frank."

"Good. I feel a lot better. You know, I knew that Weldon guy was a fake agent. Real agents never would pull that crap."

***

Frank looked at the clock. It was only a matter of time before the Feds would arrive, ready to pounce. His mind was in battle mode. Weldon was on a mission to put him away, but Frank was ready to swat anything they threw at him.

As expected, Special Agent Weldon strutted into Gallo's restaurant with a wide smile. He had put a plan together that would bring Gallo down. The maître 'd greeted him at the door with a smile. She found him a table and set down a menu.

"Would you like something to drink?" she asked

He leaned back in the chair. "I'll take a coffee. Also, could you tell Mr. Gallo that Special Agent Weldon would like to talk to him?"

She walked away and whispered into the manager's ear. She came back to the table and placed the coffee in front of him. "The manager is going to find him."

He tapped his foot impatiently. He couldn't wait to see Gallo's face as he read him his rights and to bring him out himself with the cameras rolling. The team waited outside so as not to spoil his fun.

Gallo finally emerged from the back room and walked slowly over to Weldon's table.

"Mr. Gallo, please take a seat," Weldon said, smiling. "You remember me? We had that nice conversation."

"I remember you," Frank said, pulling out a chair. "You're the fake agent that dropped by a couple of weeks ago."

"That's not going to help you in a court of law."

"Oh, I think it will."

"Enough with the small talk. Let's get down to business."

"Let's. So, what brings you here?"

"You're a good actor, Mr. Gallo. Let's start with Jimmy DeRosa. Do you know him?"

"Yeah. Good kid. He's been missing. You know where he is?"

"Mr. Gallo, playing stupid with me isn't going to get you anywhere. But I expected it. You have any idea

202

what Jimmy DeRosa was doing in Paul Ryland's home last night in Belmont, Massachusetts?"

"I can't help you."

"Well, he was killed by one of our agents we'd placed there in case you decided to go after Paul Ryland's family. Lucky for us we had someone there; otherwise, I think the outcome would have been different. There was an exchange of gunfire, and our agent was hit. He's in intensive care. He should make it."

"That's a nice story, but what the hell does this have to do with me?"

"You've been skirting the law for a long time."

Frank shrugged. "That's your opinion. Tell me how you think this is going to go down, Weldon."

"I'll lay it out for you," he said with a smirk. "You met with Ryland. You told him to keep his mouth shut, and you were going to make sure of that. So you sent Jimmy DeRosa to Belmont, Massachusetts, to Ryland's house."

"Really?"

"I'm not done. Jimmy DeRosa called you prior to breaking into Ryland's house; we have his phone records. Coincidence? I don't think so."

"You think a jury is going to buy all this?"

"I got a nice photo of you and Jimmy."

Weldon reached into the side pocket of his blue blazer and pulled out a picture. He pushed it over to Gallo who chuckled. Then his face went cold.

"And what does this prove? I was like a father figure to Jimmy, and you bastards killed him and his girlfriend. You people are the monsters, not me. This is all flimsy circumstantial evidence that will never hold up in court."

"Well, when Ryland hears about this, he might just come clean. But a jury will hear all the evidence and decide the outcome. It really doesn't matter what I say."

Frank leaned back, ready to play his cards. "You ever play chess, Weldon?"

"I'm not a chess player."

"Well, let me give you a crash course. "You made a move that you thought was checkmate, but you didn't think it through completely. What you did at Ryland's home? That's no FBI move. I know. More like a rogue CIA agent working undercover."

"Your opinion doesn't matter, Gallo."

"True. I got something for you though." He opened the folder in his lap, pulled out a photograph, and pushed it across the table."

Weldon's eyes widened.

"*That's* what I call checkmate," Gallo said with a smug smile. "I think it's a good picture of you. What do you think?"

Weldon didn't respond; he couldn't believe what he was looking at.

"I went to see Ryland in prison," Gallo continued. "We basically talked about how his own people had screwed him. Then he mentioned that he thought his wife was having an affair. A man knows when his wife is having an affair, you know what I mean? So he asked me if I could do him a favor and check on his wife. So the night you decided to pull your little stunt, we were there, hence the nice photo of you in a rather compromising position. And the idea you had an agent protecting Ryland's family seems a little farfetched since I have photos of this agent banging Ryland's wife."

Weldon was now on the defensive. And the day had started off so promising. "What are you going to do with that photo?"

Gallo smiled. "I'm going to make a thousand copies." He laughed at the panic in Weldon's eyes. "I'm just kidding. I'm a fair guy, so it's really up to you. I'll put that in the vault with the original and forget about it unless you do something stupid; then the world will know. It's that simple."

"How do I know this won't get out?"

"I guess you'll have to trust me."

"You're a real bastard, Gallo."

"*You* think *I'm* a bastard. That's what they call ironic. Anyway, unless you have something to say, we're done."

Weldon got up and stared down at Gallo. 'This isn't over," he warned then walked out of the restaurant.

Marty came over. "I see the agent left with his tail

between his legs."

"Yeah, but I don't trust that bastard; he's a very dangerous man. When the time is right, we're going to kill that bastard for Jimmy."

Chapter 27

Frame cottages, sprawling vineyards, and rolling farmlands lined the countryside along Lienz, a small village in southern Austria on the border of Italy. Peter Sanderlin sat sipping a hot cup of tea with Eric Steele next to him in a small café. Ed Farley walked in wearing a dark blazer and gray slacks. He was escorted to Sanderlin's private table off the main area. The men got up and hugged like long-lost friends, uttering pleasantries to each other as they sat down.

Sanderlin snapped his fingers at the waiter. "Mark, get my friend a cup of tea."

"Yes, sir," the waiter replied then disappeared.

"How was your travel?" Sanderlin asked Farley.

"I forget how beautiful it is out here. You age like fine wine, Peter."

"It's from breathing all this clean air. I come here once a week with my father and enjoy a quiet cup of tea with him." Sanderlin put down his cup and folded his hands. "It's good to be away from the world sometimes, and this place lets me get back to my roots and reminds me how important our jobs are in making the world a beautiful, loving place."

"Most people don't see what we see," Farley sighed. "And it's our responsibility to make them understand the importance of unity. We know that's the only way to move forward for the world, and yet there are people who want to hold on to the old ways."

"Speaking of old ways, how did your conversation go with Mattison?" Eric asked.

The waiter came back with a small cup of tea, placed it in front of Farley, then left.

Farley took a sip before answering. "He didn't buy that his brother died from a road-rage incident."

"Well, I didn't expect him too," Sanderlin said. "We asked him to give us Bolton, and he decided against it. So his brother paid the price."

"He gave me the usual conservative political bullshit, but he knew all about me," Farley said. "I don't know if he was just fishing or if he really knows we're controlling Atkins."

"How would he know that?" Eric asked.

"Somehow Bolton knows what we're doing."

Sanderlin shook his head. "There's no way Bolton would have a clue. I think Mattison is throwing bullshit out there."

Farley frowned. "I don't know. He knows about the dark pools."

"If this is really true," Sanderlin said with concern, "it makes it even more imperative that we find Bolton and, more importantly, who he's working with."

"Well, Mattison made an interesting offer."

"What type of offer?" Steele asked.

Farley smiled. "He's willing to give us Bolton, after Bolton puts a bullet in you."

"So Mattison believes I had something to do with his brother's death."

"Well, to be fair, you did," Sanderlin pointed out.

"I guess there are no bridges to mend here," Steele said.

Farley took another sip of tea. "I told him I'd get back to him."

"What do you mean, you'll get back to him?" Steele retorted.

"I already got back to him, Eric; I made the deal."

At his panic, Farley and Sanderlin laughed, making Steele think it was a joke.

"Good one, Ed."

"No, I'm not kidding, Eric. I talked to Peter about it, and we both agree it's a good trade."

Eric stared silently.

"We need to use you as bait," Sanderlin explained. "It will never get that far."

"Bolton killed seven guys in Canada. He survived Seattle and God knows what else. He's dangerous," Steele said.

"What the hell are you worried about?" Farley asked. "We gave him your hotel room at the Washington Center Hotel. You'll have a security team."

"I don't care what I have. That guy is capable of anything."

"We had to make it as real as possible. Mattison would have smelled it out."

"Bolton will never get that far," Sanderlin repeated. "We're going to tip off the FBI, and they'll take him out prior to him getting anywhere inside the hotel or close to you."

Steele remained nervous. "Why does Mattison want to give up Bolton now?"

"Maybe because Bolton won't give him the information he wants, or maybe Bolton has nothing that can really do any damage," Farley said. "Lighten up, Eric. Everything is going to work out just fine."

"It's easy for you to say. That's what Oz thought too, and he's dead."

Farley changed the subject. "How'd your conversation go with Sam?"

"I just let him know that we're pulling the strings now. He didn't like it, but that's reality."

"We own him, and he knows it," Sanderlin added. "He might not like it, but he'll do what we want, or we'll get someone else. We're so close."

"We're close," Farley agreed. "But we can't let up now. The next election is the big one. We can finish what we started. It's been a long thirty years."

"You should get most of the credit," Sanderlin said. "Your idea of how to break America was absolutely brilliant."

"The Constitution is just a piece of paper and is only

as good as the people who believe it or defend it. Once you break the people's will to defend it, you win. It all started with downplaying religion in schools, breaking the Pledge of Allegiance, having people focus on gender issues, women's issues, removing history and painting the forefathers as bad people, and have people rise up against the flag. If you hammer it home long enough in today's world, the sheep just go along with it. Controlling the Supreme Court will finish the NRA and allow us to change the Constitution to our way of thinking."

"As long as Ethan White doesn't rain on our parade in the next election," Sanderlin said, referring to the senator from New Hampshire. I think we should assume he's running. What are our options to discredit this guy?"

"He will be a tough opponent," Farley acknowledged. "He has no baggage, is a good talker, ethical, a people's guy, a former vet, and a family man. You got some ideas, Eric?"

"Men are weak. Couldn't we plant some hot woman to seduce him?"

"I know the guy; he won't bite on that. The problem is he was born to be a president."

"Maybe we should just kill him," Steele said, half-joking. "That would solve the problem."

The conversation suddenly stopped. It was like a light went on. A man who couldn't be beaten had to be removed by any means possible. It was all about power and the world vision

"It's a good idea, Eric," Sanderlin said.

Farley agreed. "Brilliant."

"I wasn't serious," Steele said.

Sanderlin leaned in. "Our first option should be for White to have an unfortunate accident. Do we agree? And the sooner, the better. Once he declares he's running, it'll be much harder because he'll then have Secret Service protection."

"I agree," Farley said. "Why don't we draft a plan to take him out? We can't take any chances of losing the next election."

"Eric, I want the best group of trusted people you have to work out a plan," Sanderlin said.

"I'll take care of it."

Chapter 28

The auditorium at St. Elizabeth College in Concord, New Hampshire, was three-quarters full as the emcee stepped out from the curtain and grabbed the microphone.

"Hello everyone. Welcome to the Third Annual Guy Rogers Patriot Picnic. I think you're going to enjoy the people who are speaking today. So let's get on with it, because I don't think you came to listen to me. Okay, maybe my wife did…She's shaking her head no."

He smiled at the smattering of polite laughter. "Our keynote is a great role model and family guy who has done an excellent job for the people of New Hampshire in the Senate. Please help me welcome to the stage my friend and someone who I know is going to impact your life greatly, Senator Ethan White."

Loud applause and a standing ovation greeted White as he came onto the stage. He stood tall with a gray suit that matched his salt-and-pepper hair, his smile infectious. He took the microphone.

"How's everyone doing out there? Let me tell you a little about myself for those of you who don't know me. I've been a two-term senator thanks to the good people of New Hampshire. I have two hard-working teenage daughters, and there, sitting in the front-row, is my beautiful wife. We met in college, and it's been love ever since, right, honey?"

She rolled her eyes but smiled.

"I have to thank her for where I am today," White said. "She believed in me when nobody else did. We make a good team."

He gave the crowd his background: after graduating from Harvard he joined the United States Marines, where he decided he wanted to pursue politics to help implement what was best for the country. He gave his opinion about the money spent deploying US military to conflicts in the Middle East and elsewhere, inefficient and ineffective money management by the government, the federal debt, immigration, the dangers of big government, the need for unity, improving employment through better training, and his support of the Second Amendment.

He finished by saying, "The one thing I try to do is treat people the way I would want to be treated. The world needs more love. We need to work together. And when you get home today, don't be afraid to say hello to your neighbors and hug your kids. One last thing: just remember the Constitution is only as good as the people who support it. Our brilliant forefathers created this document to allow individuals to be self-empowered and free from tyranny, which they understood all too well. My fear is that over time each generation loses the ability to see tyranny, and that in itself is perhaps the biggest threat to America. Thank you for being a great audience today."

He left to another standing ovation. James Mattison watched as he sat in the front row. He had listened to White's talking points with great interest. He was certain the senator had what it took to win the next election; the trick was talking him into running. He was the perfect candidate: a politician with the ability to make anyone he talked to feel important.

***

Ethan hugged his wife in the VIP tent behind the stage. "So how was I, honey?"

"Okay."

"Just okay?"

She brushed back her curly blonde hair and buttoned up a white sweater that wrapped around her petite frame. "I just don't know if telling it like it is helps or hurts."

"You know me: I always tell it like it is. I can't sugar coat it. I just want to send a message of self-empowerment; people are in control of their own lives, so they need to avoid the path of dependency."

"You're an honest soul, Ethan White. That's why I love you."

James Mattison walked in. "I'm not interrupting anything, am I?"

"Not at all, James. How're you doing?" he asked, shaking Mattison's hand. "You remember my wife,

Sarah."

"How could I forget her?" James smiled. "That was a good speech, Ethan. We think a lot alike. This next election is very important. That's why I'm here. This election is probably going to be the nastiest race in American political history."

"They say that every four years."

"You remember the last one. It wasn't fun."

"It wasn't fun because we lost."

"I'm sure that had something to do with it. I don't want to take up too much of your time, but I just wanted to reiterate how much we need you to run. You can win the next election. We can raise a war chest for you."

Ethan smiled. "Thanks for the kind words, James, but there are no guarantees. You know that. The polls like you one week and hate you the next. So I haven't made up my mind yet. A lot depends on what Sarah and my daughters want. It's a big drain on the family. And I really don't know if I want to bring them down that path where there's so much negativity. We like our life now; it's relatively quiet."

"So, I should be buttering up, Sarah," James said with a sly smile. "Is that what you're telling me?"

"Well, it would be a good place to start," he joked.

"Keep me out of this," Sarah said. "This is Ethan's decision."

"To be honest with you, James, I don't know if I'm ready. It's a big commitment."

"Think about it," James said. "I'm sure you'll make the right decision when the time comes."

Chapter 29

After the standard frisk and search, Donna Ryland, wearing jeans and a black sweatshirt, with her hair in a loose bun at the nape of her neck, walked into the prison visitor's area. She sat down across from Paul and gave him a half smile.

He grabbed her hand. "I heard what happened. You okay?"

"Yeah."

"Where were the kids?"

"They were at my mother's. She likes seeing the boys; you know that. I didn't think a little me time was a big deal. You're looking at me like I'm a bad mom or something."

Paul controlled his demeanor. "No. Why is it lately that every time you come to see me we end up in a fight, and the boys are never with you?"

"It's you, Paul. You always have this look, like you're angry at me for your situation."

"When I'm talking to you, it's like you're just going through the motions. How do think that makes me feel?"

"That's just your imagination."

"Really? So maybe you can explain what happened last night."

"You said you already know what happened. Why do

I have to rehash it?"

"You were there. I'd like to hear what exactly happened. The news doesn't always have the facts of the story."

"I rather forget about it, okay?" she asked, raising her voice.

"There you go. Somebody broke into our house, and you don't want to talk about it. What should I think? Should I just forget about it? You don't really like me asking you about the boys. You never tell me anything about what you're doing. Any problems. Everything is great. You don't mention how you're looking forward to my getting out of here soon. I don't see the little notes and the homemade cookies. I haven't heard the words *I love you* in quite a long time. I'm just wondering what's going on out there." He paused, giving her an opportunity to respond. When she didn't, he took another approach. "So how's Alex doing? He was one of my best friends. Do you know he hasn't visited me in a year? Maybe if you see him, you can tell him I would like to see him."

"Maybe he's busy, you ever think of that? I know his mother's been sick."

"Really. It was a good thing he was there when this guy broke into the house last night. I'm really grateful that Alex was there to protect you."

"The FBI assigned him to the house because they thought maybe Gallo would do something. He took a bullet for God's sakes."

Paul leaned back in the chair, holding back his anger. He knew his wife was having an affair with his best friend; he didn't exist in his wife's mind as anything more than garbage on the side of the curb. She was in damage-control mode. She couldn't even tell him the truth. He was so glad he had never told her about Tripp. He almost had once, thinking they were on the same team.

"That sounds like Alex, taking one for the team. I would like to thank him personally for maybe saving your life because I don't know what I would do without you. Maybe I haven't appreciated you standing by me these last few years. It would be tough on any woman. I'm sorry I put you through all this."

"You should be. This has been tough on me and your boys."

"Our boys, Donna."

"Yeah."

"You in a hurry? I notice you keep looking at the clock. Like you can't wait to leave."

"There you go again. I'm going to leave."

"I've had enough of the games, okay? I was hoping you'd have the guts to tell me that you're having an affair with Alex, but I guess not."

She paused. It was like the air of a balloon leaking out. "It just happened. I didn't plan it."

Paul exhaled slowly. "Why should I be surprised?

You've always been self-centered. And Alex…he took advantage of the situation and moved right in. It's like I don't even exist. You want to talk about damaging to the boys?"

"Don't come off like you're some angel," she said, her eyes starting to well up. "You worked all the time. You never had time for me or the boys. And you knew the consequences of this stupid Bolton thing, but you couldn't walk away. You were going to be a superhero and stop all the bad guys. I begged you to get out, and you wouldn't listen until it was too late. This is not how I planned my life."

"That's a great argument, but last I checked Alex worked for the FBI, so I'm thinking he works long hours too."

They coldly stared at each other. Donna finally said, "You win the argument, Paul."

He shook his head. "You've never looked better. I now know why."

"I'm leaving."

"I'm sure you'll have a happy life together. You're both the same self-centered assholes."

She walked out without looking back.

Chapter 30

Jack and Art checked into a Motel 6 outside of Washington, D.C. A plan had been drafted to take out Eric Steele at the Washington Center Hotel. Their inside man would notify them when the time was right. He had also arranged their escape. Like any plan, all this was reliant on execution and trust.

Jack had no confidence in any of it. He's was a Lone Ranger, with no Brian covering his ass, no Navy SEALS knowing each second counts, and, of course, no back-up. He didn't trust anyone he was currently associating with.

Jack lay awake on his bed playing out the mission in his mind. Art was sleeping on the adjacent bed. There'd been no real banter between them. He felt like he was being fed to the lions. He had become a person he never wanted to be: a hitman, taking lives with one pull of the trigger. Tears slowly rolled down his checks. He couldn't control these bouts of emotion that would come out of nowhere. But he was more determined than ever to destroy the people who had destroyed his life and hurt the people he loved.

The next morning at 7:00 a.m. Jack got dressed in a pair of jeans, sweatshirt, and sneakers. The few hours of sleep he had managed would have to do. Jack went into the bathroom and took a hard look into the mirror. He splashed water on his face. Unbeknownst to Mattison and his henchmen, there was a plan B. He had used Chip's encrypted phone to make plans under their noses. He was sure that Mattison's henchmen were lurking in the shadows.

"Hey, where you going, Jack?" Art asked, springing up from the bed.

"Breakfast."

"I'll go with you." He hustled out of bed, looking for his pants.

"I don't think so, Art. It's going to be an all-day breakfast."

"You know what Mattison said. He wanted us to keep a low profile and stay put."

"I don't care what Mattison said."

"Jack, you're wanted by the FBI. There's an award out for your arrest. I don't think it's a good idea to be running around Washington."

"Nobody will recognize me with this scrub on my face. Just relax and go back to bed and enjoy the day. I'm sure you can catch up on some of your talk shows."

Art frowned. He remembered what Mattison told him about keeping Jack in his sights at all times. "Come on, Jack. Let's just stay put. I don't want to screw this up."

"And miss out on all the exciting sites in Washington? I don't know when I'll be back again."

"You just make everything so difficult."

"No, I just make it difficult for you and Mattison. There's a difference. Have a good day, and don't worry about me."

Jack left and headed to the SUV.

Art got on his phone. "He's leaving now; keep track of him and let me know where he goes and what he's up to."

***

Jack turned onto Ohio Drive SW, not far from the Jefferson Memorial. He drove like he was being followed. They weren't going to let him out of their sight without knowing his agenda. And he had one, which included keeping Mattison at arms-length. He was sure they too had a plan that didn't include him.

Jack pulled into a parking lot adjacent to East Potomac Park, located on a manmade island, along the Potomac River. He stepped out and a man with a dark complexion wearing a leather jacket approached him. Jack passed him the keys, and the man drove off in the SUV.

The morning air held a chill. The sky was clear as joggers, bicyclists, and people walking their dogs enjoyed the colorful foliage. After walking about one hundred yards, Jack arrived at a park bench offering a view of the Potomac. He sat down and waited for the players to arrive. He looked around and noticed some couples; it was tough watching them smiling, holding hands, and bantering back and forth. He'd had all that and, in a snap-of-the-finger, it was all gone.

Connor Harris's cold, hard face, silver hair, and business suit made him look like a high-level executive about to close a deal. He smiled when he saw Jack sitting on the bench. They shook hands.

"You sure nobody is watching us, Jack?" he asked as they sat down.

"With today's technology, who the hell knows? But I think we're good."

"A beautiful day in the world's political cesspool."

"That's a good way to put it," Jack agreed.

"So, we have a plan."

"Yes."

"Chip filled me in on the details. I brought my Bible. We might need some intervention from God."

"Whatever works."

Connor studied Jack's face. "You don't seem too worried."

"That's because I have nothing left to lose."

***

Carlos walked along the river as if on an espionage mission. Half an hour before Jack had arrived, Carlos did a quick study of anyone who entered the park. He'd kept a low profile since arriving in America but had been close friends with Brian Butler from their days in Mexico.

Carlos ran a small underground business in Washington, D.C., creating forged documents for desperate people or people who were dependent on documents to survive in America. He dabbled in narcotics, just selling to people he knew. He helped the illegals from Mexico, getting them settled in. All of it was a lucrative business niche that was small enough to stay off the radar of the authorities. But dealing with Jack, the stakes were much higher. He couldn't afford to make a mistake.

Carlos wore a black suit that matched a black bag held in one hand. He looked like a funeral director. He slowly strolled up to the bench and stood in front of Jack and Connor.

"Good to see you," he said with a slight accent.

"I didn't recognize you," Jack said. "You look pretty suave in that suit."

"That's what the women say," he said with a wink. "I didn't want to take any chances; like the last time I saw you when they shot Brian, I walked the area. I'm confident that we're alone."

"That's good. This is the man I said would be with me. Connor this is Carlos."

"I heard a lot about you, Carlos," Connor said. "I hear you're good with papers."

"And the women," he said, then grew serious. "Jack, it's a damn shame what happened to Brian. And I'm truly sorry to hear about your girlfriend. Mayhem seems to follow you."

"That's an understatement. But life goes on. Do you

have the documents?"

"Wait a second; I have a call coming in." Carlos answered, listened, then hung up. "As you expected, Jack, we found a GPS tracking device on your car. We're going to take that GPS for a ride that should keep your watchdogs busy. Meanwhile, once my guy hooks up the new GPS tracking device, we can test it here."

Carlos's phone buzzed. He read the text. "It's all set. So, let's give it a try." He opened an app on his phone and a GPS map popped up. "He's on the Fourteenth St. Bridge, heading this way." He flashed the phone toward Jack and Connor. "It's on a battery system, which means you'll have ninety-six hours at best, and then it will run out of juice. Of course the more you use it, the less time you'll have. So just leave it alone until you really need it. We put the GPS tracker in a rear storage section. It's a push system, so it will give the location within ten feet every ten seconds as you request it."

They downloaded the app on Connor's phone and made sure everything worked. Carlos also gave him a brief tutorial.

"I'm good," Connor said. "I'll practice using it while you're here."

Carlos reached down into his bag of goodies. "And for you, Jack, another new identity."

"I've done this so much, I'm starting to forget my real name."

"I'm running out of ink," Carlos said with a chuckle.

Jack took a good look at his new license and his shiny passport.

"You like your new name?" Carlos asked.

"Jack McGee. It'll have to do."

"I like it," Connor said

"I have one more document for you, Jack." Carlos pulled out a rectangular FBI ID with Jack McGee's name, a badge number, and a sealed hologram."

Jack stared at Carlos. "Where the hell did you get an FBI badge?"

"I was playing around one day with some plastic and ink. I didn't know what to do with it, and then I thought of you."

"I don't know what I'll do with it."

"It's not just any FBI badge. You notice the small gold cover?"

"Yeah."

"Well, you're now a special agent."

They all erupted in laughter.

"You're amazing, Carlos," Jack said.

"Honestly, anything can be forged with today's technology." He handed Jack some glasses.

"What am I going to do with these?"

"Put them on."

Jack made a face as he eased the glasses in place.

Carlos smiled. "There. Now you now have the look of a special agent."

"The car is in the parking lot," Connor said. "I think

I'm getting the hang of this."

Carlos closed his bag. "My work is done here. I wish you luck, Jack."

"Thanks for all your help."

They walked out to the parking lot. The keys to the SUV were handed to Jack. Carlos drove off in another car.

"Stay close, Connor. We're waiting for the word to go forward."

"Okay, Jack. I got your back."

"I'll be in touch."

They shook hands and went their separate ways.

***

Jack walked back to the bench and took a seat. It wasn't long before a man in a brown trench coat wearing shades and a baseball cap walked up.

"Jack."

"Greg."

Jack smiled as Greg sat down. "You look more like a guy on a black op than a journalist."

"I would say this is as covert a mission as it gets in my line of work."

"I guess you could say that. Seriously, I appreciate you meeting me. Just talking to me puts your life in danger; I hope you fully understand that. Everybody associated with me in some way seems to have an untimely death."

"I understand what I'm getting into, Jack. This is the

kind of story a reporter waits their entire career for. So yeah, I understand the potential consequences and accept them. The juicier the story, the higher the risks."

"As long as you understand that, I'm good."

"It's ironic that the whole world is looking for you and you're right here under their noses. I was surprised to hear from you, especially after what happened in Maple Creek."

"I don't want to think about that. I'm moving on."

"Who do you think killed Costa?

"What did you say?"

Charlie Costa had helped Jack kidnap the group of frat guys who had gang-raped his sister, Nicole.

"You didn't know? Somebody shot him in his driveway a few weeks ago."

Jack's heart sank and he looked up at the sky, rage pulsing in his veins. "They killed him because of me. It's never going to end until I'm dead. Or they all are."

"I'm sorry."

Despite the sense of darkness looming over him, Jack was even more resolute. "I'm here in DC for a reason, and if it doesn't work out, at least I have somebody who can identify my body at the morgue."

"So I should stick around?"

"I'm not going to say anymore."

"Can I ask you just a couple of questions?"

"Go ahead; make it quick."

"Did you kill CIA Director Gus Banner?"

"The answer is no. I was there, but he jumped all on his own from the top deck. Banner told me I was there because they wanted me to be there."

"What do you think he meant by that?"

"Whoever killed Brian knew how I would react."

"Do you know who did it?"

"I'm not sure who, but I have some ideas. At first I thought Banner ordered it, but after our little conversation that night, I'm convinced he had nothing to do with it."

"If Banner didn't initiate it, then who did?"

"That's it with the questions for now, Greg."

"Okay. You said you had something for me."

"I do, but it's not about me. It goes to the basic foundation of our democracy."

"Former Special Agent Ryland gave me a file of the connection between President Atkins and Laura Weston," Greg said. "It's quite the story, and it's probably legit, but they would run me out of town if I wrote it. I just don't have enough. So, whatever you have, it has to be factual with actual proof, not hearsay."

Jack sighed. "It's sad what they did to Ryland, locking him up like he's some sort of criminal for allegedly colluding with me. I met him only twice. The first time was when my sister went missing, and I'd turned to the FBI for help. The second time, I saved his life."

"What do you mean by that?"

"I had a flash drive that implements Banner and then Senator Atkins in a crime. Ryland tracked me down near the Canadian border, and he had two choices: kill me or let me go."

"So he let you go?"

"If he had killed me, he wouldn't have made it far himself with that drive. Why do you think they are trying so hard to kill me? It's not about Atkins's son."

Greg now understood why they had silenced Ryland. "He's lucky he didn't have an accident."

"Yeah."

"So what proof do you have?"

"You will be getting an encrypted file that will blow your mind. It uncovers a deep state conspiracy."

"When will I be getting this file?"

"When I finish my mission or am killed in the process. The password will be sent to you by email."

"Can you give me a hint what this file is all about?"

"Ed Farley and some powerful globalists are running the country via a shadow government."

Greg didn't seem impressed. "I need a smoking gun."

Jack stood. "I'll let the file tell the story. We're done."

"Okay. I'll be anxiously waiting for that file." He got up and shook Jack's hand. "When this ends, I hope I can get an exclusive interview with you."

"I think it's going to end just one way, Greg."

"Just stay safe."

Jack started to walk away then stopped. "Where are they keeping Ryland these days?"

"FMC Devens. Why, are you planning on visiting him?" Greg joked.

"Why not?" Jack replied with a wicked grin.

***

Jack arrived back at the hotel in the early evening. Art jumped off the bed.

"Where the hell have you been."

"Does it really matter?"

"Mattison is pissed."

"I don't give a crap. I'm here now; that's all that matters. I'm here to take care of Steele. That's it. After that we're going our separate ways."

"You're the boss. I talked to Mattison; tomorrow's the day."

"Good. I just want to get this over with."

Chapter 31

President Atkins stepped out of the White House and got into a black SUV, which took him to his son's grave twelve miles away. He made an effort to visit John's grave every week; it gave him the opportunity to clear his mind. The vehicle passed through the cemetery gates then drove to a side road. A group of secret service agents fanned out on the cemetery grounds.

Gray storm clouds had turned the afternoon dark as Atkins walked the worn path to John's grave. He stood looking at the headstone, imagining what his son might have become. He had never gotten over the loss, but it was Jennifer's stinging words that hit home. He *had* failed as a parent. The cost of striving to be president at any cost had taken a toll on his family. His losses were all self-inflicted. He had allowed his selfishness and womanizing ways to tear the family fabric apart. His wife looked the other way at his sins, which just emboldened him more. He felt like a man on an island; he didn't know where to turn.

Another SUV pulled up behind the president's. FBI Director Shone Williams emerged and walked the same worn path.

"Sam," he said.

The two men embraced. They had been friends for

more than twenty-five years. Their fathers had also been close.

"Good to see you, Shone," Atkins said softly. "I haven't seen you in a while."

"I've been on vacation."

"You're probably wondering why I asked you out here. I like the serenity. I listen to the crows. They're absent today, probably because a storm is coming. This weather is ominous, and something is coming for me too. I sit in the Oval Office, and it's a pretty lonely place. I can't make a decision without pissing someone off. Being president is a lot harder than I thought it would be."

"You're doing a fine job, Sam."

"Maybe on the surface. But there's more going on than any of us know."

"What do you mean?"

"It wasn't fair of me dragging you into the Sanderlin Group tactics. I put you in an uncomfortable position. I should have never done that. But I couldn't trust anyone, Shone. When Banner was around, he had a network of people who could take care of problems quickly and efficiently."

Williams's phone buzzed. "Excuse me, Sam." He walked away a few moments, speaking in hushed tones. He came back and said, "We got a reliable tip: Bolton is right here in Washington. He's going after Steele at the Washington Center Hotel. This evening. We can take him down before he enters the hotel."

Sam rubbed his chin. "No."

"Why not? I thought you would be elated."

"We're just being played. I want you to stand down."

"What do you mean?"

"How would someone know this precise information?"

"I don't know."

"Did they mention the reward?"

"No."

"Let him go after Steele. Then take him down after he comes out. I want to see him. I want him alive, you understand?"

"I don't think that's a good idea."

"Shone, it's not your job to think here," Atkins snapped.

"Okay, Mr. President. You don't have to get upset about it."

Atkins sighed. "I just want this to end. I see it all so clearly now. You know when Brian Butler was killed, Steele anticipated how Bolton would react. Bolton followed the script and took care of Banner, and Steele got exactly what he wanted."

"What do you mean?"

"Banner was a loyal, cut-throat soldier. With him out of the way, I was vulnerable to being blackmailed by Steele, Sanderlin, and Farley."

Williams tilted his head as if he was having trouble

hearing. "I'm confused."

"There's no question I brought this on myself. I had a conversation not long ago with Steele, right here in front of my son's grave. He informed me that it was Farley who pushed for me to be the chosen one. They knew about my baggage and got me elected because there was a bigger plan. Farley needed someone who they could blackmail and control to carry out his world agenda."

"What world agenda?"

"The goal is to change the Constitution. A world with no borders. Steele wants me to take in three hundred thousand refugees, and get the Trans-Pacific Partnership passed, to name just two."

"He can't dictate to you."

"That's not all they want. They want me to give amnesty for twelve million illegals."

"That's crazy."

"No, it's not. They also want to disarm America in due time. Take the guns away."

"They never would get the votes."

"The more they change the country with people who don't understand America, the easier it will be to change America. Steele told me I would go down in history as the greatest president if I just play the game the way they want."

"And if you don't go along with what they want?"

"Farley and his criminal cartel will take me down,

and it's possible I could go to prison for a very long time, Shone. I'm just a puppet, and Farley is the puppet master. They've taped every conversation. You remember a month ago out in the boat? That's just one example. I'm sorry, Shone, but if I go down, you will too." He looked at his friend. "I never told you, but seven years ago I had Laura Weston kidnapped and taken to a Mexican cartel."

Williams went pale. "Why?"

"I had an affair. She got pregnant. I couldn't run for president if the public found out. Getting an intern pregnant was never going to get me elected, so Banner arranged the kidnapping."

"You had her kept captive for years?"

"I know. Stupid. But I can't change the past. And Farley knows he can use that against me anytime."

Williams was stunned. "I don't know what to say."

"There is nothing to say except I've dragged you in. I'm sorry."

"There must be something we can do."

Atkins shook his head. "Farley's been planning this for a long time with the Sanderlin Group and his EU allies. Farley's people are all still here in Washington. I call it a silent army. They're in the DOJ, the State Department, NSA, CIA, IRS, and any other department you want to name."

The FBI director looked like he might be physically ill. "I can't believe it."

"I had a chat with my father about it and asked what he would do. He said he would kill Farley. I think he was joking. My father was pretty upset with me. He did say my carelessness brought it on myself, and now there's no Banner to fix the problems."

"So, he didn't have an answer."

"There aren't any good answers when the other side has your playbook."

Chapter 32

Pizza boxes littered the coffee table. Jack sat in a chair by the window dressed in dungarees and a sweatshirt. The afternoon sun had broken through the dark clouds, brightening the room. He dampened the end of a toothbrush with some solvent and vigorously scrubbed carbon deposits off of the barrel hood and feed ramp of his gun. He wiped the exterior of the barrel down with a solvent-dampened rag.

Art watched him cleaning his weapon. "Probably a good idea."

"Old habits are hard to change," he said. And once again there he was, sitting around waiting for a green light to start an op. "I always thought the real bad guys just lived in other countries, but those looking for power and money are just as bad as the ideologues we fight on the battlefield."

"That's just the way the world works, Jack. I find a way to work within the system that benefits me."

"Robbing banks and working for Mattison is what you call working within the system?"

Art grinned. "I've learned not to rock the boat. It's worked out pretty well for me."

"You just think it has. Karma eventually catches up to people like you."

"What does that mean?"

"Maybe you're living on borrowed time."

"I don't think so, Jack. I think you're the one on borrowed time."

Jack laughed. "Karma has already done a number on me."

It occurred to Jack this was the longest conversation they'd ever had. But it was a fragile, temporary alliance. Art was the type of guy who didn't forget. His eyes gave it away. He was right at home taking out lives. He was just waiting to kill Jack to avenge his brother's death. Art's brother had been robbing a bank in Seattle and got caught up in the middle of Gallo's men and the FBI. It was Jack who fired the fatal shot that took down Art's brother, but he did it to protect Ryland whose gun jammed at the wrong time in the chaos of the running gun battle.

Art grabbed a whiskey bottle and poured some into a shot glass. "Here; this stuff will help calm your nerves."

Jack shook his head. "I'm good."

Art cracked his neck and stretched out his arms. "Suit yourself." He downed the shot.

"I think you enjoy all this. You're a killer. But I've never done anything to anyone unless they had it coming. There's a big difference."

"Revenge makes it okay, is that what you are telling me?"

"Don't waste your time giving me a lecture of what's

morally correct."

"Oh, I'm the last person who could do that. Mattison wants us to get along for this job, so I will. But you shot my brother in Seattle, and I'm just supposed to forget about it? Why are you smiling?"

"I said the same thing to Gallo on the phone before I shot his son."

Art took another swig of whiskey. "You had no remorse because he raped and killed your sister. He had it coming, right? Why is that any different from what happened to my brother?"

"It wasn't intentional. I was shooting back in self-defense at where the bullets were coming from. It never was personal."

"Well, it was to me."

Jack held up his hands. "I can't bring your brother back. You and I both know that there was chaos in the streets that day. Everyone was shooting at everyone."

"It don't matter now. It's the past. I never really discussed my childhood with anyone, but I want you to hear it."

"I got time."

Art told him about growing up in a small rural town in Texas and how close he was to his brother. His father was an abusive drunk, and his mom one day left and never came back.

"I couldn't really blame her. Who could live under those conditions day after day?"

His father then took out his anger and frustration on his sons, who joined the Army the second they were of age to escape.

"A few years later they found my father hanging from a rafter. He died a lonely man. You know how many people were at his funeral? Two. Me and my brother. We took his ashes and just threw them out the window driving down the highway. That's one of my best memories. So my brother was the only family I had. I've never had a relationship. To tell the truth, I don't feel remorse for anything."

"I had a brother as a kid too; he fell through the ice and slipped from my hand. My folks died in a car crash. My sister was raped and murdered. I had love in my life as a kid, but I lost all of them. I wanted a family, and Kelly and I were beginning that journey. I'm angry because the people in power took that away. I hate this life."

"Nobody took anything from you. You did all this to yourself. You made those decisions, they had consequences."

"That's true. And you and your brother chose to rob banks."

The phone vibrated on the nightstand next to the bed. Art picked it up and stepped out of the room. He came back a couple of minutes later.

"It's on. We'll be getting our hotel uniforms shortly. They order room service around 7:30. We'll make sure

Steele is there. And then we'll deliver the evening grub and catch them off guard. Once we're done, we have a good escape plan. The Mattison organization is quite thorough."

"Good. I feel much better now," Jack said, not displaying his true thoughts. He finished putting his gun back together. "I heard that Charlie Costa was shot in front of his house. Any idea who'd do that?"

"Charlie was shot?" he asked, feigning surprise. "What the hell is the world coming to? Charlie was a good guy. Is he okay?"

"He's dead. So you know nothing about it?"

"I'm shocked like you," Art said, finishing off the whiskey.

Chapter 33

Weldon oversaw the FBI operation and was giving marching orders. "Don't grab Bolton until he comes out of the hotel, and take him in alive."

The FBI Director had reiterated that too many times to count. Weldon felt handcuffed again to his job. He knew it was a risky proposition considering what had happened in Seattle. Weldon had positioned snipers with night vision on the surrounding roofs along Thomas Circle. He had men on the ground in plainclothes. He had agents in the lobby of the Washington Center Hotel. So many times before Bolton had eluded him; but he wasn't going to escape Weldon's grasp this time.

***

Jack rolled the SUV to a stop between two cars in a parking spot along Thomas Circle in the heart of Washington, D.C.

Art turned to Jack. "You ready for this?"

Jack exhaled as he screwed the silencer onto his Glock 17. "No different than Mexico. It's always the unknown that I fear."

"We got a good plan; we'll get out of there. Let's go."

They stepped out of the SUV dressed in white and black attire as if they were waiters going to work. They both wore lightweight black jackets to blend into the night. As they walked, Jack scanned everyone regardless of their shape or size. He had a bad feeling, as if a thousand eyes were watching him and he'd be ambushed by a group of Feds before he could finish the job.

They walked about a half-mile until their target destination was in sight. No words had been spoken. As they approached the main lobby, Jack paused.

"Why you stopping?" Art asked, putting the phone to his ear.

"The Feds are here. I can feel it. They know. We're being watched."

"Trust me, Jack; we're going to get out of this." Art listened for a moment and then informed him, "Justin is waiting for us on the second floor where the restaurant is. We'll take a right when we get to the top of the main stairs that lead into the restaurant kitchen. Steele's group just ordered room service. It's on. Let's go; stop worrying."

The two entered the hotel, Jack's eyes were wide, looking for hostiles while walking through the lobby. The place was as crowded as Grand Central Station; that at least gave them cover. The Feds would be foolish to attempt to bring him down while endangering civilians. Then that bad feeling rolled around in the pit of his stomach that maybe this was how it was going to end. A bullet he never saw, like Brian; one minute you're breathing, the next minute it's lights out.

They walked up the wide lobby stairs and took a right to the restaurant kitchen. Justin greeted them and shook both their hands.

He took them to a small room off the main kitchen. "Okay, here's the cart. Underneath it is a secret compartment. Put the gun in there and just practice pulling out the compartment."

"Do you think they'll pat us down?" Art asked.

"I did a trial run yesterday evening. They pat you down at the door. Check the trays. They even taste the food, but they don't check underneath. They boot you out pretty quick, so you're going to have to act fast and pull the compartment out and start firing. That's my advice. But I'm sure I don't have to tell you guys your business."

"What's the best escape route?" Jack asked.

"You'll like this. Follow me."

He led them from the small room to a corner spot in the open kitchen, which was hopping with activity churning out food. Justin stopped in front of a door. "This leads to the wine cellar where there is a boarded-up door. You can't miss it."

"We won't have time to break a door down," Art said.

"Don't worry; I've loosened the boards. Just pull them off. There's a flashlight on the right on the ledge. Again, you can't miss it. Open the door, walk through a brick corridor about fifty feet, and you'll come to a stairway. Take the stairs, go through the open door at the top, and it'll lead you right into a bar called Buchanan's, and you're home free. By the time the authorities figure it out, you'll be long gone. Simple as that."

"I like it," Jack said. "The hard part will be getting back here."

"You'll have eight or nine minutes once a call goes out before the DC police show up."

Art nodded. "That should be plenty of time."

"How many security people?" Jack asked.

"Steele is in 416. He has five security guys. Good luck."

"What about you, Justin?" Jack asked.

"You're worried about me?" He smiled. "No one usually gives a shit about me. I appreciate your concern. But this is my last day. I'm not real. That's what the FBI will find out in their investigation. You, on the other hand, are very real. So, do your job and forget about me."

Jack grabbed the cart with plates of food strategically placed. His gun was neatly tucked away in the secret compartment. His adrenaline was pumping at an abnormally high rate. He just wanted to finish it.

Jack and Art stepped onto the elevator, and other people squeezed in. It stopped on the fourth floor. They rolled the carts down the corridor until they came to their destination. Jack knocked on 416 while Art knocked on 417. The moment of truth had arrived. Jack thought of Kelly and pushed away his regrets.

The door opened as a large man with broad shoulders and big biceps, wearing a brown tee-shirt with a gun holster across his pumped chest greeted Jack. He blurted out, "It's about damn time."

"I'm sorry. I'll tell my manager you don't like the service."

"Stop! Let me check you." He patted him down quickly and opened the lids. "The food looks good. He's clear," he hollered loudly then pointed. "Just wheel the cart over there then get your ass out of here."

"Okay."

Jack rolled the cart, taking a mental picture of the room.

"What the…" the big guy said, no longer leaning against the open door. He'd heard the shots next door, just as Jack had, then went to investigate. Jack heard another shot go off. A second security guard stayed with Jack with his gun drawn and lost focus for a split-second when Jack reached underneath. Another shot was fired and the security guard dropped.

"That's how it's done, Jack," Art boasted loudly with a sick grin. "No hesitation. Welcome to the jungle. Now go find Steele, I'll wait out here. Make it quick."

He saw the real Art in action. A stone-blooded killer, who had no empathy. It was like stepping on ants to him.

There was no doubt now he killed Costa. Jack exhaled then reached underneath the cart, pulled out the secret compartment, and yanked the gun. He entered the bedroom, using one hand to pull open the closet door, the other holding the gun. There in the corner was Steele, hiding under some clothes.

"Get up." Jack pulled him up by the tie and threw him on the bed.

"I had nothing to do with killing your girlfriend," he pleaded.

"You're like all the rest of those spineless bastards."

"Wait! Please! I beg you."

Jack pointed the gun at his head.

"Wait, I can help you, Jack. Mattison set you up."

"That wouldn't be surprising, Steele. Just another day for me."

"He made a deal: you for me."

"How can I believe that?"

"You're not supposed to be here. There was a call to the FBI. They know you're here. They were going to grab you."

"It looks like there was a change in the plans. I'm sorry, Steele. Maybe you'll see Oz in your travels."

Steele continued to beg. Jack saw a desperate man willing to give away everything or anyone just to dodge death.

Art yelled from the other room, "You okay, Jack?"

"I'm fine. I'll be there in a minute," he yelled back.

"Hurry up; I don't want to be shooting my way out of here."

"I'm running out of time, Steele. I have to finish this."

Steele put up his hands to shield his face. Perspiration engulfed his forehead. "Look, remember that Keller guy, the boyfriend of Laura Weston?"

"What about him?"

"They're going to kill him tonight."

Jack couldn't believe what he heard. There was no end to their madness.

"I don't care about Keller. Sorry."

"No, I got something else. I can give you Sanderlin."

Jack liked that idea, but he knew the man was guarded by a battalion of security. "I'll never get close. Nice try."

"No. Sanderlin takes his father every Tuesday at nine o'clock to a small café called Hofburg in Lienz, Austria. It's on the southern border of Italy. He has minimum security with him."

Jack rubbed his chin. "Even if you are telling me the truth, I don't know if I'm going to get out of here alive. I'm sorry Steele, but you guys had no mercy on my girlfriend."

"I'll disappear, nobody will ever see me again." He pleaded loudly. "I promise."

"I got to go." Jack pointed the gun.

"And they're going to kill Senator Ethan White,"

Steele blurted.

Jack's curiosity got the best of him. Time was getting short. He was cutting it close. He could hear Art in the background yelling for him to finish the job or he would.

"Why?"

"They're afraid if he runs for president he could win."

Jack was taken aback. "You know something, Steele. I believe you."

Steele seemed to relax just before Jack fired two shots into his head. Steele slumped and fell over. Jack raced out of the room.

"What the hell were you doing in there?" Art said. "Come on."

They ran out into the corridor and raced toward the stairwell. Jack stopped and pulled the fire alarm. A loud siren echoed throughout the building and worried guests came streaming out of their rooms. Chaos was their friend.

***

When the alarm went off in the lobby, Weldon started swearing. The place quickly became a circus. Within minutes the police and firetrucks arrived. Weldon tried to take charge but could feel it slipping away as more people came down the stairwells on both sides of the hotel. How was he supposed to bring Bolton in alive with this? He barked out orders to his agents to check every individual leaving the premise, but the madhouse was making it extremely difficult to observe everyone. Once again Bolton had figured out a way to change the odds.

Weldon's phone buzzed as he scanned everybody passing him. He was at the foot of the lobby stairs. He picked up his phone.

An agent reported: "There are dead bodies in room 416 and 417."

"Check every room; they're here somewhere."

He hung up in frustration and ordered a perimeter at the exits. Nobody was getting by. He knew there was no fire; it was just a ruse to escape. As he glanced up the stairs, he saw Bolton staring at him with cold eyes, then he disappeared. Weldon yelled at his agents to join him as he ran up the stairs. He drew his gun, waving people out of the way. When he got to the top of the stairs, he took a right and cautiously entered the kitchen through a set of swinging doors followed by a group of agents who spread out through the area.

Bolton wasn't there.

Weldon turned around to access the room and spotted a door in the corner. He pointed and approached the door then waited as one of the agents returned with a tear gas canister and gas masks. He slowly turned the knob. There were stairs leading into pitch blackness and the light switch didn't work. He tossed the canister down into the darkness and listened. Nothing. He waited a couple of minutes then pulled on the mask and cautiously walked down the stairs, holding a flashlight against the gun. He stepped onto a cement floor and glanced around. It was a wine cellar.

Slowly walking through the cellar, his flashlight illuminated another opening. He pulled it as the agents behind him pointed their guns and flashlights into a dark corridor. Weldon realized his biggest fear was coming true. He moved forward through the corridor until he came to a stairwell and yet another door. He pushed it open and peeked out, startling a woman heading to the bathroom. She let out a small scream.

"I'm sorry I scared you." Weldon took out his FBI badge and a picture of Bolton. "Have you seen this man?"

She shook her head then rushed into the restroom.

Weldon frowned and followed the short hallway into the main area of the very crowded bar. Music was playing; there was a football game on the TV; and people were happily drinking, talking, or playing pool. A few patrons gave the agents curious looks, but most ignored them. The agents exited through the front door. Weldon looked up and down the street, shaking his head in disgust. Bolton was long gone.

Weldon went back to the hotel and met with the fire chief who told him it was a false alarm and everyone could go back to their rooms. He then made his way to the crime scene on the fourth floor. The forensic team was already taking pictures and accumulating specimen samples. Weldon stared at the large guy in the hallway. It was obvious that the man never knew what hit him.

After stepping over the body, Weldon went to the living room and saw two more guards. Then he went into the second unit, stepping over another security guard body and then entered the bedroom, he found Eric Steele, the latest casualty of Bolton's revenge tour. Weldon wondered what the point was of a forensic report: Bolton was the guilty party; it wasn't a mystery.

The phone buzzed and Weldon answered.

"Did you get Bolton?" FBI Director Williams asked.

"No."

"What the hell happened?"

"You guys didn't want to take him out before he walked into the hotel. That's what the hell happened."

"You lost him in the frigging hotel?"

"It was an inside job. Somebody gave him the layout. There was a nice shortcut in the wine cellar. Who knew? He's long gone."

"Shit," Shone said. "What damage did Bolton cause?"

"Just the usual; he killed Steele and his security team."

"Write me up a report and have it on my desk tomorrow morning."

"Sure thing," Weldon said with frustration.

Chapter 34

Jack and Art hustled back to the SUV. The hit went without a hitch. No scrapes or bruises. No wild shootout with the Feds. No collateral damage. The plan had been perfect.

Jack eased the SUV out of the parking spot into traffic. In the distance an array of blue and white lights could be seen.

Art laughed. "I'd love to see the faces of the Feds when they figure out how we got out of there. So, what the hell was taking you so long?"

"I was jotting down his last will and testimony."

Art laughed. "No, really."

"Men who are desperate sometimes tell you things that are very relevant."

"Did he?"

"Time will tell."

Jack focused on the road, his mind working overtime, filtering through the trove of information that Steele was so willing to give up. The first piece of business was to get rid of Glover. The job was done, and it was time to drop him off. What he learned from Steele just confirmed that Mattison was as bad as the rest of them.

"Time for you to go, Art. It was real fun, but I have other plans."

Art felt he had played his part like an Academy Award-winning actor. It was time to end the facade.

"No, *we* have a change in plans."

Jack turned toward Art and saw the gun aimed at him.

He shook his head. "You're pathetic, Art. You have no moral compass."

"Don't start with the bullshit. This is just the way the game is played. I'll direct you where you're going. Give me your gun – slowly."

Jack handed his weapon over. "Since I now know where you stand, let me ask: did you kill Charlie?"

"Yeah, I shot Charlie. He was a nice guy. Had a family. But you know what, Jack? I didn't feel a thing. I just shot him and walked away. It was easy. And I killed Chris, too. He wasn't living life. He was just drowning in his sorrows."

"You're a piece of work. You have no soul."

"No, I'm a survivor, Jack. Just like when I was a kid. Maybe that's why I've been able to last in this game while others don't make it. I'll ask you the same question I ask everyone: ever read Machiavelli?"

"No."

"Well, basically he said to keep your enemies close. And you get rid of them before they get rid of you. You should have killed me when you had your chance."

"Why spoil all the fun? Like I said before, Art, karma is eventually going to kick you in the ass."

"Let me worry about that."

"So, what's the plan?" Jack asked, hoping that Connor was on their trail.

"The plan is to turn you over to Sanderlin's henchmen. I'm sorry about that. I just take orders."

"So Mattison sold me out."

"I guess you could look at that way. I don't care."

"I get rid of Steele, and you turn me over to Sanderlin."

"That was the deal. These guys aren't going to be so kind to you. I'm thinking you're going to wish you were dead."

"I've been there before. I have a high tolerance for pain."

"Well, you're gonna need it. You seem pretty calm about all this. You hate me, don't you? I can see it in your eyes."

"Yeah, I do. I don't like people who kill my friends, but I'm at peace. No point getting upset. It's just the game, right? Why fight it? I'm tired of all the killing, being on the run." Jack played it like he was at a poker table bluffing the guy with the good hand, but it was all dependent on Connor having his back.

"You can't trust anyone in this game, Jack. After a while the lines become blurred. You don't know the good guys from the bad guys. You just do what they tell you. Unfortunately, you chose to be a lone wolf. It doesn't work in this game."

"Thanks for the advice, but where are we going."

"We're heading for the Potomac Mills Mall. That's where I get off. Take 395 South."

Jack focused on the road, hoping that Plan B was in play.

Art directed him to pull over. "I got to make a call. Don't try anything cute."

Jack just smiled.

Art dialed a number while remaining focused on Jack. "Hi. Everything went as planned. I'm now on my way to the mall to drop off Bolton. You know where to send my money." Art ended the call. "I think we would have made a good team, Jack."

"You chose the wrong team."

"I don't think so. Take this exit coming up to the Prince William Parkway, then turn left onto Worth Ave."

A few minutes later they entered the Potomac Mills Mall.

"Where do you want me to go?"

Art pointed to a dark, empty area at the far end of the mall. "Park away from the cars and back the car up against the curb."

The SUV rolled to a stop, facing the mall. "Now what?" Jack asked.

"We wait." Art leaned against the passenger door, his gun directed at Jack.

"While we're waiting, who killed Brian?"

Art paused. "I really liked Brian. To tell you the truth

I don't know. Could have been Mattison, but then again the bullets could have been meant for you." A few minutes later a car flashed its high-beams. "They're here. Let's get this over with. Get out of the car slowly where I can see your hands."

Art stood next to Jack in front of their vehicle while jamming the gun barrel into his ribs. Three men got out of the other vehicle.

"Here you go, "Art barked. "He's all yours."

The three men moved forward when a bullet ripped through one of them, and a second one fell before he could take cover.

Art instinctively moved his gun toward the direction of the gunshots. Jack lunged at him, knocking the gun from his hand. They both tumbled to the ground. The third man sent to pick up Jack retreated to his vehicle and put the car in reverse just as a shot struck him in the head. The car rolled down the parking lot and eventually came to a stop against another car.

Jack and Art continued their fight to the death as if they were fighting in a UFC cage match. Punches were exchanged, they charged each other like rams, staggered, rolled on the pavement, got up, and kept fighting. Art head-butted Jack and pounded him as he staggered back against the SUV. Jack grabbed him and kneed him, causing Art to double over. He tried charging, but Jack hit him with an uppercut that shattered the bone above his left eye. Blood spurted, blinding Art.

Connor walked slowly toward the SUV, watching the two combatants battle it out.

"Art," he shouted, "remember me."

Art turned, wiping the blood out of his eyes. He stared at him like he had seen a ghost. "But you're dead."

"No, I'm very much alive."

"I shot you and threw you over the bridge. There's no way you could have survived. No way."

"Well, I hate to disappoint you, but I'm very much alive. And I have a score to settle with you."

Jack moved away. "Like I told you, Art – karma."

"Fuck you."

Jack walked away.

Art was bent over but found the strength to straighten up, staggering as Connor moved forward and pulled out a handgun.

Jack turned and looked toward the Mall expecting an army of police heading in their direction. Then a gunshot echoed in the air.

Connor walked over. "So, how's your night going?"

"What the hell took you so long?"

"I wanted to see who was going to win the fight. Aren't you going to tell me I should see the other guy?"

Jack rolled his eyes. "We don't have time to joke around, Connor. The night's not over. I need you to follow me."

"Where are we going?"

"To find Jeff Keller. Steele told me they're going to kill him tonight. I just hope I'm not too late.

Jack grabbed his gun from Art's limp body then he and Connor got in their respective cars and sped out of the parking lot. A few minutes later a sea of blue flashing lights converged on the mall.

Chapter 35

Jack drove onto I-95 North. He picked up his encrypted phone and dialed Chip, who was in Canada sipping his favorite whiskey.

"Connor tells me you guys are taking care of business, Jack."

"Well, I guess you can call it that."

"At least you're still alive."

"I need Laura Weston's address. Can you do that for me?"

"Sure. Hang on a second." He pulled a file up on his computer. "She lives off of West Street in McLean, Virginia. The Blue-Sky Condominiums, number eight. You got that?"

"Yeah. I'll be talking to you."

Thirty minutes later Jack rolled into the Blue-Sky Condominium Complex and drove around until he located number eight. He jumped out of the car, hoping someone was home. He gestured for Connor to wait as he approached the townhouse. Jack hesitated then knocked on the door.

"Who is it," Laura asked in a nervous voice.

"Um, it's Jack Bolton."

She peered into the peephole. "How do I know it's you?" she asked, ready to press 911.

"We talked on the plane. Buck Airlines."

She slowly opened the door then gave him a big hug. "I can't believe it's you."

From the moment they had met in Mexico, she had felt a connection with Jack. Maybe it was the knight-in-shining-armor thing, him risking his life to bring her home. Whatever it was, she had been drawn to him and realized she still was.

Jack was surprised at the royal welcome and by how much he had needed a hug. All the killing, the hate. He was living in a world of darkness. Seeing Laura with that twinkle in her eye and feeling a woman's touch was a nice change of pace. But reality was killing the moment. He needed to get back on track and save Jeff before it was too late. As much as he wanted to catch up with Laura, time was of the essence.

"Laura, it's really good to see you." He walked in and looked around. "Where's Jeff?"

"We're not together anymore. We're not getting married. Why?"

His concern was obvious. "So where does he live now?"

"Well, he's still here, but he's moving out as soon as he finds a place."

"Do you know where he is right now?"

"Probably with Jennifer Atkins."

"The president's daughter?"

"Yeah, they're together. It's crazy. I haven't told

anybody because it's embarrassing. Your tormentor's daughter going out with your former fiancé."

Jack found it hard to take his eyes off of Laura and felt raw emotion bubbling inside him. Laura's mannerisms had triggered the thoughts of Kelly, and out of nowhere, his eyes started to well-up.

"You okay, Jack?"

"No. I hate who I am."

She walked over and held him tightly and found herself getting teary. So many bad things had happened to them both.

Jack didn't want the hug to stop. All the emotion he had bottled up was exploding. He pulled back and looked into her eyes then pulled away before things got out of control.

"I wish we could catch up, but I'm here to try to stop them from killing Jeff."

A bolt of fear shot through her. "He told me that a guy threatened his life a few weeks ago but he'd be safe as long as I kept quiet about President Atkins. We did exactly what they wanted."

"Well, I guess they've changed their minds. But if he's with Atkins's daughter, they should have Secret Service."

"I don't think so. I met her the other day, and there was no Secret Service with her."

"We need to find out where Jeff is right now."

"I'll try calling him, but he might not answer."

"Give it a try. I need to get to him before they do. Where does he hang out?"

"He likes going to Willard Tavern. It's on 19th Street NW in DC."

"Okay. I'm leaving. Here's my number. Keep trying to call him. Do you have Jennifer's number?"

"I do."

"Try to call her. I probably should take your number as well. I'm sorry I have to cut this short. I would love to stay and talk. Maybe another time."

"I would like that, Jack." She wrote down her number and handed it to him. "Be careful. And here." She opened a drawer and pulled out a snapshot of Jeff. "This might help."

"Thanks."

They shared an embrace goodbye and then he rushed outside to the SUV, once again in soldier mode.

Laura watched him go, hoping that their paths would cross again.

Jack plugged in the tavern's address on his GPS then took off with Connor following. He arrived at the bar twenty minutes later. After parking, he quickly explained the situation to Connor then went inside.

There was a good crowd on hand. In the corner a man played the piano. Jack sat down at the counter and ordered a beer. He scanned the patrons, carefully looking at each face. If Jeff wasn't there, he couldn't protect him.

Jack texted Laura, hoping that she had some news, but she had nothing to report. Time was running out, or maybe he was already too late. He checked the patrons again but didn't see Jeff. He stared at his beer. He felt defeated. Maybe Steele had told him a bunch of bullshit to buy time, but he didn't think so. Plus Steele had been right about Mattison double-crossing him. Either way it was time to move on; he had to find Senator Ethan White. The Senate was on recess, so he'd likely be back home in New Hampshire.

Jack made a call, working out the details with Buck, his favorite covert pilot. They would meet at Virginia Highlands Airport in the morning and fly to New Hampshire. Before hanging up, Jack also asked Buck to find him transportation to Europe.

Jack put away his phone and drained the last of his beer. As he got ready to leave, he looked across the bar and stared. It was Jeff. He was still alive. Jack ordered another beer. The soft piano music played in the background while a young crowd – some in suits, some in jeans – bantered back and forth.

He studied the crowds again, this time to identify a killer among them. One thing about associating with killers, he thought, you can sense them. He looked around until he fixated on two individuals sitting at a table not too far from Jeff. Two suits that looked out of place, watching and waiting for the moment to strike.

Jack watched as Jeff made conversation with the

bartender and the people around him, oblivious what was in store. Tonight he'd be Jeff's guardian angel. He studied the two men. He wasn't wrong; he could feel it. He debated whether he should just take them out and end the story or wait for them to show their hand. Both had risk. Like what if he was wrong?

***

Jeff got up and maneuvered past people. He felt something against his side, and then someone said in his ear, "Time to leave, Jeff. You try anything funny here, I will put a bullet in you."

Jeff followed the instructions.

Once out the door, Jeff was panicked. "What do you want from me?"

"Just walk. Let's go to your car," one of the hitmen said.

"I did everything you asked," he pleaded.

"It's just business," the second man told him. "Get over it. Keep walking."

When they got to Jeff's car, he was near tears. "Please, just let me go. I won't say anything. I give you my word."

"Jeff, get in and drive."

Before Jeff could move, he heard two quick *thwups* and the hitmen dropped.

Bolton walked up. "You okay?"

Jeff was shaking, paralyzed with fear.

"Do you know who I am?" Jack asked.

Jeff shook his head.

"I'm Jack Bolton. Now help me get these bodies in the back seat."

Jeff opened the door, staring at the dead men in shock.

Jack grabbed one under his arms then looked up. "You going to help me or just watch?"

Jeff helped Jack push the bodies into the car then kept staring at them.

"We don't have time to stay here," Jack told him.

"I just haven't seen dead bodies before," Jeff said in a whisper.

"Trust me; you get used to it."

"They were going to kill me."

"Yes, they were. Throw me the keys."

Jack hopped into the driver's seat and directed Jeff to get in the passenger seat. Connor pulled up next to them. Jack signaled him to follow.

Connor rolled down the window. Jack did the same. "What about your car?"

"I'm going to just leave it; the feds will probably be looking for it soon enough."

Jack eased the car out on to the main road and sped off.

"Are we going to the police station?" Jeff asked.

Jack glance at him. "That was a joke, right?"

"There are two dead bodies in my back seat. Shouldn't I report this? I have enough going on in my life."

"What are you going to tell them? That you just happened to be walking down the street and two thugs came up to you and luckily this Good Samaritan just happened to come by and save the day."

Jeff was quiet for a moment then asked, "What's your plan?"

"First we have to dump the bodies. Then my buddy Connor is going to take you to Wyoming."

"That's your plan?"

"You don't like it?"

"Oh, I just love it," he said with sarcasm. "I always wanted to go to Wyoming."

"I'm sorry. That's the way it's going down. You'll be safe there until this all blows over."

"What about my family? My girlfriend? They're going to think I'm dead."

"I hate to say this, but I don't care. If you want to stay alive, you'll do exactly what I say."

Jeff looked out the window. "My life is a mess anyway. I'm driving around with two dead bodies, my former fiancée threw me out, I got another woman pregnant, and my job sucks, but other than that just another normal weekend," he muttered to himself He turned to Jack. "How did you know I was in trouble?"

"Someone told me. Doesn't matter who."

"How did you find me?"

"I talked to Laura."

Jeff was quiet, trying not to feel resentment, remembering how Laura had talked about Jack and how brave he was. *Of course he's brave,* Jeff thought. *He's a killer.* But a killer who had saved both his life and Laura's.

"Why did you want to exchange yourself for me back a few years ago?" Jeff asked.

Jack hesitated. "I read a story about you serving time in prison and had good reason to believe you were innocent. And I felt guilty about what I'd done to avenge my sister. I deserved to be in prison for rest of my life. I figured if I could get you out, at least someone's life wasn't going to be ruined."

"Who are the people coming after me?"

"Probably the best way I can put it is they are monsters. Now, let's get rid of these bodies and send you off to Wyoming."

"Wyoming, huh," Jeff muttered, rolling his eyes.

"Probably not my place, but let me give you little advice: When you find a good woman, don't lose her."

"Jack, what the hell do you know about love?"

"Yeah, you're probably right, Jeff. What the hell do I know? I've been trying to live a normal life and I always get sucked back into a life I hate. I just want to be like everybody else. Forget about it."

"Hey, I'm sorry man. I didn't mean what I said. I've just been through a lot myself. Thanks for saving my life back there."

Jack half-smiled. "I understand." Jack pulled off I-66 and drove until they found an isolated, deserted old mill where they could dispose of the corpses; Connor pulled up behind him.

"What if someone finds them?" Jeff asked.

"Somehow they'll probably tie it back to me, so you shouldn't worry about it."

With Connor's help, they pushed the bodies down an embankment behind the mill. Jack then turned to Jeff. "Connor here will take care of you going forward. And if I'm successful, you'll get your life back. But you will need to get a new car."

Jeff just nodded. "I don't know how to thank you."

"Don't worry about it."

They shook hands then Jack said farewell to Connor and drove off.

Chapter 36

After several hours of driving, Jack rolled into Clayton Lake State Park around three in the morning, leaned the seat back, and fell asleep. He woke up around 7:00 a.m. to the sounds of birds chirping He couldn't get far enough away from Washington, D.C., a place he now despised. He didn't want to turn on the radio and hear about all the mayhem he had caused and the authorities announcing over and over again that he was armed and dangerous and anybody with information should contact the FBI immediately.

He gazed out the window and enjoyed the quietness. Not a human being in sight. He got out of the car and stretched. There was a cold breeze, yet the numbness of the previous day had set in so he didn't feel it. The trees were barren. The sun broke through and gave hope of a better day. He followed a path and sat against a maple tree overlooking the lake while watching the clouds form patterns in the sky. He sat and reflected. He had been on the run for three years. His dream of a life with Kelly was lost forever. He never would experience the love of a wife or the joy of being a dad: the first words, the training wheels coming off the bike, the laughs, and the hugs – all the craziness of bringing a kid into the world.

He had desperately wanted that. Now he was so deep into the depths of a black hole that there was no sanctuary at the other end. He was lost forever. Everybody he was close to was gone; it was as if he was the last dinosaur to walk the earth, and it was only a matter of time before his own extinction.

The park was beautiful at this time in the morning. He skipped a rock into the lake and reminisced how he would do that with his little brother or race him to the house. Jack always won. His little brother always looked up at him. And the pain of losing that would never go away. He stared out at the lake letting the tears fall. He was a mess. He just wanted to throw the gun into the water and never touch one again, but it was his lifeline until he had finished the job.

He got up and walked over to the gazebo and put his hands on the railing, wondering how many people had gotten married there. He walked further along the lake and came to a beach and plopped down on a bench. He missed Brian – the one guy he could trust. He was a great partner in crime, always cracking jokes and never worrying about the situation. Even when they were in the claws of the Garcia Cartel, Brian could find humor in it. Seeing Brian in love was unexpected. He had been ready to settle down but never got a chance.

The world saw him as a rogue former Navy SEAL gone bad. He would never be able to change people's opinions. They had no idea what was happening under the surface. Their country was fighting an invisible war that only he could see. The next victim on their hit list was Ethan White, an ethical, strong-willed politician who was a danger to the plans of the new world order. He had no idea what was coming. Jack had to inform him. But to win at this game was to expose the game and slay the dragon. That's what he decided to do. He gathered his last thoughts and walked back to his car to make the hour-and-a-half drive to Virginia Highlands Airport.

Chapter 37

Jack pulled into the airport parking lot at 11:30 in the morning. The place was so small that it would be easy to miss if a passerby blinked.

Buck had given him instructions to sit tight in the parking lot. Fifteen minutes had passed when a tall man with a long, gray ponytail, wearing a dungaree jacket headed his way.

Jack got out of the car, and the two men embraced like lost souls.

Buck stepped back and sized up Jack. "I hate to say this, but you look like hell – and that's probably an understatement. But we can talk on the plane. I'm sure you can't get out of Virginia soon enough."

"I see you're still rocking that silver ponytail."

"The women love it."

Jack chuckled then grew serious. "What about security?"

Buck laughed. "What security? That's the great part of flying small planes. There's no security at these small airports. And us small time pilots are one big family. I have connections all over the country. So, when I want to fly from one part of the country to the other, it's easy."

He led Jack onto the runway. "The plane is fueled

and ready to go."

Jack carried a duffle bag with a strap wrapped around his shoulder. He stepped into the Cessna 208 Caravan with Buck following, settling into the pilot's seat with Jack as his wingman.

Buck put on his headphones. "Cessna 208 clear for takeoff runway 28 left, make left closed traffic." He glanced over. "Here we go."

The engines roared as the plane began to roll down the runway, picking up speed until Buck pulled the nose upward. The plane climbed at 110 knots between nine hundred and one thousand feet per minute until it settled into a cruising speed of 180 knots.

"Okay, now we can talk," Buck said with a calm smile. "How you holding up? What's it been? Three years on the run and the Feds still haven't been able to catch you."

"Just lucky, I guess. What about you?"

"The Feds tried to take me down, but at the end of the day the federal prosecutor had no case, so he dropped it. But bringing Laura Weston back after being held six years by a Mexican Cartel as a favor to the president wasn't a career move. You know what I mean."

"Yeah."

"But now you, Jack," Buck chuckled. "You have too many enemies to count. Between the Feds, the Mafia, the Moreno Cartel, the CIA, and God knows who, I don't know how you're still standing."

"I think I have more enemies than that. Looking back at it now, I wish Brian had just left me in prison."

"How you holding up?"

"Not so well, Buck. I have these surges of grief out of nowhere. This isn't the life I signed up for. But it is what it is. I'm killing people, and I don't feel anything. I have a lot of hatred in me, and it doesn't take much to unleash it."

"Blame the government. They trained you for that. I flew many bombing missions over North Vietnam; I just didn't see the human damage. I'm sure if I'd seen the devastation, I might have had second thoughts and real nightmares."

Jack shook his head. "I was just a Navy SEAL fighting the bad guys, and I found out there are really bad people everywhere."

"I know you want to fix it, Jack. You can't."

"I feel guilty for everybody who's died because of me. I have to live with that." He rubbed his eyes. "It's getting harder, Buck. I don't know how long I'm going to last."

"Look, you've done a lot of good. You saved a lot of people. Hold it together. You risked your life to bring Laura back from Mexico."

"I also brought Joe Cap's corpse back to his father. The past haunts me. There's just too much pain. And now other people – some innocent, some not – are dead just because they knew me."

"Let me tell you something, Jack: The past shapes the future. Character matters. Karma has a strange way of showing up. It's not where you started, it's where you end up."

"Thanks for the words of wisdom. You sound like life coach, but I don't know, Buck. It doesn't seem to be working out that way for me."

"You're too hard on yourself. Here, I have something for you." He reached into a black bag and gave him an envelope. "You wanted a way to Europe, so I've set it up."

Jack looked through the envelope. "Wow, that was fast. Thank you."

"Forget about it. I have a buddy who flies chartered flights to Europe. He'll fly you from Maine International to Venice Marco Polo Airport. You'll need to have a good fake passport; security is a bigger deal overseas. All the information is in the envelope. And you can always call me if you have any questions."

"My new IDs should pass muster."

"Good. I'll have someone meet you at Marco Polo in Venice, and he'll drive you to wherever you need to go. I've also arranged for the flight back."

"I'm going overseas to finish it, Buck. I don't want anybody getting pulled into this."

"Don't worry about it. You just do what you need to do. Also, I got a car for you to drive to Maine. The plane is scheduled to leave in two days. I'm just worried you'll have too much free time to get into trouble," he quipped.

"That's perfect. I have some errands to run. I have to get rid of my money. I'm going to open a safe deposit box at the first bank I see. And in case something happens to me, I want you to have it. I'll send you the information once I have it."

"That's kind of you, Jack, but I'm all set. I just like flying, and I would get in trouble with it. I'm sure there's someone else out there who could really use the money."

"Okay. How much do I owe you?

"Nothing. You make life interesting. The people in power are chasing you; I like being part of it. And what would an old guy like me be doing anyways?"

Jack smiled. "You are crazy, Buck. And having way too much fun."

They both laughed. In less than an hour, they were on final approach to land at Nashua Airport.

"Buckle up. And thank you for flying Buck Airlines."

Jack smiled wide. "Don't ever change."

Chapter 38

Special Agent Weldon left one crime scene to visit another. He'd had no sleep. He held a coffee in one hand as he exited his car and surveyed the carnage at the Potomac Mills Mall. A man with an overcoat walked up.

"You Special Agent Mike Weldon? I'm Detective Ron Johnson."

"Nice to meet you." They shook hands. "Did they tell you the FBI is taking over?"

"Yeah."

"You got any ideas what happened here, Detective Johnson?"

"I don't know. It looks like a highly-skilled player took out a few people. This is not a gangland type thing. It looks like some business transaction that went bad."

Detective Robinson directed him first to the vehicle with a dead body slumped over the steering wheel. "He was shot in the head. Looks like a sniper rifle. Whoever did this was definitely trained, most likely military experience."

Weldon just observed not saying much. He had seen this too many times since he had been tracking Bolton.

The detective then led him to the bodies on the ground just as the morning sun broke through the clouds. Weldon lifted the tarps to gaze at each individual. When he got to the last body, he stared.

"What is it?" Detective Johnson asked.

"I've seen this face before. I just can't place it."

"Well, we'll know a lot more when we get fingerprints and DNA samples."

Weldon kept staring, then it hit him – the cemetery in Maine. He'd been with Butler. He knew Bolton. He must have been with Bolton at the hotel. The security video would prove it.

Weldon straightened up. "I know this guy. I just don't have a name. I'm going to have to wait for the forensic team to give a report. He was with Jack Bolton last night; both are suspects in the murders at Washington Center Hotel."

"What do you think happened?"

"That's a damn good question. Hey, Gary," he called out and pointed to the body. "Can you start with this guy? I need a name as soon as possible."

"I'll get right on it, Mike."

"I'm chasing a ghost, Detective. Let me ask you something."

"Sure."

"If you killed a bunch of people, what would be your first instinct?"

"I don't know. Probably get out of Dodge."

"Exactly my thoughts. So why would they come here?"

"Maybe to trade cars, figuring the car they were driving was caught on a surveillance camera."

"Maybe. But something is fishy here. If Bolton was with this guy, he's either dead, or he orchestrated it."

"What do you mean?"

"Like a backup plan. Bolton is working with someone. At this point I doubt the guy trusts anyone. There are too many people who want him dead." Weldon stretched his neck. "I need some sleep. The coffee isn't working. Detective Johnson, thanks for your assistance."

"No problem. If there's anything I can do, just let me know."

"Thanks, but we'll take it from here."

Chapter 39

Shone Williams was sitting in a chair in front of his desk when Mike Weldon walked in. The large windows allowed the afternoon rays to brighten the room

"You get some sleep, Mike?"

"Not much." He planted himself across from Shone. "I'm on my third cup of coffee."

The director leaned back. "How's the investigation going?" he asked with a hint of sarcasm.

"You know, Shone, we would have had him if you didn't tell me to stand down. When you get an opportunity to take down Bolton, you do it. The man has a way of just disappearing."

"If you had the whole damn place covered, how could he have escaped?"

"I'll tell you how: he had inside help. Someone knew about an ancient wine cellar that just so happened to have a convenient passage to another restaurant next door. Old plans from back in the day. Who knew?"

"The president isn't happy."

"I'm sure he isn't. But if you had let me take care of business up in Canada the right way, we wouldn't be talking about it now. I mean the idea of sending assassins…really, Shone? You sent a bunch of assassin thugs under Steele's command and are surprised when

Bolton comes looking for the ringleader? Pretty predictable."

"Easy for you to say. You've had your chances, and I don't see Bolton back behind bars."

"We had him. It was you who told me to stand down. Why?"

"Not my call; let's just leave it at that. So where do you think he's heading?"

"I don't know. A normal person would be heading out of the country."

"He's not normal."

"No, he's not."

"He's heading into the storm," Williams said.

"What do you mean?"

"He's not running anymore, Mike. He's killing now."

"I know, Shone. I have dead bodies all over the city. But he's going to make a mistake. I'm going to track him down if it's the last thing I do."

"He has an agenda. Steele was on it."

"Maybe you're on it, too," Weldon baited.

"That's not the way Bolton works."

"How did he know about Steele?"

"I don't know. What scares me is what else does he know? The president is concerned. He's running amok out there, almost mocking us to find him."

"I've been doing this for a long time. I had faith in Banner; he knew how to play the game. He brought me in to do whatever was necessary, now you guys hold me back from doing the job."

"Mike, I have people to answer to. It's not the frigging Wild West, okay?"

"Who are you answering to? It's becoming a pretty short list. If you want Bolton, let me do things my way. Banner was good at that. Tripp knew how to get things done as well. I get this feeling I'm on the outside, Shone."

"I tell you what you need to know. It's for your own good."

"You're wasting my skills."

"You just worry about Bolton. That's an order; you got it?"

"I get it, Shone. But something changed since Banner's been gone. Steele was suddenly getting involved with Bolton. Can you explain that to me?"

"I don't have to answer to you, Mike."

"Let's not forget that you signed off on me coming to the FBI. You know what Banner's intentions were. You can't play the neutral party here. You're in as deep as I am, so don't get cute with me. There's something more going on. I'm like a guy driving a car in the dark with no headlights. I can't work this way."

"Are you done whining?"

Weldon's phone buzzed. "Excuse me. I need to take this. I'll be right back."

Mike stepped outside Williams's office, listening. "I got it," he said then hung up. He walked back into the director's office.

"I guess somebody called about Jeff Keller being missing," Weldon said.

"And?"

"Surveillance video that we captured on 19th Street NW shows Jeff Keller being escorted by two men out of Willard Tavern. They drop and, out of nowhere, up walks Bolton. Keller helps Bolton put the bodies in the back seat of his car and off they went."

"He's become a real problem," Shone said in frustration.

"Yeah. But apparently somebody has now decided that Keller is expendable. Is it a coincidence that Bolton just happened to show up in the nick of time to save Keller?"

"I don't know."

"I think I do. I think Steele told Bolton before getting shot in the head."

"I don't want to talk about it."

"This affects me directly, Shone. A few years ago, when someone took out Bolton's partner in crime, Butler, Bolton retaliated and killed Banner. That wasn't by accident. Then last night I had a chance to take out Bolton, and you tell me to stand down. Now I'm thinking Atkins wanted Bolton to take care of Steele. Without Banner, Atkins is at the mercy of those globalists who know all about his dirt and are demanding he put forth their agenda. Am I missing something, Shone?"

"That's above your pay scale," Williams snapped. "Just focus on Bolton."

"Come on, Shone; we're well beyond that. Banner left you out in the cold for a reason. Maybe I should fill you in."

"I don't want to know."

"I think you should; there's a lot at stake for both of us. The Phoenix Project, for instance."

"Atkins mentioned it."

"I'm sure he did, but I'm going to give you my take, just in case something got left out. I worked with George Cap and a few others on that in Iraq. Banner gave an order to move the pallets of cash to Atkins's brother's bank in Seattle where it would be laundered. It was eventually dumped in a Cayman Island account. It was a directive by Congress to give the Iraqi people their money, but Banner had other ideas. He thought it should be used as a small down payment for the war. Who would care what happened to the money over time?

"But George Cap and a few other people didn't agree. They were going to rat out the whole scheme. So one by one they all had accidents. George was scared; he knew too much. So he headed back to the States where he had an accident too. But Banner wasn't satisfied. We monitored Cap's house day and night and followed his brother Joe everywhere. Nothing until one day we stumbled on this group of ex-SEALs having a reunion.

No big deal, we thought. We had no idea they were planning Bolton's prison break."

Shone sat stone-faced. He didn't want to hear it. "That's enough, Mike."

"No, Shone, you need to hear it all. This group of former SEALs along with Joe Cap broke out Bolton. As we all know, Bolton went after Atkins's son, but shortly after that they all met up in Texas and from there went to Mexico where they hit a bank run by the Moreno Cartel. Who knows how much money they stole, but somewhere along the ride, we assume Cap gave something to Bolton before he died."

"And how do you know that?"

"We had tracking devices on their vehicles used to break Bolton out of prison, and it wasn't too long after that we find Bolton in Seattle where the flash drive was in a safe deposit box at a local bank."

"If you had tracking devices, why didn't someone stop Bolton from shooting Atkins's son?"

Weldon shrugged. "It was a screw-up for sure; nobody expected it. But we tracked Bolton and Butler to a hotel in Virginia after they got back from Mexico. We grabbed Bolton when Butler wasn't there and took him to an abandoned warehouse."

"How do you know all this?"

"Banner gave me the play-by-play before I stepped into this shit. Anyway, weeks later we pick up a phone call made to the Cap's residence looking for a safe deposit box payment from a bank in Seattle. Banner sent a few agents; Bolton had just beaten them to it."

"So you're telling me that Bolton is in possession of something that can implicate the president?"

"Nobody knows for sure, but they think it's a flash drive about the Phoenix Project."

"How do they know it's a flash drive?"

"Because he dropped it right under the agents' noses before they realized who he was. They gave chase, but he was gone."

"This is a real mess, Mike."

"It gets better. I've saved the best for last."

Shone sat straight with his hands folded, feeling sick, realizing his friendship with Atkins had led him down a dark path with no return.

"You know the story behind Laura Weston. Pretty damn crazy if you ask me. But one of the guys who kidnapped Laura Weston had an epiphany."

Williams feared what was coming next. "What do you mean?"

"The guy gets cancer, and he's going to make all his wrongs right. Well, this guy gets in touch with Greenburg, Keller's attorney. Remember him?"

"Yeah, he was murdered, but Keller beat the charges."

"Banner had a conversation with Atkins. They decided to close all the loopholes, which included Ryland, but they thought Ryland might be useful in getting Bolton's attention, but it never came to fruition. Ryland probably knew as much as Greenberg. So Banner discredited Ryland and built a trumped-up case to put him away, and amazingly it worked. You look like you're not enjoying this, Shone. We took care of the leaker, but like a leaky boat more holes kept popping up. I mean at some point you just lose control. Just remember, Shone, we were doing all this to protect Atkins."

Shone shook his head.

"We made up the story of some connection between Keller's father and Bolton selling secrets to the Chinese. It was endless. I could see this was all wearing on Banner. He was tired. Then there was Jennifer Atkins's psychiatrist. Jennifer told her about her father's affair with Laura Weston. She told her about photos of the two together and said she sent them to Greenberg. The psychiatrist couldn't leave well enough alone. So, Banner had the problem fixed."

Weldon leaned in, hands on the desk that separated the two of them. "It didn't stop, Shone. Greenberg took the information from the informant and hired a private eye, and he didn't hire some stiff; he hired one of the best. The guy was good; he found her. He told Greenberg she was still alive. Banner worked with Tripp, and they devised a plan to end all the leaks. Banner wanted to get rid of Weston, but Atkins wouldn't have it. They couldn't afford Laura Weston coming home telling her story. So Tripp arranged for Keller's escape, timing it with Greenberg's murder, but it got screwed up. Keller escaped his handlers, but it didn't matter, the storyline worked fine. Who do you think killed Greenberg?"

"What do you mean?"

"I took care of Greenberg."

"You killed him?"

"That was the order from Banner. Greenberg sure was surprised when I stuck a shiv in him. It was a great plan. We had Keller's fingerprints on it. Banner made sure the Moreno Cartel was aware that a private eye team was looking for Weston. They found them and executed them. Problem solved. They even told Moreno who stole his money and where they lived. Moreno sent hit squads to kill everyone involved. Butler survived because he had made friends with some psycho, who I think is now lying dead in the Potomac Mills Mall parking lot."

Williams could not believe what he was hearing. "I don't know if I should throw your ass out of here, Mike, or arrest you for your confession."

Weldon smirked. "Shone, you know and I know that we're in the same boat. You never liked bringing me on, but your signature is on the paperwork. Banner lent me to you. What the hell do you think I do for a living? I'm not a boy scout. I do the dirty work that needs to be done."

"I can't believe this shit. And I don't need it. I think you enjoy it. I think you're the psycho. Deep down you're a stone-hearted killer."

"I'll take that as a compliment," Weldon said with a grin. "I'm not a nice guy, Shone; that's why Banner brought me in. I have a job to do, and I'll do whatever it takes. Now, we've got another group of clowns trying to take Bolton down, and it just complicates everything. Banner always said keep the circle small; the bigger the circle, the bigger the fall."

Shone leaned forward. "What are you looking for?"

"I want my old job back in the CIA. I miss the dead drops. I miss walking down dark alleys on moonless nights gathering intel from dead-men walking. I miss living in the shadows. I sometimes forget where I am. I was only supposed to be here on a temporary basis. This job is too dangerous now. Atkins is working with the wrong people. I'm expendable and so are you, Shone. I know these people."

"You think these people would kill us. I'm the frigging FBI director. I'm close to the president."

"Please. We're part of Atkins's baggage. Someone might decide we know too much. I came here to get Bolton, and it's personal to me now. Once this is resolved, I want out."

"That's fine with me."

"I want to spend the remaining time in my capacity tracking down Bolton, nothing more."

Shone leaned back. "I don't have a problem with that."

"Good."

There was a knock on the door. "Come on in," Williams called out.

"I'm sorry to interrupt," the agent said, standing at the door.

"Come on in, Butch. We were just finishing up."

Weldon got up.

"You might want to hear this, Mike," Butch said. "We've had an APB out on Keller's car. It's been spotted at a small airport in Abingdon, Virginia."

Weldon paused. "Bolton has a pilot friend, the one who brought Laura Weston back. Buck Mason. I'll bet the FAA can track his plane. I wish I'd thought of that sooner."

"He's probably one of the few friends he has left," Williams said. "It's worth a try. Let's get on it. Thanks, Butch. Good job."

Chapter 40

Jack sat in the rental car and pulled his docs out of the duffle bag. He exhaled a deep breath. Just the sight of the barbed-wire fencing and prison-guard attire gave him a shiver down his spine. Hell, he wasn't sure why he was doing this. Maybe to thumb his nose at the authorities. He had a plan, and he was checking it off as he went.

He had picked up a nice suit along the way and looked like a "real deal FBI agent" according to Buck. It had been a long time since he was well-dressed. He got out of the car and looked down at his sparkling black shoes. He took one last stare into the side mirror and straightened his tie. He was looking sharp. As he walked, his shoes squeaked, and his thoughts drifted to Kelly. She surely would have complimented him and then joked about his *super-secret agent* outfit.

It was quite the ballsy move to be mocking the system, but at that point what did it matter? It was a minimum-security prison. Security would be lax. He had the advantage; nobody would expect this. Of course, impersonating an FBI special agent was just another violation of the law, he thought. The list was adding up, not to mention he was already supposed to be serving a life sentence. He straightened up and then entered the FMC Devens facility. He put his best acting skills forward and walked to the security desk.

He popped out his FBI badge. "I'm Special Agent Jack McGee; I'm here on official business. I would like to talk to Paul Ryland."

The head security guard at the desk had seen this too many times; it was almost routine that the Feds wanted to talk to Ryland. He glimpsed at the badge then buzzed the steel gate open.

He called out, "Sal, show Special Agent McGee to the meeting room."

For a split-second Jack felt like a real special agent. This was actually fun, playing the role of a Fed. He followed Sal into a quiet room with no windows, a table, and four wooden chairs.

"Just take a seat," the guard said. "Ryland will be here shortly."

Jack sat down, leaned back, and put his feet up on top of the table. He was just missing a cigar. The door opened and Ryland entered. Jack pulled his feet down and made little eye contact.

Ryland sat down. "What the hell do you guys want now?"

Jack lifted his head. "I'm Special Agent Jack McGee, and you are probably wondering why I'm here today."

Ryland stared like he was dreaming. "What the hell?" he muttered. "I don't believe this. You are one crazy bastard. You know impersonating a federal agent is a crime," he added in a wry tone.

"Just add it to the list, Paul. I was in the area. I heard you got put away for a few years. I wanted to see you. I feel a little bit guilty that you're in here because of me."

Paul shook his head. "It wasn't you. The agency is corrupt. The FBI and Banner's merry band of henchmen pretty much destroyed my life. I haven't seen my boys in a while, and my wife is having an affair. I don't know what I'm going to do when I get out." He hesitated then added, "I heard about what happened in Canada. I'm sorry to hear about Kelly."

Jack looked away. "Thanks."

"I met her, you know, when Gallo's men took you from the hospital. She was a really nice girl. I went up there to investigate and I got lucky finding her and I interviewed her. She was pretty shook-up. She really cared about you though. I kept it quiet from everyone. I was scared for her."

"She told me about your encounter. I told her if she needed to talk to the Feds, you were the one person she could trust."

Ryland just nodded with sad eyes. "Anyway, I happened to be walking by the TV and saw you're all over the news today. They were talking about you in connection to what happened last night at the Washington Center Hotel. Did you kill Steele and his men?"

"They did it to themselves when they sent a team of

assassins to kill me up in Canada and killed Kelly, our baby that she was carrying, and my dog. She did a pretty good job of defending herself before they shot her. I finished it for her. But I didn't come here to talk about last night. There's a lot going on that the American people have no idea about."

"We live in crazy times," Ryland agreed. "So why *are* you here?"

"I have a few things left to do, and I'm not sure how it's going to turn out. I have a safe deposit box registered as Jack McGee, and you're the beneficiary of the box."

Ryland stared at him. "Why are you doing this?"

"You have three boys, right? They'll need a college education someday. And, like you said, what are you going to do for work? I don't think employers are going to be lining up to hire you once you get out. I'm not planning on dying, but I'm a high-risk candidate."

"I'm afraid to ask how much is in the box."

"About a million and a half."

Ryland nodded slowly. "Cartel money?"

"Blood money. But the money isn't important anymore. I'm far beyond that. You might find this amusing. Atkins isn't really running the country. Farley never left. He's deep in the shadows, pulling the levers."

"What do you mean?"

"Farley and a group of elite globalists are using Atkins as a puppet to get their agenda through."

"How do you know all this?"

298

Jack shook his head. "Do you know who Senator Ethan White is?"

"He's the senator from New Hampshire."

Jack leaned in and said in a low voice, "If my information is correct, Farley and his group are planning to make sure White doesn't run for president. Permanently."

Ryland ran his hand over his face. "Like get rid of him literally?"

Jack just nodded.

"Unbelievable. Let me ask you one question. What's on the drive?"

"Long story short, $18 billion that was earmarked for Iraq disappeared and ended up in a Cayman Island bank account. Banner orchestrated it, and the money was laundered through Atkins's brother's bank in Seattle."

Ryland sat back, stunned.

"There's more," Jack said, "but the story of how the money is being used is for another day." He stood. "It was good seeing you, Paul. We should go out for drinks when you get out. If I'm still breathing."

"I'm sure I'll have some free time," he said with a bitter laugh.

They shook hands and Jack left.

On his way out of the prison, he took a deep breath of fresh air then slowly exhaled. Now for the hard part.

Chapter 41

Jennifer Atkins met her mother inside the White House residence for breakfast. She sat down on a stool across from her, trying to hold back the tears that were bubbling up.

Her mother looked at her. "Honey, what's wrong?"

"Nothing, Mom."

"Come on, Jennifer," she said in a soothing tone. "I think I can tell when something is wrong."

"Jeff is missing."

"What do you mean *missing*?"

"He's missing, Mom. Nobody knows where he is."

"I'm sure it's nothing. He's probably out with his friends or something."

"Mom, he told me somebody threatened his life a few weeks ago. Dad is behind this; I know it."

"Your dad?" Mrs. Atkins shook her head. "Really, honey…."

Sam walked into the kitchen wearing a gray suit with his hair slicked back. He was feeling good after hearing about Steele's unfortunate death. Seeing Jennifer broke his good mood. He looked at her distraught face and shook his head.

"What drama are you embroiled in now?"

Jennifer coldly stared. "You're a bastard. Mom

should have left you a long time ago."

He exhaled. "I don't have time to listen to your bullshit this morning, Jennifer. You aren't going to ruin my day. You should learn some respect."

He grabbed a coffee and headed toward the door.

"You've always been good at walking away, Dad," Jennifer said. "Did you have Jeff killed?"

He turned back. "What the hell is wrong with you? Why would I care about that loser?"

"I know you ordered it. I know it."

Her mother stepped in. "Stop it, Jennifer. I know you're upset, but don't take it out on your father. He has a big job, please."

Jennifer turned to her mother. "You've protected him your whole relationship. You've always looked the other way about everything. But I know he's responsible."

She got up and strode out of the room, vibrating with fury.

Chapter 42

Weldon sat in front of Laura Weston's townhouse. He had been going nonstop with very little sleep for the past twenty-four hours. The phone buzzed in his pocket, and he pulled it out. He listened as an FAA official gave him the lowdown of Buck Mason's flight plan. Buck's Cessna had left Virginia Highlands Airport at 1:00 p.m. and landed at Nashua Airport around 2:30 p.m.

He wondered where Bolton was going. If Shone was right, he wasn't running anymore. Was he going after Gallo? He made a call and arranged for a flight that evening to Nashua. Then he got out of the car and slowly walked to Weston's front door and knocked. The front light turned on. He saw a shadow pass over the peephole.

"Who is it?"

Weldon pulled out his badge. "Special Agent Weldon. I have some questions I'd like to ask you."

The door clicked, and she opened it a crack. "What do you want to know?"

"Can I come in?" he asked with a smile. "I won't be long. I promise."

She reluctantly opened the door. "Okay."

He stood in the living room, pulling a pen and notepad from his trench coat pocket. "You reported this morning that your boyfriend Jeff Keller was missing."

"I did, but he's not my boyfriend."

"Did you have a conversation with Jack Bolton?"

She wasn't expecting that. She hesitated. "Um, no."

"Ms. Weston, I know you've been through some rough times, and I'm not here to grill you, but my job is to get Jack Bolton behind bars. The man is a fugitive, and he has continued his murderous ways. It's a crime to lie to an FBI agent. Do you understand that?"

She nodded. Her heart was racing, and her mouth had gone dry.

"I'll ask that question again: did you talk to Jack Bolton?" There was silence then she said yes in a low tone. "See, that wasn't so hard. I'm trying to help you find Jeff. So, what did he want?"

"He told me that Jeff was in danger. And asked if I knew where he might be."

"And?"

"I told him he might be at the Willard Tavern."

"That was the extent of the conversation you had with Bolton."

"Yes."

"And since that time there's been no other contact with Bolton. I can get a court order to check your phone records. And if we find you had some contact, I could charge you with false statements. You understand?"

"I swear to you. I've had no further conversation with Jack. I haven't heard from Jeff either."

303

"You know, I believe you. Bolton found Jeff outside the Willard Tavern. There was just one problem. I guess there *were* people looking for Jeff. Do you have any knowledge about that? Does Jeff have some enemies?"

She held her story. "I don't know of any."

"But Jack Bolton did, right?"

"Yes," she said, her voice quivering.

"The circles that Bolton is running around in now, it's hard to understand where he would get this information."

"I don't know."

"The good news is I think Jeff is still alive."

She exhaled a sigh of relief.

"From what was recorded on surveillance cameras in the area, Bolton's information was quite accurate."

"What do you mean by that?"

"What I mean is Bolton's very good at what he does. He shot two men like others eat popcorn. The funny thing is, Jeff helped him put the two dead bodies in the back of his car as if they were partners in crime. And off they went."

Laura was in shock, trying to hold it together. She was suddenly frightened of the man grilling her. These people were capable of anything.

"Are you okay, Ms. Weston? You look pale."

"I'm not feeling well. Are you done with the questioning? I don't know where Bolton went."

"Just another question or two and I'll be on my way.

Where would Jeff go? You said you two are no longer a couple. I'm sure there's another woman involved here. That's usually what happens when guys get thrown out."

She paused, anger replacing fear. "Are you done, Special Agent Weldon?"

He raised his brows. "I now see how you survived all those years in captivity. You have a tough side. But you didn't answer my question. Where might he go? I need to talk with him; he's the last living person to see Bolton that we know of."

"You really want to know?"

"That's why I'm here."

"You're right, there is another woman. Her name is Jennifer Atkins."

Weldon was caught off guard. "Any relation to POTUS?"

"That's right, Special Agent Weldon, she's the president's daughter. Now I'm done answering questions. Please leave."

Weldon walked to the door. Before leaving he said, "You should learn to control that little temper of yours if you want to keep a man around. Have a good night, Ms. Weston."

Walking to his car Weldon smiled. He had learned something new. The president's daughter. How was that for irony? But he would deal with that little lead later. It was on to Nashua to find Bolton.

Chapter 43

After a good night's sleep at a local motel, Jack wandered down a busy street in downtown Nashua looking for a place called Micks, a popular twenty-four-hour café that served breakfast any time of day or night. He'd read that Senator White made it a point during his downtime from Washington to reconnect with his working-class constituency.

White had announced his first senate run while sitting at the breakfast counter, a brilliant move that immediately connected him to the middle class. Once the senate campaign was over, he continued to stop by Micks and interact with the townsfolk as a regular guy.

Jack wore an old black jacket with a baseball cap as he strutted past barren trees and red brick buildings under low-hanging gray clouds. He found the area charming with its old mills that had been remodeled into shops and eateries now dotting the landscape. He opened the door to Micks and went to an empty seat at the counter, bypassing the hostess. The place was busy; the waitresses were running around keeping the customers happy while the busboys cleaned the vacated tables.

Jack sat on a stool watching the cooks flipping pancakes, eggs, and home fries on the grill. It brought back memories of him and Kelly eating at their favorite breakfast place. He observed the patrons, couples and families chatting about life, their plans, kids, and future endeavors. These people were oblivious to what was happening to their country. As far as they knew it would always be the good old US of A. Nobody ever sees it coming, he thought, and then one day it's gone.

He studied a picture of Senator White on his smartphone then looked around. He didn't see him, but it was possible he was in one of the booths.

The counter girl came over to him. "Can I get you something?"

"Sure. I'll take a cup of coffee to start."

She brought over a pot of black coffee and poured it into his mug.

"Can I ask you something?" he said.

"Sure."

"Is it true that Senator White usually comes here?"

"Yeah, he's a regular. He's here right now."

"Really?"

"He's in that booth over there by the windows," she said, pointing.

"Wow! Thanks. Maybe I'll say hello."

Jack watched as people talked with the senator. He waited until he saw his opening and walked slowly over to the senator's table. He walked past it like he was heading to the men's room then turned and acted as if he was a huge fan.

"Senator White!"

"Can I help you?" the senator said softly.

"I can't believe it. It's actually you. I voted for you."

"Well, I can always use the votes."

"Hey, can I sit down. I don't want to bother you or anything. I just have something I need to ask you. It will be quick I promise."

The senator tilted his head. "Do I know you? You look familiar."

"I get that a lot. But can I sit?"

"Um, sure. I guess. I've got a few minutes."

"Great." Jack sat down across from him.

"So, what is it?"

"Do you know who I am?"

"No, but you look familiar."

"I'm Jack Bolton."

The senator sat up straighter. "What do you want? I wouldn't do anything stupid here."

"I'm not here to hurt you," Jack said, as two police officers entered the diner. "It's not what it looks. I'll get to the point. Your life is in danger."

"How would you know that, Mr. Bolton? If I have my facts straight, you could be the one endangering me."

"But I'm not. They want to kill you."

"Who's they?"

Jack looked over and noticed one of the police officers walking in his direction. "A police officer is walking over here. Just be yourself, Senator, please. Nothing stupid."

The officer stopped at the table. Jack put his head down, almost habit by now. "Senator White, how are you?" he said enthusiastically, looking at both of them. "I'm sorry if I interrupted something."

"It's fine, Wayne," White said. "This is Jack; he's a friend from the old neighborhood. One of the little kids who liked to follow me around."

Wayne smiled. "Nice to meet you, Jack."

"The same." Jack took a long swig of his coffee, keeping away from eye contact.

"The family well, Wayne?" White asked.

"Yeah, can't complain. We're expecting another kid."

"Congratulations," White said with a wide smile.

Jack just went along with it though it brought back hurtful memories of Kelly being pregnant.

"Thanks. Well, I won't keep you. I just wanted to say hello. It was good to see you, Senator White. It was nice meeting you, Jack."

When the officer left, White leaned in. "So you think there are people out to kill me. I'm curious where a guy like you would get that information."

"I got that information from Eric Steele."

"The man you killed? What happened? You pointed a gun at his head and he tried to negotiate for his life by saying something he thought you'd want to hear?"

"You have no idea what's going on, Senator. Why don't you check with the people who killed my girlfriend and tried to kill me up in Maple Creek? They were assassins, and it wasn't the FBI. Why do you think they've kept it a secret what happened up there? And, Senator, just for the record, I've never hurt anyone who didn't hurt someone I loved. I'm not the boogieman."

"So now you're trying to be a hero and make up for all the bad stuff you've done?"

"No. I'm trying to stop more killing. I already saved Jeff Keller. Now I'm trying to save you."

White folded his hands on the table. "Okay, let's say I believe you. You haven't answered the question of who wants me dead."

"The Deep State."

"What the hell is that?"

"They're the ones running the country right now. Atkins is just a puppet for Ed Farley."

White chuckled. "Come on; I know Ed, and he's not running the country from his garden. You have quite the imagination."

"I know this is hard to digest. Atkins has a lot of baggage, which I don't have time to explain. Farley is working with the Sanderlin Group, pushing their agenda."

White leaned back. "Sorry if I'm skeptical. Plus, I'm not even running for president, so I'm not sure why they would want me dead. I'm just a little old senator from

New Hampshire. I doubt the deep state, as you call it, is really worried about me."

"That's the point. They are afraid that you will win the election. They want to get rid of you before you announce and get a secret service detail. Don't you see that, Senator?"

Even though it was unbelievable to White, something about Jack's demeanor sent off red flags. "I don't know...a deep state?"

"You're probably going to have an accident, and it's going to happen very soon."

Out of the corner of his eye, Jack spotted a familiar foe; obviously they were hot on his trail. Weldon was heading in his direction, and Jack kept his head down as he passed on his way to the men's room.

"I have to go, Senator. Please trust me; your life is in danger."

The senator shook his head. "I just can't believe – "

"Go talk with former Special Agent Paul Ryland. He's still in prison at Devens because they framed him for aiding and abetting me. Quite a ruse. He can vouch for what's happening behind the curtain, but you don't have much time, Senator."

After landing in the early morning hours, Weldon was directed to Micks after he'd asked the best breakfast spot in Nashua. He stood at the urinal, thinking how the man talking to Senator White looked a lot like Bolton but dismissed the thought; no investigator could be that lucky. Besides, what would White and Bolton be doing together anyway? That would make no sense. But his instincts were telling him otherwise. He burst out of the bathroom and stared at the booth. Jack was standing up ready to leave. They made eye contact and reached for their guns at the same moment.

Senator White jumped up in between the two rivals, pushing a waitress to the side into a booth, trying to stop the madness before any innocent people got hurt. There were a few screams as the two men pointed their guns at each other, but Jack had to worry about the two police officers at the counter. Both officers were caught off guard by the sudden mayhem that erupted in this peaceful local diner.

"Put the gun down, Bolton," Weldon ordered. "I'm Special Agent Weldon. It's over."

Jack grabbed the shoulder of Senator White, slowly backing up. "Weldon, put the gun down, and nobody gets hurt."

The customers were frozen in fear, most too afraid to move.

"I'm not putting the gun down, Bolton. There are two officers with their guns drawn over there. It's over. Now drop it. In minutes the place is going to be surrounded. Make it easy on yourself."

"Go to hell." He fired a shot above Weldon who ducked and people screamed. The two officers aimed their guns wildly with no clear shot.

"Whoa!" the senator yelled, holding up his hands. "Put down the gun, Special Agent Weldon. I'm going to go with him. That way nobody gets hurt. You too, Wayne. Put your gun down along with your buddy."

Weldon stared with cold, intense eyes, then shook his head in disgust as he slowly put the gun down on the floor.

"Now kick it over here," Jack said.

Weldon kicked the gun over; the senator picked it up and handed it to Jack, who glanced at the two policemen.

"Officers, put your damn guns down now. Don't be heroes."

"Do what he says," the senator repeated in a loud voice. "Do it, damn it."

Wayne put his gun down on the floor. The trainee held fast, not letting go of his gun.

Jack backed up with the senator in tow, using him as a shield, not letting go of his shoulder, all while watching the room and keeping his eye on Weldon and the trainee. Jack had an open shot of the trainee, who was getting in position, trying to be a hero.

"Wayne, take the damn gun away from him and put it on the floor," the senator yelled.

Jack had managed to get to the door. Wayne grabbed the gun from his partner, just as the senator and Jack turned onto the street. A police cruiser skidded to a stop twenty yards in front of them, and two police officers jumped out with their guns drawn. Jack just grabbed the Senator, using him as a shield as they scampered down the street. Then another cruiser came flying around the corner almost hitting another car.

Jack held the senator at gunpoint as they leaned against the corner of a brick building on the main street, facing the first of many police officers. Weldon had come out of the diner looking for a gun. Jack could hear a trove of sirens in the distance.

"Jack, just give up. You can't run forever," the senator said calmly. "Where are you going to go?"

"I'm not finished yet. Thanks for jumping in there."

"I didn't do it for you. I did it for the innocent people inside."

"That's why the other side is so afraid of you. Look, just believe me, Senator White. Your life is in serious danger."

The senator stood still against the building for a moment, thinking Jack was still behind him, holding a gun. Then he realized he was gone. But something kept him from letting the police know. An extra minute would give him the time needed to slip the police.

Jack ran a block and ducked into his car as two state police cruisers zipped by. He started the car and turned it around, driving away from the fracas.

When Weldon found the senator, he quickly ran forward studying the landscape, realizing quickly that Bolton had once again eluded capture.

Chapter 44

A crowd of media descended on Senator White as he tried to slip away after giving a statement to police.

"Senator White, customers of the diner are calling you a hero," the reporters yelled out.

"I'm no hero," he said with a smile. "I was just trying to diffuse the situation without any innocent people getting hurt. That was all."

"What happened to the suspect?" another reporter called out. "Was it Jack Bolton?"

"You'll have to ask the authorities," he said, waving goodbye then getting into his car.

***

The secure phone buzzed as Farley sat in a leather chair in his den, sipping a cup of coffee while watching the latest news. He picked up the phone and pushed it against his ear.

"How are you, Peter?"

"We've got a problem," Sanderlin snapped.

"I know; I'm watching it now."

"It's now in play."

"Good. I don't think we have a choice."

"I agree. It'll be done soon."

"The sooner, the better. We can't take any chances."

"We'll talk offsite when the job is done."

"Sounds good." He hung up and leaned back in his recliner thinking, *One more obstacle to remove and one step closer to the ultimate goal.*

Chapter 45

The White family was just like everyone else shuffling through the security line at Boston's Logan Airport. Their bags were scanned. They gathered their belongings and headed to a private plane at Gate 6. The chartered flight was scheduled to leave at 9:00 a.m.

Ethan and his wife, Sarah, and their two teenage daughters boarded a Learjet 55 for a private charter to Fort Meyers, Florida. They were greeted by the captain, and he directed them to their seats and gave them a quick overview of the set-up and encouraged them to help themselves to the snacks and beverages. The plane had seven comfortable, spacious seats. The girls sat down laughing and joking, excited to get the flight underway.

Senator White chatted with the co-pilot and the captain then took a seat next to his wife and gave her a small kiss on the cheek.

"Is this legal?" Sarah asked. "This isn't some favor."

"No. We're paying this out of our pocket. I can't be bought, remember?" he said with a wide smile.

"That's what I was afraid of. A private jet."

"It's fine. We can afford it. We'll have a good time, and the kids are looking forward to it. Good time of year to go to Florida."

"I think we all need it."

He turned to his daughters. "You ladies ready to go?"

They giggled and smiled.

The pilot announced that they would be leaving the gate in fifteen minutes. There was a short delay.

Ethan's phone vibrated. He picked it up, walked around, then planted himself back down, still talking as the plane was getting ready to jettison to its destination.

***

The G650 landed at Cameri Airport, outside of Milan, Italy. Jack went through customs and passed with flying colors. The small airport catered to private airplanes of the rich and famous.

He stepped out of the arrival area with his small carry-on, wearing a baseball cap embossed with a big B in front. Just like Buck had promised, a black sedan slowly maneuvered into the pick-up lane and rolled to a stop in front of Jack.

The passenger window came down. "You Jack McGee?" a well-dressed man asked in an Italian accent.

Jack bent down. "Yes."

"Get in the back seat."

Jack opened the back door and slid in, pushing his carry-on to the side. The car sped into the departing lane.

"Where to?" the driver asked.

"Lienz, Austria."

The driver looked at his watch. "That will be about a five-hour drive."

"What's your name?" Jack asked.

"Adamo."

"How do you know, Buck?"

"I don't. I was told to pick you up and help you out. Here; they said you would need this." Adamo reached into a duffle bag then held up a Glock 17. "They said this is your gun of choice, yes?"

Jack reached forward, took the gun, and placed it on the seat next to him. Adamo then handed him some magazines full of ammunition.

"The gun has been cleaned."

"You know guns, Adamo?"

"Yes, that is a good choice, Mr. McGee. Good reliability. Seventeen rounds in a magazine, low weight – just what you need in high-pressure situations."

Jack leaned back in the black leather seat. This guy wasn't just a driver. "Call me Jack."

"Okay."

"Do you know who I am?"

"Should I?"

"No. Who do you work for?"

Adamo occasionally glanced in the rearview to make eye contact. "I'm an independent contractor. I don't care what you're here for. I'm just here to drive you and do whatever is necessary. I get paid to get you to where you need to be and back safely."

Jack just shook his head. Adamo had no idea what he was walking into or that one of the most powerful men in the world was on the hitlist. *I hope they're paying him extra*, he thought with a laugh.

"So how did you get into this line of work?"

"I'm in what you call the export, import business, and your friend does favors for the people I work with. In return, we do favors for him. That's how it works, and that's all I am going to tell you. So sit back and no more questions."

Jack got the point. "Okay," he said and shut his eyes.

Chapter 46

Kelly was smiling, with Sampson by her side, greeting him at the door. They hugged and then they shared a long, passionate kiss. She grabbed his hand and led him out to the patio where they filled their glasses with wine. They couldn't take their eyes off of each other and couldn't stop smiling. The day was beautiful. The temperature perfect. The rolling hills could be seen as far as the eye could see. As he looked at Kelly, the wind picked up, the sky turned dark, and she began to slide away. She gripped Sampson as Jack reached out and grabbed her hand, pulling her closer, and her hand slipped out of his, and she was gone.

He bolted upright in a cold sweat.

Adamo glanced into the rearview. "You okay?"

Jack rubbed his eyes, getting his bearings as the dream faded. His heart still racing, he leaned back in the seat. "I'm fine, Adamo. How long to go?"

"An hour."

"I slept for four hours?"

"Yes."

When they arrived in downtown Lienz, Jack said, "I'm looking for the Café Hoffmann."

Adamo nodded and they drove another mile before rolling to a stop in front of the café.

"Let's get a bite to eat," Jack said. "I want to check the place out."

He took some duct tape from his bag and put it in his jacket pocket before leaving the car. Once inside they were seated by a hostess. After ordering, Jack got up and took a look around, checking out each room. He went into the men's room and closed the door to one of the stalls. He took out the tape and wrapped it tightly around the Glock 17 then pushed it flush against the back of the toilet bowl. It couldn't be seen, and it was high enough to not be in the way of any cleaning crew. He returned to the table and sat back down.

"You find what you're looking for?"

"You worry about driving, Adamo. I'll worry about me."

He smiled. "You're the boss."

The next morning around 7:00 a.m. Jack emerged from the hotel. Adamo greeted him.

"I'm all set, Adamo. I'm going back to the Hoffmann Café by myself for some breakfast."

"I'll drive you."

"No. You stay back here. I have some business to attend to."

Jack walked down the main street. The temperature was a cool forty-seven degrees. He gazed at the picture-perfect town as if he was part of a postcard. He had no idea if Steele's information was accurate, but he had been right about Keller. As he walked, Jack could feel his nerves, the butterflies in his stomach, the unknown, the idea that in a short time he might not even exist. The closer he got to the café, the fancier the cars parked on the street were. A couple of men in London Fog coats leaned against black sedans. They stirred with intense eyes as he approached. And as he was about to enter the café, the bigger of the two men ranted something in German and made a gesture indicating he was a threat.

Jack now knew the target was inside. The game was on. It was like a beehive where the outside bees warn the approaching bear that it's a bad idea to move forward, but a bear usually ignores the warning; it just wants the honey. He only understood the German word *schnell*, as the other man came around and greeted him.

"What the hell is this?" Jack asked in aggravation.

The man spoke English. "I'm sorry, sir, but the only way you are going inside is if we check you."

"Really?"

"Really. It's your choice, sir."

Jack put up his hands and let the man pat him down.

"He's good," the large man said.

The second man nodded that it was okay to go in. "We're sorry for the interruption, sir."

Jack scanned the café and saw a few people seated. And there were two security guards by a closed door straight down the corridor. He was seated, and coffee was delivered. He waived off the waitress, saying he didn't want to eat. He nursed the coffee, plotting his next move. Sanderlin had a security team outside and two men inside, so Jack got up from the table and headed down the corridor and casually glanced at the two security guards in front of him before turning into the men's room to the right. He walked in and went to the sink, exhaling a deep breath, with his heart pounding and his mouth parched.

It was now or never.

He was finishing up when a man who looked like a KGB agent walked in. There was something about these people. Jack could sense with near-complete accuracy who they were. The man stepped to the sink next to him.

"Oh man, when you got to go, you got go," Jack quipped.

The man said nothing: no smile, no humor, he was all business, checking him out like he was a threat. And he was.

Jack quickly retired to the stall where he had placed the gun. He sat on the toilet slumped, facing the stall door while his hands maneuvered the duct tape off the gun. He pulled it out from the back of the toilet and quickly inserted the noise suppressor on the barrel just as the door was yanked open, and the man pointed a gun in his direction. Jack sat there calmly and fired one shot in his forehead. The man staggered back and dropped, not knowing what hit him, gurgling as one last gasp of air percolated.

Jack stepped over him and took a deep breath. All

hell was about to break loose.

He pushed the bathroom door open and turned the corner, two hands on the gun firing two shots, the one remaining security guard dropped. He kicked open the doors to find a small room with nobody in it except two men who were seating comfortably at a small table. He fired a few more shots killing the older gentleman instantly, his head slumping flat on the table.

Jack stared at the other man with pure white hair and a hard face. He put his hands up. "No, don't shoot. Do you know who I am? I'm Peter Sanderlin. I can give you a lot of money."

"Thanks for the introduction; that means I've got the right person." Jack noticed the side door. He grabbed Sanderlin by the tie and pulled him up hard. "Let's go."

They exited the café into the crisp morning air. Two security men in long overcoats greeted them with guns drawn. Jack look at each man, one on each side.

"Who are you?" Sanderlin asked.

"I'm Jack Bolton," he said, pressing the gun into Sanderlin's temple. "Tell your friends to back away and put the guns down."

"And what? I'll live if they do that? You just killed my father. You have no soul, Jack. You're everything they say you are. But I'm a businessman, and everything can be negotiated, even your life. Otherwise it's the end of the line, and you don't have much time to decide."

The two bodyguards waited for the nod to take down

Jack.

"Whatever happens to me, you won't see another day either."

Out of nowhere came Adamo in the black sedan. He screeched to a stop, got out, and started firing at the bodyguards, catching them flat-footed. They both dropped. Jack sprinted to the car while dragging Sanderlin along. Two more men came around the side of the building, Adamo fired more shots while Jack pushed Sanderlin into the back seat. Then Adamo slid into the driver's seat and floored the accelerator, wheels smoking as the car peeled away.

Adamo headed west on B100 back to Italy.

"What are you going to do with me?" Sanderlin asked calmly. "You aren't going to get far."

"I've heard that a lot. Adamo, take the next exit." The car turned off B100 onto a scenic road and then turned onto a bumpy dirt road that ran along the River Isel. Adamo pulled into a clearing and killed the engine.

"You wait here, Adamo. I'm going to have a little conversation with Mr. Sanderlin."

Jack pulled him out of the car then took him down a small incline. The sun gleamed overhead on the crisp November day. He pushed Sanderlin down against a large white birch tree on a rolling hill not far from the river's edge. Jack stood over him.

Sanderlin sat with his arms folded, his expression condescending. "Whatever you do to me isn't going to change anything, you do understand that, right?"

Jack stood listening to the softly running water, taking in the landscape. He hated every bit of what he had become, shooting people as if it was a steady job. To think he had hated guns as a kid.

"How did you know where to find me?"

Jack turned his attention back to Sanderlin. "Steele told me everything. He wanted to live."

"Well, I'm not surprised. What else did he tell you? Did he tell you that Mattison double-crossed you?"

"Yeah. Not a surprise; I had expected it. A bunch of gray-haired billionaires sitting in a boardroom figuring out what's best for mankind. You and your world order."

"That's a little harsh, Jack. It's more of a global initiative, where America doesn't run the club but is just one of the boys in it."

"It's all the same. Power corrupts."

"There's nothing you can do to stop what's going to be. Killing me isn't going to stop anything. I'll just be replaced."

"You really don't understand why I'm here, do you?"

Sanderlin gave him a blank look.

"I'm not here because of politics. I learned a long time ago that the world is a dark place."

"Then why are you here?"

"Because you are part of a group of soulless people who killed the woman I loved. Sure, you didn't pull the trigger; you guys never do. But you spread your evil at any cost. And you are the same people who are going to decide what's good for the world?" His laugh was bitter.

"I don't expect you to understand why the world has to be unified. A borderless world, where religion, politics, and cultures are meshed together all with a common goal to advance the human spirit beyond our world. It can't be America calling the shots anymore. You might not like what you're hearing, but you can't stop it. Politicians sold out a long time ago. You might think you're some patriot, Jack, but I hate to tell you it's over for the America you know. You ever hear of Bitcoin, blockchain technology? Cash won't exist, digital IDs will represent a person's way around the world, which leads to blockchain technology tracking every transaction."

"I don't care."

"Those technologies will just make America weaker. You see, everyone thinks that Bitcoin is some fast-track investment vehicle. People believe anything, especially the young people. Bitcoin is really the foundation for a world with one currency. The plans have been in place for a lot longer than you can imagine. So now you need the right politicians to execute it."

"Farley."

"Oh, he's been terrific. He's a big fan of a one world order and is still running the show. So that flash drive you have means nothing, Jack. We're already moving on."

"I know all about Farley. Just like I know about the Cayman Islands account and where all the money has been going. You look surprised."

"It really doesn't matter what you know. We control the media, the Internet. Technology companies are all in this and world leaders. The next election, it's over for America. The Supreme Court, your guns, your freedoms, are going to be like every other country."

"You are not going to win the next election. Atkins's days are numbered."

Sanderlin waved his comment away as he would a gnat. "You don't get it; we have a plan B, and Atkins isn't even part of it."

"America is different," Jack said, tired of Sanderlin's bullshit.

"Your politicians are all crooks," he laughed. "Half your population is dependent on your federal government. They need people who promised them a free lunch. I know this is hard to digest, but you'll accept it. Your Constitution is just going to be a piece of paper. It was a great document, which took a long time to crack. Your forefathers were a brilliant bunch."

"You think you can destroy America."

"Jack, it's already being done from within. No bullets, no uprising, like a covert operation. You know about those. You get in, you get out before anyone knows what happened."

"I told Senator White that people wanted him dead. If he runs, he can win."

Sanderlin smiled with a wicked grin.

"What?"

"I agree with you that Senator White could win, but I guess you haven't heard. His private plane crashed yesterday. Everybody on board died. I'm sorry. A mechanical failure I'm sure."

"You fucking bastard; you killed him." He bent down and grabbed him by the throat, pushing his head against the tree then let go.

"You can't win; let it go." Sanderlin straightened his suit jacket.

Jack knew Sanderlin was enjoying rubbing this all in his face. "Why are you telling me all this?"

"Because there's absolutely nothing you can do to stop the inevitable. So getting rid of me changes nothing. This is much bigger than either of us. You are just a pebble on a beach."

A wave of calm came over Jack. He looked at Sanderlin with pity and said, "You see this tree you're sitting under? It didn't need any fertilizer, it didn't need anybody's water, it survived storms, harsh conditions, and here it stands strong and beautiful. That's America. There are the people like you who hate what America stands for, the ability for the average guy to be empowered, to have his own opinion, to strive for a better life. It's called freedom. The people you represent are pure evil, who want to force their will on people through technology, some fake ideology, or whatever psychological method you rats are using. I fought that. I saw that, I felt that in my travels. So I guess I do have a purpose after all. Good will prevail. You won't win. None of your cohorts are going to win."

Sanderlin's tone was smug. "Like I've said. you are already too late."

Jack squatted down and spoke softly. "I know all about the Cayman Islands bank account and how it's funding your master plan. When the first domino falls, they all do."

"You're a dead man, Bolton."

"I think you have that backwards. I'm the good guy. You're the dead man."

He pulled the trigger, and the silencer sent a soft echo off the trees. Sanderlin's head slumped onto his chest then his body fell over.

It was done. Jack looked out at the river. The country, his country, was under siege, and nobody knew. He walked slowly back to the car where Adamo waited, leaning against the door.

"You okay?"

"I'm exhausted. I'm sad, and I'm scared for the future." Jack slid in the back seat. "You weren't just supposed to be my driver, were you."

"They told me to watch your back."

"Well, thank you. Time for me to go home, Adamo."

331

Chapter 47

The chilly wind whipped old leaves around the cemetery. President Atkins stood in front of his son's grave in a long overcoat, his hands deep inside the pockets. He still felt a deep pain in his heart that John had died before his time. He'd believed he was the most powerful man in America, and yet he could feel the tide pulling him in.

As he stood in a dreary early November morning, he could see a car in the distance being allowed through by the Secret Service. He was surprised to see Shone Williams emerge from the SUV and walk to the gravesite.

"Hello, Mr. President."

"Knock off the formal bullshit," he said with a grin. "How did you find me?"

"Nobody had seen you. So I figured you were over here."

"Good guess. How you've been?"

"Could be better."

"I know what you mean. Our little problem is still a problem. It's very frustrating to continue to meet out here, and my son's killer is still roaming free."

"I understand your frustration."

"No, you don't, so don't act like you do. I just want

the bastard dead. How damn hard is that? Is there anybody out there who can do it? I'm hearing that Bolton took out Sanderlin in Austria. Couldn't happen to a nicer guy. What have you heard?"

"The same thing except I have some good news."

"What might that be?" he asked, skeptical. "The only good news is when Bolton is actually dead. Until then, it doesn't mean anything."

"We got some intel that Bolton is heading back to the States."

"Is it reliable?"

"I don't know. I'm going back to set up a unit to take him down."

"No."

"What do you mean 'no'?"

"If you know where he's coming in, I just want it done quietly. Have Banner's guy do it. Just him alone. Nobody else. You understand?"

"What, kill him?"

Atkins stared, eyes dead. "Do I need to spell it out? This has been going on far too long. I don't want to talk about it anymore. I have other problems to deal with. Once it's done, ship him back to wherever he came from."

"Okay."

Atkins looked away. "I'm not sure I'm in their plans for the next election. Farley is a problem. A very big problem. Banner was ruthless; they feared him. Me they don't fear. If they bring up my old baggage, I don't just have to worry about impeachment. I might get a prison sentence. That means unfortunately it isn't going to work out for you very well, either. I'm sorry; you're a good man."

"I did this all on my own, Sam."

"Remember years ago when we would head to Banner's cabin up in Maine and go fishing and drinking all week."

"Yeah, that was fun."

"We all had such big dreams. Banner was already moving up the political ladder in Washington, and I wanted to be president someday, and here I am. Amazing."

"I was going to be the head of the FBI, and it all came true."

"We both had powerful fathers, so we just had to play our cards right. And we did. And now Banner is dead, and you and I are fighting an invisible enemy that can pull the plug at any time."

"We'll get through it; we always do."

"Maybe you're right."

"It's horrible what happened to Senator White and his family."

Sam snorted. "Do you really think that was a mechanical failure?"

Williams stared at his friend. "Are you saying it was an assassination?"

Atkins's silence spoke volumes.

"Who would do that?"

"The same people who want to control me. Senator White was a threat in their eyes to win the next election."

Williams kicked at the ground. "Banner's guy tracked Bolton to a restaurant in New Hampshire and guess who he was last seen talking to?"

"Senator White?"

"Yeah."

"So Bolton talked to Senator White and then coincidentally also found out where Sanderlin ate breakfast. Connect the dots – Steele."

"You think Bolton warned Senator White his life was in danger?"

"I think that's exactly what he did. But it didn't save the senator."

"We should look at this as a crime."

"No, we should just be quiet. Farley's silent army is everywhere in Washington. These people are capable of turning the tables on me at any moment. Or maybe that's been their plan all along. I don't know. Just let the NTSB do their job."

Feeling as if the world was slowly closing in on him, Williams said, "I have to go, Sam."

As he walked away, Atkins called out, "Just finish it, Shone."

***

Frank Gallo sat at his usual table reading the *Wall Street Journal* and the *New York Times*. He wore reading glasses, his belly hung over his belt. He sipped on a coffee as Marty took a seat.

"Hey, Frank. I got some info I think you'll like."

"Wait a second." He showed Marty the front page. "Bolton?"

"Yeah, he's on a killing spree. I guess he's hell bent on getting back at the people he thinks had something to do with killing his girlfriend."

"These are international people, Frank. Why's he after them?"

"I'm good with hunches, and I think there's more going on here. You remember how close we were to putting a bullet into his head?"

"Yeah."

"And remember when Bolton offered me $20 million to let that college kid go?"

"Yeah. He was just saying that, Frank."

"No." Frank folded his arms and shook his head. "I know people; he was sincere. That's one thing about people like Bolton: they don't bullshit you with a bunch of manure. I do respect Bolton in some ways. He's a man of character and loyalty. I respect that. It doesn't mean I don't want him dead though. Anyway, he's into something or knows something. I first thought that Deal Maker was only interested in killing Bolton because Atkins wanted revenge, but there's something more

336

going on here."

"Yeah, you're probably right."

"Ryland probably knows; maybe I'll ask him sometime. I'll offer him a job. We hire felons, right?"

Marty laughed. "They're our best hires, Frank."

They both started laughing.

"So, what good news do you have for me?"

"We found out where that FBI agent lives. It's a nice quiet street in Newton, Massachusetts."

Frank's eyes lit up. He brought the cup of coffee to his lips, enjoying every drop. "How did you find him?"

"Good detective work," Marty said, proud of himself. "Do you want me to put a hit out on him?"

Frank leaned back in his chair, rubbing his chin. "Yeah, I want him dead. This is for Jimmy. Just remember that."

"I got it, Frank."

"I want outsiders, people that can't be tied back to us. You got that?"

"Yeah. I know a few people who will get the job done right."

"Good. Marty, don't screw this up."

"Don't worry; I won't, Frank. I liked Jimmy like a brother. I'm going to enjoy this one."

Chapter 48

Paul Ryland had followed the news the last few days. Bolton had now made the international reports. He was on a tear, well beyond rehabilitation. It was just a matter of time before his enemies or the authorities caught up with him.

Ryland had finished the standard work detail and had settled down for breakfast in the cafeteria. His mind wandered, counting the days until he would get his freedom back, unsure what he was going to do for a job once he got out. If something happened to Bolton, there was a large stash of money in a safe deposit box waiting for him. The most important concern was to get back his boys and be there for them as a dad and forget the ugly past.

A prison guard walked over to him. "You got a visitor, Ryland."

"Do you know who it is?"

"I don't," he said, shaking his head.

He took a seat in the visitor's room. Probably another fed looking for answers, he thought. A disheveled, unshaved man with bloodshot eyes and uncombed hair wearing a sweatshirt and dungarees walked in. Ryland had no idea who this homeless-looking person was.

"I don't know you," Ryland said. "I think you have

the wrong person."

"No, I have it right," he said, sliding into the seat opposite Ryland. His fingers tapped the table. "And you do know me."

"Help me out."

"I'm Senator Ethan White."

Ryland was confused. "Senator White was killed in a plane crash."

"No, Mr. Ryland, I'm very much alive. Why? I don't know. Your friend Jack Bolton warned me there were people who wanted to kill me. Went out of his way to tell me. So here I am, a dead man, asking you what the hell is going on? Is it a coincidence? I mean, planes do crash from mechanical failure. It couldn't have been an assassination – or could it? Some guy that's wanted by the FBI, has more enemies than a Mafia kingpin, tells you people are going to kill you – can that be real? He told me about you, so I want to hear it from you. Was this an assassination or a mechanical failure?"

Ryland sat there in complete disbelief. He exhaled, dreading bringing the senator into this dark conspiracy that ripped people's lives apart. "Senator, I don't think it's a good idea to go down this path."

"It's a little too late for that don't you think?"

Ryland sighed. "I guess you're right. How are you alive?"

"It's nothing more than fate. For some reason, I wasn't supposed to be on that plane. I went over it and over it in my head, why me? There's no answer, though. There never will be."

"I understand; you don't have to explain it to me."

"I was on the private plane. I had a few laughs with the pilot. I hugged my wife. I talked to my daughters; they were all excited for a week away in Florida. Life was good you know. It was just the other day that I'd had the crazy encounter with Bolton. The media built me up as some type of hero. I'm no hero. Anyway, I was on the plane when I got a phone call from my brother that my mother was in the hospital, she'd fallen and might have broken her hip. I decided at the last minute to see my mom at UMass Memorial Medical Center in Worcester. I told my family to go ahead, I'd fly down that evening, no big deal. My wife agrees and off I go."

He fought back tears.

"I'm so sorry for your loss."

"It's slowly sinking in that I won't ever see my family again." Grief and guilt shadowed his face. "Anyway, I rented a car and rushed to UMass Memorial, which is a two-hour drive. About halfway there the radio was on, breaking news. *Senator Ethan White's private jet has crashed*. I pulled off to the side of the road. It was surreal. I didn't know if I should cry or call someone. No one prepares you for this. There's no manual. You're supposed to be this strong person, and you're crying like you haven't since you were a little kid. I've seen soldiers die in battle right in front of me, close relatives lose the battle against cancer, but this...my first instinct was to rush to the crash scene. But something stopped me. I started recalling what Bolton was trying to tell me, and the more I thought about it, the angrier I got. What if these people actually did this? So, Paul, explain it to me, damn it," he pounded his fist on the table.

"I don't know where to start, Senator. I was going to break this case wide open. Instead I ended up in prison and basically lost my family. That's what these people do. We're at war, Senator. We can't be beaten from the outside, but we can lose from the inside, and that's what these people are doing. They are slowly taking over America with stealth-like precision, one step at a time, and once people like you realize it, it'll be too late."

The senator leaned forward. "Who the hell are these people? I want to know who's behind this plot. In your opinion, was it President Atkins?"

"Bolton told me that he learned of a plot by Farley to kill you."

"Farley? It makes no sense. Why would Farley want me dead?" He stared at Ryland, waiting for an answer.

"From Bolton's words, he's behind the scenes pulling President Atkins's strings. He's deep in the shadows pushing his agenda, which is connected to some sort of world order driven by billionaire industrialist Peter Sanderlin and his group."

"I'm supposed to believe that Farley is running a

shadow government, and Atkins is just going along with it."

"There's a lot you don't know, Senator."

"What do you mean?"

Ryland exhaled. "Why do you think I'm in here? I know too much."

"Please tell me."

"Do you remember the story about Laura Weston held in captivity for about seven years by a Mexican cartel?"

"Yes."

"When President Atkins was still a senator, he had an affair with Weston, who was an intern. She got pregnant, so he had her kidnapped and held by the Moreno Cartel."

"Come on, Paul. Did Bolton tell you this story?"

"No, Senator. It's very real. He had an affair with Laura Weston, and she got pregnant. But she wouldn't give up the baby. So he decided to make sure that his indiscretion never got out. His henchmen then framed her fiancé, Jeff Keller, and he was sentenced to life in prison."

"How do you know this is true?"

"I saw it firsthand. I know President Atkins's story very well. In fact, Jeff Keller's Attorney, Aaron Greenberg, actually talked to one of the men involved in the abduction, and he told Greenberg what happened. They were going to kill her and then the plan got changed at the last minute, and they brought her to Mexico until Bolton and a few former SEALs rescued her."

White held his head, trying to grasp the enormity of the conspiracy. "I'm not in my right state of mind at the moment, but couldn't we get a grand jury to get these men to testify against President Atkins? I mean, if this is true, how can it just not be prosecuted? The girl could testify as well. I must be missing something here."

"You are, Senator. Greenberg and the informant are both dead; Laura Weston is too scared to tell her story. And there's no physical proof."

The senator leaned back in his chair. "This is unbelievable. You're saying these people are capable of pretty much anything and getting away with it."

"There's more. You remember the legislation that was passed to give eighteen billion in Iraqi funds back to Iraqi?"

"Of course. I also remember the money somehow disappeared, and nobody knew where it went."

"Bolton has a flash drive that lays out how the money was disbursed."

"Where did it go?"

"Gus Banner, the CIA Director at the time, managed to move the money to President Atkins brother's bank in Seattle where it was laundered then stashed in a Cayman Island bank account."

"You have got to be kidding me." White's face

flushed. "How could nobody know? How did Bolton get this information?"

"I'm not quite sure, but I believe it came from the brother of one of his SEAL buddies who worked for the CIA and was killed in another so-called accident."

"An accident, right."

White stood and paced the room, running his hands through his hair.

"There's more."

He frowned. "I don't have time to hear the rest; I get the big picture."

"Look, I don't know what you think about Bolton, but he's smart, elusive, and has good instincts. He's an honest guy caught up in a riptide that he can't break free from."

"Yeah. I know character. That's why I'm here."

"So, what's your next move?"

"I could go to the FBI."

"It's compromised, Senator. That's why I'm in here."

"So, you're saying I'm all alone out here?"

"Pretty much. Keep in mind, Farley's people are entrenched all around President Atkins."

"I'm sure Farley knows all about Atkins's baggage, which means he can basically blackmail him," White reasoned.

"If I remember correctly, he was a big advocate for President Atkins in the past election."

"Yeah."

"Bolton said Farley is the man behind your assassination."

For as much as White didn't want to believe it, everything was starting to make sense. "I appreciate your time, Paul. I hope things work out for you."

"What are you going to do now?"

White took a moment to gather his thoughts, pushing the weight of his grief aside. "If these people thought this was going to be a deterrent from me running, they are sadly mistaken. They took the most important things in my life away. The only way I know how to live is to get up and fight back, no matter how difficult something might be. Later today, I'm going to announce that I'm seeking my party's presidential nomination."

Ryland stood and shook the senator's hand.

"When you get out, Paul, if you want it, I could use a good security guy."

Ryland was taken aback. "Thank you. Let me think about it."

"Okay. When I get what's left of my life together, let's talk again."

Chapter 49

He slid his gun into a side holster as he waited for a call. Weldon looked out his kitchen window for the last time at his Newton residence. The townhouse was on a lease. Banner had set it up prior to his arrival a few years ago, but now Weldon had an airline ticket to Aruba for when the job was done. The inside of the townhouse was barren other than the staging furniture. It was like nobody had ever lived there.

Shone had been tipped off by a European intelligence agency, Five Eyes. Jack Bolton was flying into Logan International Airport on a private charter. This no longer had anything to do with the FBI. He had a new identity. This was now a hit job. Just take him out then disappear overseas with a new assignment.

It had come down to this: no rules, no regulations, and no laws – just end it. Bolton wouldn't know what hit him.

Weldon's phone buzzed. He picked it up.

"Hi, Shone."

He wrote the instructions down, Shone expressing confidence that they had reliable information.

"I've got it. Two o'clock. Don't worry; I'll be right there waiting for him. Yeah, I got the flight ticket. It was an experience working with you. But no more contact after this call."

He hung up and shrugged into his overcoat, arranged his tie, and massaged gel into his crew cut. He looked into the mirror for one last time then stepped out of the townhouse into the fresh air and walked toward his car. He looked down the short driveway and saw a car blocking the way. It looked like someone had pulled over to talk on their phone.

"Hey!" he yelled. "Move your damn car." He was in no mood to be delayed.

A petite young woman with blonde hair got out of the car and clumsily pushed up the car hood, looking helplessly at the engine.

Weldon walked closer.

"I'm sorry," she said in a sweet voice. "The car just died. I think it's the battery. I can't get through to my boyfriend. Maybe if you give me a jump, I can be on my way."

He rolled his eyes. "The best I can do is roll you out of the way," he said brusquely. "I have an appointment I can't be late for."

"I'm so sorry," she repeated.

"Maybe you should get Triple A, you ever think of that? Just get in the car and steer," he said, exasperated.

He shut the hood and looked up to see two men wearing leather coats pop up from the back corner of the car shooting in his direction. Before he could react, his body was riddled with bullets. He staggered and fell hard onto the street. The men jumped into the car, and the woman floored it and sped off.

Weldon lay on the street in a pool of blood, his dream of taking down Bolton a fading brain pulse.

***

Palm trees lined the circular driveway where George Atkins emerged from the back seat of a black sedan. He waved the driver off. He looked up as two Secret Service agents greeted him. They patted him down like he was a criminal.

"Really, boys?"

"Just protocol, sir."

He was escorted into the foyer of the large beachfront estate on Siesta Key in Florida. In the corner of the deck, Ed Farley sat enjoying a glass of red wine. He got up, and they shook hands.

"George, so good to see you. It's been a while."

"You've got a beautiful place here. The view is spectacular."

"This place is my sanctuary. I love Siesta Key's white sand. You want something to drink?"

"I'll take a beer."

"Any particular type?"

"No, surprise me."

"Okay; I'll be right back."

The temperature was in the high seventies with a light ocean breeze. The sun shone brightly. Ed walked back out on to the deck.

"Here you go, George."

"Thanks. You've got those Secret Service guys trained well."

"I'm sorry about that. They harass everyone. I've got them for life. I guess you need them with all the kooks out there. So what brings you down here? You must be proud of Sam."

"President is pretty good. I just don't like how he got there."

"What do you mean?"

"Associating with you. Bad move."

Farley's smile was frosty. "I don't want to disappoint you, but Sam wouldn't have been elected without me. The people loved me in office. And the truth is, if I could have run another term, I would have won. So me backing Sam got him over the top. I'm probably not going to change your opinion on this, but that's just the reality."

"Okay, politics are a blood sport, and some people are better at it than others. Some know how to manipulate the sheep better than others. I'll give you that."

"I learned it all from you, George. You were the best at it, but you kept your eye on the ball. Not like you didn't fool around, you just did it intelligently. Not like Sam. Women and politics are a bad combination. They eventually get you in trouble."

"You were no angel."

"I never said I was."

"Why did you back him? You already knew his baggage."

"I'm not going to try to bullshit you; that would be insulting. I needed someone who had baggage, who had a powerful name, and who could win the election. Sam was the perfect candidate. It gave me the leverage I needed to make sure my legacy continued, my agenda moved forward, and the global objective wasn't deterred. It's that simple."

George took a slow sip of beer. "Is that the first time you've ever been honest?"

"Can't bullshit a bullshitter, now can I?"

"Your agenda has nothing to do with America. It's about some crazy dream of a world without borders."

"Change is hard for people like you, always holding onto the past. Sometimes change is good. So why are you really here, George? To threaten me? I accepted your request to come here because I knew you wanted to figure out where I was going with your son."

"I told him it was a bad mistake to get caught up with you. You used my sons to get that $18 billion back to the States."

"You know all about that, do you?"

"And don't think I'm not wise that you were behind Banner's demise. Bolton was just a pawn." He took another sip. "But he seems to be paying you back now."

"Bolton is just a nuisance, nothing more. He'll be

dealt with. Banner was a thorn, but I had nothing to do with that."

"Yeah, I'll bet you didn't."

Farley shrugged. "It's the past; I'm only looking ahead to the future."

"I'm sure you are."

"I think it would be a good idea for everyone if you could convince Sam to just work on our agenda. If he does, I will personally make sure that he gets another four years in office. Not a bad deal."

"For you or him? Is that why Senator White's plane went down?"

"That was unfortunate."

"Just like it's unfortunate that Sanderlin is missing."

"George, you're rooting for the wrong team. Talk to your son. The world is changing. Technology is taking over; you need a different perspective. The conservative party is gone. The world united will be able to do great things. The Constitution is obsolete."

"You really expect me to believe that bullshit that snake oil salesmen sell?"

"Just think about it. As technology moves forward, it makes more and more jobs obsolete; we need to plan for that. Don't look at it as some diabolical plot. It's not. It's just a way to enhance the human experience and advance as a civilization."

"You've been drinking some bad Kool-Aid. You think by reducing America's influence the world is going to work together. You are delusional."

"I understand as people age they get fixed in their ways. Change is hard. I just think the world working together can do great things."

"And you know what's best for the world?"

"It's a process, George. It doesn't happen overnight, and we're getting closer every year to that final destination."

"And we'll all sing *Kumbaya*."

Ed just smiled. "I know I'm not going to change your opinion, but for Sam's sake, just talk to him."

George got a ping on his phone. He took it out and saw there was breaking news. "Well, look at that. Senator White isn't dead after all. He wasn't on the plane that went down. And he's just announced he's running for president."

"What are you talking about?" Farley was no longer smiling or smug. "Let me see that."

George leaned over and flashed the phone.

Ed read the headline with glassy eyes then leaned back wondering how this had happened. They had been given confirmation White was on that plane with his family.

"You've gotten awfully quiet, Ed. Something bothering you? Senator White is alive. That's good news, right."

"The crash was yesterday. So what's he been doing for a day and a half?"

"I don't know; everybody grieves differently."

Farley stared out at the beach. "You know, in thinking it over, it might be a good idea if Sam thinks about not running for reelection. He has a lot of baggage, which could be a problem. He might face impeachment."

"What the hell are you talking about?" Atkins asked in a low voice.

"Hey, it's better than a prison sentence. I mean, the idea he could kidnap a girl and have a cartel hold her for seven years, that's pretty brutal. I would hate that to come out, wouldn't you?"

Atkins's face flushed deep red and the vein in his neck pulsed. "Who the fuck do you think you are, Farley?"

"I'm sorry, George, but I'm not sure Sam is up to the task. Senator Ethan White is going to be tough to beat. We need a better candidate. It's time we end our conversation. I have things to do."

"You're a snake, Farley. I see right through you."

"I'm sure you do; you were always good at that. Do I have to call security?"

George shook his head and stood. But his fury exploded, and he charged Farley, grabbed him by the throat, and broke the beer bottle over his head. Blood ran down the side of Farley's face.

"You think you can destroy my family, you bastard," Atkins yelled, blind with rage.

Farley tried to fend him off, but Atkins was bigger and much stronger. He pushed Farley to the balcony then grabbed his ankles. With superhuman brute force, Atkins flipped him over the railing. Farley hit the concrete deck below face-first, a pool of blood quickly spreading around his head.

Atkins grabbed onto the railing, in shock over what he had just done. His heart was pounding, his face now bright red, his breathing labored. He wiped his forehand with a trembling hand. He watched as Secret Service agents raced to the deck. Atkins gazed at the ocean.

The first secret service agent to reach the patio asked, "What the hell happened?

Atkins just stared at him in complete silence.

Chapter 50

The president called Shone into the Oval Office. He wondered what the urgency was? When he walked in, the room was quiet. Sam was standing up behind his desk looking out the window.

"Shone, take a seat." His demeanor was sullen. He turned from the window and sat behind his desk.

"You okay?"

"Ah, to tell the truth, Shone, I've seen much better days." He looked around. "Did you ever think you and I would be sitting here one day?"

"No, I didn't, Sam. We did joke about it, though."

"Yeah, we did, and here we are. We're just missing Gus. How's our little problem?"

"I haven't heard."

"Well, I won't hold my breath. But I have more pressing problems today. Remember when I said a storm was coming?"

"Yeah."

"Well, the storm is here."

"What's going on?"

"I wanted to tell you before it hits the media."

"Tell me what?"

"About an hour ago my father killed Former President Farley."

Shone stared, his eyes wide. "As in murdered him?"

"Yeah," Sam said in a low voice.

"Why?"

"He didn't really say. I'm sure it had something to do with Farley's vision of the world and the pressure he was putting on me to carry out that vision."

"Is he going to be charged with murder?"

"I'm sure. If you kill someone, don't they charge you for murder?"

"He could be charged with manslaughter. Depends on the circumstances."

"Murder is murder. There's been a lot of that lately. But that's not the only issue for today."

"What else is going on?"

"This evening renowned reporter Greg Wilson is going on Charlie Thompson's show to break some bombshell about me and my administration."

"Can't you stop it?"

"We've tried, saying it was all a bunch of bullshit, threatened to sue, but they're still airing it."

"Could this be Bolton's information you've been so afraid of?"

"Maybe. I never fully explained the $18 billion earmarked for Iraq. Farley was behind it, but his fingerprints are nowhere to be found."

"Weldon told me everything."

"He did? Well, then you know if it comes out, it's possible I could get impeached or worse, they could try to press criminal charges. I feel like my presidency is slipping away. I'm sorry, Shone. It's going to be a mess. They'll get a special counsel and dig into everything. They will subpoena everyone and drag us all through Senate hearings and turn everyone's life upside down."

Shone felt numb. He rubbed his hands over his face, his mind in a total uproar. His phone conversations, the Weldon connection, the illegal surveillance. Who knew what they'd find? They'd remove him as director. They might even prosecute him for working around the law to take out Jack Bolton. He knew enough to be taken down. After what had happened to Ryland, anything could happen.

"You look like you're in pain, Shone. I'm really sorry. You might think about resigning before the sharks start to circle and smell blood."

"I'll be okay, Sam. We're in this together."

"You might change your mind after Wilson's revelations come out."

"Well, thanks for the heads up. We'll get through this."

Shone walked out, knowing they weren't going to get through it.

Chapter 51

Shone Williams arrived at work earlier than usual. His office was quiet. He looked out the window then slid into his seat and turned on the computer and scanned the Internet. Every news outlet was in a frenzy. The writing was on the wall; nothing could save Atkins. There would be all types of investigations. A special counsel would be appointed. Impeachment and criminal charges would undoubtedly follow.

Investigative reporter Greg Wilson had appeared on Charlie Thompson's show and set the world on fire. The stolen $18 billion was just the tip of the iceberg. Wilson revealed everything, along with a detailed blueprint of how the account was being used to undermine the American government. He named organizations and individuals. He exposed the deep state. This time there wasn't going to be the usual deals made. This was the Super Bowl of corruption, and the fact that there had been foreign involvement would unleash a manhunt for the people behind the sabotage of American ideals.

Shone's relationship with the president would be dissected. There was no place to hide. He would be indicted. The FBI and the CIA would be put under a microscope with plenty of collateral damage. The murder of former President Ed Farley, the presumed murder of Peter Sanderlin, and the attempted assassination of Senator White just added to the intrigue and helped connect the conspiracy dots.

Bolton was suspected in the disappearance and suspected death of Sanderlin. But Shone knew he was the architect behind Wilson's information. The guy who had lost everything had found a way to bring the whole conspiracy to the American people. He was the only one still standing. Weldon's bullet-ridden body had been found at the end of his driveway. Nobody had seen a thing. The investigation would lead back to the FBI, which would lead to questions that he couldn't answer, like who exactly Special Agent Weldon was.

Greg Wilson has also made sure that the world knew that Jack Bolton was the hero behind the curtain.

Shone made a phone call to Atkins, but there was no answer. Dark thoughts consumed him. His career was over. He didn't want to go through all the hearings, the investigations, the testimonies, the lawyers, the media shaming, and then passing by Ryland on the way to prison. Karma really was a bitch.

Shone gazed at a group photo of Gus, Sam, and himself in better days and a beautiful picture of his loving family. Tears began to roll down his cheeks. He had disgraced them. He didn't want to add to their shame by putting them through the storm that was coming, as Sam put it. He took a piece of paper out and wrote a letter that drained his soul. After he finished, he opened his bottom drawer and took out his Glock 22. He popped in a magazine, put the gun to his head, muttered that he was sorry, and pulled the trigger.

His secretary came running in. Everyone else came running when they heard her horrified scream.

Chapter 52

Business was brisk at Gallo's, and Frank was in a jovial mood. He went around making sure his customers were getting first-rate service. He then took his usual seat, grabbing a coffee and scanning the daily papers.

Marty came by and plopped in the seat next to Frank with a plate full of food.

"You paying for that?" Frank asked with a straight face.

"Sure, I'll pay, Frank."

"I'm just kidding, Marty," he said with a grin. "Enjoy it. It's a great day."

"Yeah, we got that fake Fed guy," Marty boasted.

"Payback for Jimmy. It looks like they have no idea who did it or who the hell was shot. I'm sure they'll figure that out eventually, but the FBI is going to be too busy eating its own for a while."

"Why? What's going on?"

Frank shook his head. "How the hell do you walk the streets with no idea of what goes on in the world?"

"I have my own problems, Frank."

"I'm sure you do. Well, let me fill you in." He told Marty about Greg Wilson's report.

"So we could have been rich?"

"Yeah. Hell, I might have spared Bolton's life if I

knew he had access to an $18 billion account."

Marty chuckled.

"That frigging Deal Maker, offering me $200,000 in chump change. Now I know why they wanted Bolton so bad. And how they were using that money."

"What are you talking about?"

"Forget about it, Marty. You're too busy feeding your face."

"I'm hungry, Frank."

"You know this whole thing with Bolton these past few years, it's funny how we're the ones still standing while the whole bunch of crooks are either six-feet under or going to prison."

"We're smart, Frank."

"No, *I'm* smart, Marty. Even Ryland, who I like, ended up in prison."

They both broke out in laughter.

"You see, when you take matters into your own hands, you control your own destiny," Frank said with a wicked grin. "Don't forget that, Marty. A perfect example is Bolton; the bastard beat the crooks at their own game."

"He's still on the list, right?"

Frank's eyes burned. "He's never getting off the list. I'll never forget what he did to my son."

***

James Mattison stood in his study, looking out at the wild horses roaming freely. He couldn't believe how everything had fallen into place with plain dumb luck. Greg Wilson's scathing disclosures had given his political party new life. Senator White coming back from the dead and now running for president and revealing that he believed the plane crash that killed his family was an assassination attempt just added to the intrigue.

Luke walked in with two coffees and placed them down on the desk. They engaged in a strong handshake as if someone on the team hit the winning shot with no time left

"What a beautiful day," Mattison said with a wide smile. "It couldn't have gone better."

"I know, James. Bolton came through."

"He just didn't come through; he exposed the whole corrupt system. Atkins is history, Sanderlin is more than likely dead. And George Atkins took care of Farley. We couldn't have planned this better ourselves."

"I know."

"The irony is that Sam and George Atkins could be sharing the same prison cell." Mattison laughed out loud.

"What about Bolton?" Luke asked.

"He's a problem, but we'll deal with that at another time. For now we can only thank him; he did us all a big favor."

Luke's phone buzzed. He answered it, listened, then put it down. "The Feds are here, James. They have a search warrant."

"For what?" he asked, annoyed.

"They are going to search the premises for Bobby-Jo Graham," he said.

Mattison relaxed. "As if we would leave that piece of shit's body lying around. No, this is just a frigging message from Bolton. We'll find that SOB when the time is right. Show the agents around, Luke."

***

There was a knock on the door. Jennifer looked through the peephole and couldn't believe her eyes. She flung open the door and wrapped herself around Jeff so tightly he almost couldn't breathe.

After a minute Jeff leaned back. "Jennifer, I missed you so much."

"Where you've been? Why didn't you call or text? Something."

"I couldn't. He said it was too dangerous."

"Who's *he*?"

"A friend of Jack Bolton's. He never gave me his full name. He said it was better that way. Some men tried to kill me near Willard Tavern, and Jack Bolton came out of nowhere and saved my life by shooting both guys."

"Oh my God, Jeff."

"I know, I was scared shitless."

She hugged him again. "All that matters is that you're here and safe."

He led her to the couch. "I had a lot of time to think

while I was away. This guy that I stayed with said he had found God, and it was the best thing that ever happened to him. He would read scriptures to me from time to time and the words were so powerful. I asked myself what I was looking for in my life and kept thinking of you."

He took her hands, his eyes welling up. "I've been so unhappy these last few years, trying to be something I wasn't. I'm so sorry, Jennifer. I haven't been fair to you. You mean the world to me. You were always there for me during some hard times. You're just a wonderful person, and I love you with all my heart."

"Jeff, I love you too. I feel the same way. I've thought of you every day. I missed you so much. I didn't know if you were dead or alive." She leaned in and kissed him.

"I have one other thing to say." He knelt in front of her and held out a ring. "Jennifer Atkins, will you marry me?"

"Oh my God, yes, yes, and yes!"

Jeff gently pushed the ring onto her finger. "I'm not going to screw this up. I want to elope, just me and you and the baby," he said, rubbing her baby bump.

"When do we leave?"

"How about right now?"

***

Laura Weston went for a jog and returned to an empty condo. Her life was as empty as her home. After watching Greg Wilson's tell-all revelation about

President Atkins's corruption, his days in the White House seemed numbered. She was going to add fuel to the fire, finally telling the story of her affair with Atkins.

She reflected on her past. The highs and lows of her relationship with Jeff. The first engagement at the piano bar with the Potomac River in the background was one of her happiest moments. Jeff went down on one knee and proposed, and she said yes so many times that the patrons clapped as if they were at a sporting event. A ten-day trip to Italy followed, and they had such a wonderful time. Life was good.

Then ten months later they had their worst moment at the Woodstove Restaurant, where she confessed she was pregnant with another man's baby and couldn't marry him. The ugly stares, the argument that followed. Their worst sides exposed. The last night she would see Jeff for almost seven years.

She saw now that the dream they would somehow live happily-ever-after getting engaged a second time was delusional. But they had played the perfect power couple. They fooled everyone. It was such a great love story – separated for more than six years then reunited, all forgiven – everyone wanted to believe it. Including them. But the truth was the same issues that broke them up the first time were still there. Jennifer was a blessing in disguise; her relationship with Jeff was doomed to fail.

Even so, it made her sad. She wanted to start a family;

all her friends were now married. Some were even working on their second marriages. A mistake made many years ago still haunted her, but it had tested her morality and her inner strength. She gained so much from it, turned a negative into a positive lesson: Don't let people define you, and when it looks the darkest, just maybe the sun will come out when you least expect it.

Then her mind reshuffled the board, and Jack came up. She had liked him the first time she saw him. She saw inner strength and confidence. He was in mourning, but she felt a real inner connection and was sure he felt it too. Their connection wasn't a mistake. She picked up her phone and dialed his number. The phone rang on the other end, but nobody answered.

***

President Atkins sat in the oval office. He hadn't slept. His world was in turmoil. The media smelled blood.

His chief of staff walked in with a concerned look. "Mr. President, you need to answer these allegations from Wilson. There's a horde of media expecting a press conference. We could spin it as some fake hit piece by our opponents."

"I don't need to answer anything. Screw them all," Atkins said. "You can tell them I'm going to sue the bastard."

"We need to get in front of this," his chief of staff pressed. "Mr. President, there are already rumblings

367

about impeachment and maybe even criminal charges. We need a Cabinet meeting to figure out a game plan to deal with this."

"I said tell the media to go to hell; I need to be alone. I can't deal with this right now."

"I don't advise that, Mr. President. This isn't going to blow over. If we don't answer this, it's going to get worse."

The president's secretary knocked and said from the other side of the door, "It's Dorothy."

"The president cannot be disturbed," the chief of staff shouted.

She opened the door. "I'm sorry. It's urgent, Mr. President. Shone Williams took his life this morning."

The chief of staff put his face into his hands. Atkins slumped in his chair, knowing in his heart the end was close.

Epilogue

A few months had passed since Jack's European adventure. He took his shades off as he entered Molly's Bar and Grill in Canton, Massachusetts, and scanned the room. He saw Paul Ryland sitting on a bar stool in the far corner, sipping a small glass of bourbon, making small talk with the bartender.

When Ryland saw Jack, he popped up to shake his hand. "What you drinking?"

"I'll just have a Bud Lite."

The bartender nodded, and Jack slid on the stool next to Ryland. "What's with the blue blazer and the baseball cap?"

"The uniform for guys on the run," Jack chuckled.

"Well, it must be working; the Feds haven't caught up with you yet."

"I had you on the inside."

"That's not even funny, Jack."

"You're right. But you did let me go."

"I did a lot of things during this whole nightmare that I shouldn't have done," Ryland said.

"You and me both."

"You're okay?"

"I don't know. I think of Kelly every day."

"It's funny now, when I met her she tried to tell me

you two were just friends. I didn't believe it, of course. But as I said before, I made sure no one knew about her. I was afraid of what these people were capable of."

Jack nodded. "I know. How you doing?"

"I've been in limbo since getting out of prison. Hey, we have something in common."

"Except I did it illegally."

They laughed softly. Paul signaled the bartender for another round then said, "I'm in the process of a divorce."

"Sorry to hear that."

"It's always the so-called best friend that stabs you in the back. I'm not complaining though. I see my boys, and I'll recover. The good news is I got a job with Senator White's security team."

"That's great."

"Hey, if he becomes president, maybe you'll get a pardon."

Jack chuckled at the thought. "I don't know about that. But I'm glad you got a good job."

"I never thanked you for saving my life in Seattle."

"I don't deserve any credit. I just reacted the way I was trained. I felt like I was back in Afghanistan."

"It was mayhem up there. Let me ask you something. Who saved your ass the night Gallo had you?"

"Have you heard of James Mattison?"

"The industrialist?"

Jack nodded. "He grabbed me and had his own

political agenda. He was the one who helped us locate Laura and get her back. He wanted me to work for him. He wanted the flash drive. In the end, I didn't want to be part of it. Then he tried to kill me."

"Quite a friend."

"He's like all the rest of them. They all want control and power. I was just a pawn to be used and discarded at a moment's notice. They were just worried about my little flash drive, which Greg Wilson presented quite nicely."

"You destroyed President Atkins's presidency," Paul noted. "It's not going to end with his resignation; he's facing criminal charges."

"He destroyed himself a long time ago."

They sat and selectively shared information, filling in blanks and missing pieces that put the years-long conspiracy into clearer focus and provided insight into both men's actions. Jack was intrigued to hear that Special Agent Weldon had been shot multiple times."

"Do they know who did it?"

"No. The bureau is in disarray since Director Williams' suicide. He just got caught up in all this; he wasn't a bad guy."

"So much shit has hit the fan over the last few years," Jack sighed. "I could write a great novel with all that's happened."

"Well, how would it end?" Paul asked.

"I don't know. Maybe with someone firing a bullet

from hundred yards and I'd never see it coming."

"Let's talk about other things," Paul said.

"Okay, how're your boys?"

They talked for hours, rehashing the past some more, their regrets, and what the future might bring. At midnight Jack slid off his stool. "I've got to get going, Paul. I hope everything works out for you."

"I hope it works out for you too." The two men hugged goodbye. "Where are you going?"

"I'm going to disappear, Paul. Take care."

Jack walked out, and Ryland felt melancholy as he swirled the bourbon in his glass. He drank it then motioned to the bartender for another. A familiar sound ricocheted outside the building as the bartender poured him a fresh drink.

Ryland pushed the glass away and walked slowly to the door. He drew his concealed weapon and went outside.